ROLLING IN THE DEEP

Arthur Kevin Rein

Published by Open Books

Copyright © 2022 by Arthur Kevin Rein

Interior design by Siva Ram Maganti

Cover image © Natalya Erofeeva shutterstock.com/g/erofeevanatalya

ISBN-13: 978-1948598583

For my parents Jack and Marge. And to the kids of East End Resort. There were ten of us living there. Jeff and Mick have passed but are not forgotten.

Prologue

When I was seventeen years old, on one summer's night, I destroyed a quarter million dollar's-worth of field corn and triple that amount in farm equipment. Good work for any self-respecting criminal, but that's not what I was. And usually, when I look back on the summer of 2013, the first for our family at Noquebay Resort in Walnut Creek, Wisconsin, population 969, the million dollars isn't what comes to mind. Had I been writing this from a jail cell, perhaps I'd think otherwise. No, what remains in my memory as clear as the day it happened is a midnight rap on my bedroom window, a baseball cap, and a girl called Sticks. Add to that a season crammed with hits, runs, and errors, had the summer been a baseball game, the scorecard would have been a freakish mess. But I'm way ahead of myself.

Back to the million for a moment. How so, avoiding jail? The Sheriff's Department treated the case as if it were petty theft, which was more than fine with me. I was never even interviewed. They had their reasons, most not peculiar to the public good. And now that the statute of limitations has expired, I can speak freely of that extraordinary time without fear of legal recrimination. My parents were surprised by what my friends and I had wrought, but not shocked. The malfeasance was directed at a family bent on driving us to certain and utter ruin, so that defused the nuclear response I would have expected from them had the facts been otherwise. Prior to that I had not shown signs of juvenile delinquency. Quite the opposite. One of a family of four boys and a girl, I was in most ways a typical second born, bouncing off James, my older brother by more than two years, playing tagalong to his Superman, and at the same time doing my best to be his opposite. "James will be mayor of Burlington one day." I heard that one all the time. No one ever hung that on me.

Which is not to say I didn't have friends. I did, quite a wide circle of them in fact, all of whom I left behind the month before I was to start my junior year in high school. We made the move to the resort because of James, there was never any argument about that, and *he* didn't even make the trip. I resented him for that; a fact I tried my damnest to forget. But trying to forget is like trying to keep your eyes open during a sneeze. It can't be done.

If I wasn't in open rebellion after we moved to Red Wolf Lake, then there was a smoldering defiance which managed to undermine whatever feeble attempts I made to make friends at Red Wolf High School. Besides, let's face it, teenagers are, nothing if not tribal, and by the eleventh year of school, groups have formed, best-friends-forever made. There's not an app or Facebook keystroke that helps with "pick a clique" to help the new-at-school crowd. Then, I got lucky. Somehow, I stumbled into Max Cherhasky, a charmingly over-confident only child who came from money. I was from a large, middle-class family until the resort leveraged us to our eyeballs. A week later I met Diane Warren; a year older than either of us, she came from a single-parent family whose finances seemed always to be poised on the edge of a knife.

With them in my corner I managed most of my junior year well enough. May came. Spring, finally. Conventional wisdom was that summer started at the end of the month, on Memorial Day. But my seventeenth summer started earlier by three weeks. Max and I were doing a little fishing, a very unusual type of fishing…

CHAPTER ONE

Fishing for Finnegan's Skull

Saturday, May 4

There was a skull at the bottom of Red Wolf Lake worth five thousand dollars. If the legend was correct, it was attached to a full skeleton of a guy named Finnegan, picked clean by the fish by now. The poor guy. In the middle of the night, he went through the ice while sitting in his pick-up, nosedived through two hundred feet of water, and was never seen or heard from again. That was 1939. A toe bone had already washed up on shore, or so people said. The reward money was enough to get Max and me off our skateboards and into a boat, with the crazy idea we would snag the skull off the bottom using a Wolf River rig and a quarter-mile's worth of fishing line.

"We should be casting for walleyes," I said, dragging my rig along the bottom, two-hundred feet below where I sat. "Our chances of finding bones, much less a skull? The odds are ridiculous."

"We never catch any fish," Max said from the front seat of the boat, his feet propped on the gunwale. Max had blue eyes, a strong chin, and money—a combination that brought adoring glances from girls as they walked by him—unlike me with my glasses and unmistakable awkwardness when dealing with the opposite sex. "I remind you, Captain Ridiculous," Max continued, "zero, nada, zilch." He threw out the heavily weighted hook and line.

The boat rocked a bit with the waves. I sniffed the east breeze but got a nose full of the old outboard sitting right behind me. "Hell, if I hook even a bone, I'll know my luck has changed. I might even ask Diane for a date."

I imagined taking her out to dinner. She wasn't the most beautiful girl in the school, but the consensus was there were only two types of boys at Red Wolf, those who loved Diane, and those that hadn't met her.

"Diane *Warren?*" Max shook his head. "Ain't that much luck in the world, dude."

"Then why do I want the skull? Really?" I dragged the line again and looked at the horizon. "The bone that washed up on shore is giving me nightmares already, and it's only a toe. The skull?" I shivered my shoulders.

"There's always electro-shock therapy." Max nodded to the east. "Hey, what's with all the boats in front of the Manticore Mansion?"

I turned to look. Even from a mile away, the group looked like a small navy.

"They must be killing it over there. Meh. They can have them. Don't feel like cleaning fish anyway. Let's stay here in the boneyard. That mansion gives me the creeps."

Even from the Narrows, the Manticore place was easy to see. It looked like the Grand Hotel on Mackinac Island and about the same age, but much smaller. I'd only been living at Noquebay Resort for nine months, so I'd only seen the mansion in the off season. From what I'd heard, the family held parties there on major holidays, but no one lived there. They could afford it. The Manticores were a family conglomerate, the richest family in four counties, possibly in the upper half of the state. One of them—Steve Manticore—went to Red Wolf High. He was disgustingly lean, an inch or two taller than me, a pack of cigarettes always rolled in the sleeve of his t-shirt. On his bicep he had a tattoo of a skull holding a long-stem rose between its teeth. I didn't know much about the guy except he was a senior who, in some previous decade, had been kept back a year. We didn't share any classes, but that didn't mean I didn't know who he was.

The house was eerie in its solitude but the garage was truly strange. Max thought it looked like a skate barn. We both wanted to get a look inside.

Max reeled in some line. "Fat chance. We're not getting anywhere close."

My line was slack as well. "You know, I'm going to put that toe bone in our tavern. Big sign." I spread my arms. "'Home of Finnegan's Bones' so official-looking people'll think they're real."

Max grabbed a soda. "So, the sign is real even if the bones aren't?"

"If that don't work, just call it The Graveyard, cuz we're getting buried."

I didn't need to say that to Max. Through the school year he'd spent so much time at our place he'd become like a brother, and so he knew what was going on at Noquebay Resort.

My parents had bought the expansive property on an impulse, for reasons that were honorable, understandable and, at the same time, all-wrong. Located on the north shore of the lake, Noquebay Resort had eight free-standing cabins of questionable log construction and two additional rental 'units' attached to the back of the lodge. One of the units was converted into sleeping quarters for my siblings and me. There was a tavern out front that fit every Northwoods bar stereotype ever imagined, and created a few more of its own. We came in the fall, the worst time to purchase a vacation business in northern Wisconsin, and rode out the winter on a wad of cash from a hoard of late-November deer hunters who overran the place. We made it, barely, and were now waiting for summer and the tourist season.

"Give it some time," Max said. "You haven't been here a year. And July is when the place will be really rolling."

"I hope so. At first the idea of moving pissed me off, but then I thought, maybe leaving is good. I could get away from James' shadow. Except it's not working."

He looked back. "What do you mean? No one knows your brother around here."

"It's not that. But yeah, he's the real reason we moved here. James was everybody's friend, same girlfriend all through high school. And she was pretty. Hell, I don't even got one."

"So what?"

"Easy for you to say. I've never even had lipstick. You know, on me."

"What! From a kiss? Never?"

"Not even on my collar."

"Well, collar is probably tougher than the lips," Max said. "Girl has to be into you."

"Collar color, that's where it's at, man. I'll bet James had some of that." I tugged hard on the line. Still nothing. Then, without even thinking, I tugged at the chain around my neck, hidden underneath my shirt. "He was a straight A student, never had a bad word for anyone. An Eagle Scout, for chrissakes. All that candy-ass stuff. How am I gonna follow that?"

"Eagle Scout! Shit. Is that still a thing? Sounds like he had some swag."

"Yeah, and every class I took at school, it was 'Oh, I remember James. He was wonderful.' Captain of the football team. Every teacher was gaga, James this and James that. Till I just wanted to scream 'fuck you, I'm not James, okay? I'm Sam.' Which I never did, of course, because I'm not the chosen one, he was."

"And then he died."

———

About half an hour later, Max said to me: "I got something." He stood up, elevated his pole, and reeled in for about ten seconds, just to get the line taut. The breeze, never strong to begin with, had died to a whisper. "I'm stuck." The drag on the reel buzzed; it couldn't take any more tension.

"Grab the line with your hands." I looked closely at Max, but only for a second, because to look longer only made me lame with jealousy. It wasn't fair; Max had a guitar, snow skis, good looks, money. Now maybe he had a five-thousand-dollar skull.

He set the pole down and slowly, hand over hand, tried to break the hook free. Then he yanked once too often. The line snapped. "That's it. My snagging career is over." He reeled in the empty line and put the pole to rest. He dug a watch out of his pocket and flipped open the cover.

"Hey, nice piece. Where'd you get it?" I asked.

"My father. Family heirloom. Getting late, we should go."

I frowned. "That shouldn't be out here. It could end up in the lake."

"You sound like my old man, Jeremiah Roman Cherhasky, big time businessman and fulltime poseur extraordinaire. When he's home enough to catch me, then he can talk."

My hand spun the reel. It took a while to bring in the slack. "I don't think we're over Finnegan's anymore." The line tightened and then would yield no more. I elevated my rod, which was suddenly bent like a horseshoe. I grunted. "You mangy piece of crap. Don't piss me off."

I tugged the line by hand and, just as Max's had, it gave way. "Damn. I'm buying whaling rope next time."

I sat down and reeled in. The drag on the line was much less, but it wasn't zero. "I think I have something." Max snickered. "No kidding." The hook breached the surface. I had nabbed something metallic connected to a washed-out piece of cloth with stitched lettering. I set down the rod, brought the sopping fabric to my hand, and turned it over. "Hey! There are some letters here."

Max sat forward. "What does it say?"

CHAPTER TWO

Diane Warren

Tuesday, May 7

Once I turned sixteen, I got a license to drive, but in Northern Wisconsin, where very little was close by and what was close may not be what you needed, having a vehicle was the real prize. Because I had no wheels of my own, transportation became an every-day priority. If the family SUV was available, I'd drive my siblings to and from school. Unfortunately, my parents often had a greater need and on those days I would either ride the bus, which any seventeen-year-old would detest, or prostrate myself before a friend and beg a ride. Almost always, this turned out to be Max, who owned a ten-year-old BMW 3 Series four-door that was the coolest burnt red I ever saw and in immaculate condition.

Just as frequently, Max would have a girlfriend riding with him. That spring it was Sarah Crimmins who was pretty and blond and a cheerleader, of course. I didn't mind taking a back seat to her, not too much, especially when it kept me off the bus. I don't know why this fact sticks, but it was a Tuesday, school was out, and the three of us were belted snugly in our seats. Max hadn't turned on the engine.

"What are we waiting for?" I asked.

Max had a way of grinning like a wolf, and he did it then, at me, in the rearview mirror. "We got one more."

Right on cue, the door opposite me opened and in came Diane Warren. She pulled her long legs in the car, shut the door, and suddenly I couldn't breathe. Today she had her dark curls in a ponytail. I didn't know where to put my eyes or know what to say. A simple "hi" would have worked, but it never came to me. She put her purse on the seat between us and kept a couple of books on her lap. Then she leaned forward and said, "Hey you two, thanks for the lift. Sorry I'm late. Sorenson kept me after eighth hour. Said I needed to 'apply myself' or I might not graduate."

"Doesn't he keep you late like every week?" Sarah asked.

"Yeah." Diane nodded buoyantly. "It's like a date, and I dress for it. That's why I'm not worried about graduation."

A mere spectator to the conversation, I could have been put off, but I wasn't. I used the time to gather my wits, regain my breathing, and catch up with the other three. I could see what she meant by dressing for the part. In tights, a short skirt and a blouse she was dressed a cut above her usual.

"Hello, Sam bone. You're a quiet one." Suddenly, her almond shaped eyes were on me.

I probably managed a "hi" or "hey" but I don't really remember. Embarrassing? Yes, especially because I'd sat next to her in U.S. History for a few weeks. That ended poorly the day I looked up and saw her standing in front of my desk. "Thanks. My GPA is going through the roof after this one." She slapped a piece of paper on my open book. It was her test. She'd copied my answers and all she had to show for it was a D+. I had no comeback so she walked away and I saw again what I had noticed from day one: Diane Warren had the most beautiful legs in the world.

Max got on the road. Diane looked at my backpack. An economics text showed its cover. Her head flinched. "You're taking *geek-o-nomics* as a junior?" She punched her book with the side of her fist. "Like I'm ever going to use this crap. The second I graduate I'm going to forget all of it plus ten percent. If you're taking this as an elective you need help, Sam, you really do."

"Bet you're the only junior in the class," Max said.

"YOLO, Sam, YOLO," said Diane.

I hesitated, thinking of a response.

"You only live once, Sam," Sarah said.

"Yeah, YOLO. I know."

Diane reapplied her lipstick, and as I watched I recalled something I'd overheard my mother say during one of her parties, "You don't have to be beautiful to be gorgeous." I knew that about Diane like a swan knows a pond. Then her lips moved. "I have an aunt who comes to your resort. Do you know her? She has the cabin way at the end. She's very cool."

"Oh. Is her name Vander Kellen, Vander…?"

"Van Zandt." Diane spoke like a first-grade teacher. "Fanny is my aunt, and Wes is my uncle."

Okay, there was one good thing about the resort—Diane had relatives there. I pushed my glasses up my nose. "Yeah, Van Zandt. No kidding."

"I wouldn't shit you."

"I said 'no kidding,' not 'no shit.'"

"I heard you. You meant 'no shit.' So, what's it gonna be? You gonna say hi if I come over, or act all stuck-up like some highfalutin pool boy?"

I burped a laugh. "Sure, that's me. Come on over. We'll go water-skiing." We didn't own a boat or skis, but I didn't care. I just hoped Max wouldn't bust me on it. In my mind, Diane was already in a bikini.

"So sweet, living on a resort," Sarah said. "Can you even wait for summer?"

"Oh, I can wait. Pushing a mower all day, when I'm not clearing brush in the campgrounds, that is."

"What is that? Some kind of humblebrag?" Diane asked. "Drop it. You think living at Noquebay Resort is tough? Spend an hour with my mom. You'll go runnin' home, if you don't hang yourself first. Like today, she'll be taking a nap. Dirty dishes in the sink, dirty laundry in the hamper. She does it just to get me cranked.

"Check my purse." She held it up and gave it a shake. "Got compacts, keys, tons of make-up, two hairbrushes. Plop it down on the kitchen table; sounds like a bull in a bathroom. Do it every day, to see if I can wake her up. Never works."

She took the rubber band from her ponytail. She tossed her

head; hair covered her shoulders. "There'll be nothing to eat, so I do my own thing. Always cold coffee on the stove, which I heat up 'cuz it goes good with the chocolate chips."

"Now you're talking. Cookies!" I said. "But with coffee?"

"Not cookies, man, just the chips. Put them between my cheek and gum and let 'em melt. Add coffee and OMG. Make it a meal. Then I go in the living room. Got a pack of cigarettes and a lighter hiding in the couch. Sit down, light up, and listen to the heat click through the registers in the wall. Me and the mice. Top that one."

"OMG is right," Sarah said. "Are you really in high school? I would never dream of half of the stuff you do."

In my head, I was half-agreeing with Sarah. But of all things, why did Diane have to smoke? "I can't top that. What about your dad? You didn't mention him."

Diane hugged herself. "He's dead and I don't miss him, not a bit. But Ethyl, she's turned grieving into a life-long pursuit, a Debbie Downer on steroids."

"Oh, that's sad," Sarah said.

"Hey, Sam! Are we mowing lawn tonight?" Max asked. "Do I need to stay?"

"Yeah, no, we have it covered. Joe did the rider yesterday. Kevin and I can do the rest."

"Those two brothers of yours," Sarah said. "They're almost as big as you. Better watch out."

I sat back, relaxing a little. "I think I got Joe. It's Kevin might leave us all behind."

"So, Diane," Max looked at her in the rearview mirror as he drove down a county road, swamp and woods on both sides. "Didn't see you at prom last week."

She looked out the window. "Didn't go. No one asked me."

"What?" I tried to see Sarah's reaction, but she was in the seat right in front of me. "I don't believe it."

Still looking out the window, Diane said, "Not my jam. Can you see me in one of those formals, my hair up?" She thrust a bent hand in the air. "Pretty little flowers on my wrist?"

"Yes," I said. "Yes, I can."

"I'll bet." Diane clucked her tongue. "Do you believe these fields? They go on forever." We were now in farmland, acres of corn on one side, beans on the other, most of it watered by a huge irrigation system, part of which was soaking the back eighty acres as we drove by, all of it owned by one family. Diane turned away. "Fucking Manticores; they own everything."

"Do you or your mom ever hear from Junior anymore?" Max asked.

"Who's Junior?" I asked.

"The middle Manticore son," Sarah said. "He was married to Jean Warren, Diane's sister, before she disappeared four years ago."

"Six years ago," Diane corrected. She shook her head. "Haven't heard from her. Haven't heard from him. Every time I see one of their construction trucks or go by their farm, it pisses me off."

"I have the same reaction when I see their palace on the lake, and I don't even know why. That reminds me." I pulled my backpack to my lap, opened the flap, and pulled out the fishing relic. "What do you think this is?"

Diane took the buckle and cloth, turned it over in her hand and took a sniff.

Sarah leaned back for a closer look. "Where'd you get it?"

"Fishing."

"Fishing?" replied Diane.

"Yeah, last week, out by Finnegan's Hole. We were trolling the bottom."

"Why would you do that?" Sarah asked.

"Fish weren't biting, so we thought, you know, why not try to hook something interesting like…"

Diane looked up. "Like what?"

"Finnegan's skull."

Diane burped a laugh, and then looked closer at the stitching.

"Well, did you get it?" Sarah asked.

"What, the skull? No, no luck. Just this piece of junk."

"This might not be crap," Diane said.

"I said 'junk.'"

"You meant 'crap.' What are these letters?"

"I know." My fingers traced the monogram as she held the buckle and fabric, about the length of a butter knife, in her palm. "Small e, r, s. Then capital N, small u. And its light blue now but it used to be darker, I think. See there?" I looked at Diane. "There's a piece missing between the buckle and the stitching. It's from something bigger. But what?"

"I think it's a piece of crap too," Max said.

Diane's mind was suddenly somewhere else. "A belt." She handed the fabric back to me. "Have you showed it to anyone else?"

"Max. He was there when I caught it." I put it in the backpack. "Why?"

Diane's shoulders wilted. She looked down at her empty hands and said, "It reminds me of Jean, that's all. When she worked, she used to wear a belt looked something like that."

Sarah's lips tightened. Her voice rising, she said, "I'm sure that isn't hers."

"Oh, I know." Diane waved her off. "A lot of people had those belts. And trash is always showing up in Red Wolf."

I could see I had bummed her out by showing her the buckle. "Yeah, Sarah's right. Stuff is washing up on the shore all the time," I said, although that wasn't altogether true.

By the time the car approached Diane's house the catch in my throat was gone, replaced by the familiar pang I felt whenever it was time for her to leave. Max drove down the gravel driveway. At the end, a dirty, green, two-story saltbox sat alone, not a tree or shrub in sight. Diane opened the door and stood up, her mini skirt defying gravity as always. She never pulled down the hem.

Diane bent low to see us in the car. "I'm not sure if I should."

"Should what?" I asked.

"Come over and water-ski. We're back-seat buddies now. Coming over there would ruin my reputation."

Max and Sarah laughed, and then I did too. I hesitated only because I could never tell when she was kidding and when she was serious. To illustrate, I offer the "Rookie Story." Diane told me, some weeks later when she came to the Noquebay Tavern, that at the age of sixteen she had snuck into a bar on the arm of a highly-touted rookie for the Green Bay Packers and drank on his tab all night. Then, at closing time, she rejected his advances and had him call a taxi for a ride home to her aunt Fanny's place. As the story went, the jock was doing just fine until she found out he was a *fourth*-round draft pick, and *so* not up to her standards. Even for Diane, I thought the tale way too brazen to be believed, and I told her so. About six months later, I heard from two highly reliable sources that every word was true.

Max waited as she walked to the back door of the house. The words had yet to be invented to describe the sway of her ass. To look away would have caused me physical pain, swear to god. My mouth went dry as a dollar bill. She went in the door and something else caught my eye. "Hey, what's that big rig in the backyard?"

Then I saw Sarah slowly shaking her head.

She smiled. She was loyal, and kind, and she came by it with such ease. I wished I could be more like her. "You've got a crush on her."

I squeezed my lips into some kind of pinch. "No, see it." I pointed at the tubular pillar, projecting over the roofline. "Right there."

"Yeah, I know. Their well went dry. She told me. They're drilling a new one. Happening a lot around here. There's a drought, haven't you heard? Now, should I tell her you like her?"

I let go a lip fart. "Crush. Pleeease. She's got a boyfriend."

"You mean Rodney Allen? Nope. They broke up. Whole school knows."

"S'pose so, now that I've heard. As gossip goes, I'm at the bottom of the grapevine."

"Bottom a' what?" Max backed out of the driveway. "That's because you don't have many friends."

"Yeah, thanks for reminding me."

"You know she was putting you on." Sarah couldn't hide her grin.

"Me? Yeah, about half the time. About what?"

"The prom. Three boys asked her. One of them was Harry Appling."

I leaned forward. "Harry? Why didn't she go?"

Sarah shrugged and turned forward in her seat. "I don't know for sure, but I think it's because she couldn't afford the dress." She looked up. "Her aunt Fanny would have paid in a hot minute but..." A corner of Sarah's mouth creased. "Too embarrassed."

"Or too proud," I said.

CHAPTER THREE

One Man's Trash

Friday, May 10

Like random hits on a snare drum, dozens of locker doors opened and shut, signaling the end of another week at Red Wolf High. I shrugged on my jacket and in the same motion shook off the specter of my grades, which were looking like an end-of-term downer. I walked toward the front door and looked for two faces—Diane, of course, and Max Cherhasky, who was supposed to give me a ride home and spend the night. He had agreed to help us clean up and rebuild the garage that had caught on fire. We had almost made it through the winter without a major disaster and we would have had it not been for go ol' amateur wiring in the old garage. It shorted out in March and found a pile of oily rags. We were lucky to get the SUV out before the whole structure was engulfed. By the time the Walnut Creek Fire Department arrived, salvage was the only thing left to be done.

There was no sign of my friends. Max might be waiting by his car, so I went outside to take a look, but he wasn't there. I reached for the door handle to go back inside when a grimy hand with calloused knuckles thumped against the frame and stopped me.

"School's out, Robel. You're goin' the wrong way."

I smelled nicotine and got a pukey feeling in my stomach. The eerie presence of the Manticore mansion flashed in my mind. I let go the handle. "Yeah, Steve, I know. I'm looking for somebody." I grabbed the handle again and pulled.

Steven Manticore's key chain rattled as he slammed the door

shut. "What's the rush? I wanna ask you a question."

"Like what?"

He rubbed the day-old stubble on his chin. "Word has it, you found something in the lake."

My stomach tightened. Other than Max, I hadn't told anyone except Diane and Sarah about the cloth, because I didn't think it was a big deal. "A what? I don't think so." The next door over opened and I made a move. Steve slid with me, put up an arm-bar to block my way and said, "I think you did. A piece of crap from Finnegan's Hole?"

I tightened the grip on the strap of my backpack. "Even if I did, so what?"

His face moved closer to mine. "Shouldn't mess with stuff you don't understand. It don't mean nothin' to you, so hand it over"—he backhanded my shoulder—"and we're still friends."

There was a tap on my back.

"Come on, Sam. The buses are leaving. I wanna get ahead of them."

I turned, saw Max right behind me, gave Steve a tough-luck shrug, and started trotting.

"We'll talk again," Steve called.

Max and I raced to the car and got away just in time.

"What was that?" Max asked. "You and Steve friends now?"

"That horse's ass? Hell no." I got comfortable and opened my backpack. "He wanted this." I showed him the buckle and cloth. "Can't figure why he'd want it. He was acting like a Hells Angels wanna-be."

"Well, don't mess with Steve. He's spooky crazy in a fight. Rodney Allen told me he can bare hand crush a beer can, both ways."

"I'll start practicing. Hey, thanks for helping on the garage." I looked out the window as we left town. "Still can't believe the lodge didn't burn down at the same time as the garage. It's a tinder-box poster child if there ever was one. The only thing that saved it was a foot of snow on the roof."

My siblings, Joe, Kevin, and Allison, were on the bus, so they weren't home yet. Max parked under the twin pines in front of the bar next to a black Cadillac. As we walked by, the back window rolled down. An old man in the back seat drew me forward with a scratch of his finger.

"Who's that?" Max asked.

"Don't know." We both approached the car. The man leaned forward, a cane between his legs, oversized rings on several fingers, thinning hair greased back.

"Which one of you's the Robel kid?"

"That's me." I kept my distance.

"Do you know who I am?" His voice was both scratchy and sharp.

I shook my head. "No, sir."

"I'm Willard Manticore. You the one hooked the belt buckle got everyone talking?" The question blew me away. It was too much, Steve and now this guy. He snapped, "Well, are you?"

I had to think. I couldn't say one thing to his son and something else to him.

He opened the door and slowly, one foot at a time, swung out of the back seat, put his cane down, and came to a stand. For the first time I noticed a cigar in his mouth. "Come here, kid."

I stepped closer.

He leaned into me. "You deaf and dumb?" He stabbed me in the chest with two fingertips. "Parents not raise you right? I'm an adult. I asked you a question." The cigar shuffled to the corner of his mouth. "From the lake? With a buckle."

I was ready to either crap my pants or run like hell, but I did what came more naturally, I lied. "No, no I don't."

Willard grinned and looked around. His laugh sounded like he was gargling rocks. "It doesn't matter. With or without it, this little postage stamp of Red Wolf real estate will be mine soon enough." With that he slipped back into the seat, wheezing with each breath. "You best be getting on. Isn't that your mother calling?"

Max and I stepped away from the car, went inside the bar,

and barreled down the short hallway to the kitchen. My father was sitting at the head of the kitchen table, talking to someone I couldn't see, seated in another chair. Mom was there, too, on the far side of the table, a note pad in front of her, pen in hand, and facing the stranger. We were halfway down the hall when I held up my hand for Max to stop. The expression on my father's face put ice in my spine.

"Listen." Dad wedged the side of his hand on the tabletop. "Listen, Junior—"

"Call me Scott, please. Willard is my father, so I use my middle name, just to avoid confusion."

Another Manticore! He had to be the same Junior that Diane had mentioned, the guy that had married her sister, Jean. I heard a chair rumble the linoleum.

"And really, I have your interests in mind here," Scott, or Junior, or whatever his name was, said to my father. "Your reservations can't be looking very good, this being your first year. And we all know about the short tourist season up here. Hard to stretch three months of business into a year-round living."

Mom wrote something. Dad leaned forward. "And why should that worry you, Mr. Manticore?"

"Scott, please." More chair scuffing. "We want to buy your place, and are prepared to offer you more than you paid Tad Simpson last September."

"Noquebay isn't for sale."

"Everything is for sale, as they say."

Dad sat back. "We came up here to make a new life, and we're doing just that."

"With one million three hundred thousand you can make a good life right now."

"You make an awful lot of assumptions, Mr. Manticore," Mom said. "They may not all be correct." She put down the pen.

"Perhaps, ma'am. Perhaps." He paused. "Think on it and give me a call. Here's my card."

"Don't have to think. The answer is no." Dad stood up and extended a hand to shake. "Thanks for coming out."

The chair groaned the linoleum again. "I suggest you reconsider. We'll give you the weekend. But be advised, our next offer won't be so generous."

I could see the muscles flexing in my father's jaw. "Good bye, Mr. Manticore."

I turned quickly and pushed Max into the bathroom area behind us. We hid there as Dad and Junior walked by. When I heard the front door close, I stuck my head out to make sure they were gone.

I waved Max into the hall. "Can you believe that? The very same day!"

"What are you talking about?" Max asked.

"Manticores. Steve almost mugs me at school and now Junior and the old man pay a visit out here. What the hell?"

We walked toward the kitchen.

Max said, "Even though they're brothers, I doubt Junior and Steve are on the same page. Steve has always been the renegade of the family. And the old man treats him like dirt."

"After what I saw in the parking lot," I said. "Maybe he's a jerk to everyone."

Max shrugged. "You know the rumor, right?" I'm sure he could tell from my expression I didn't know what he meant. "About Steve. He doesn't look like his brothers, so the story is that the Old Man is not his old man."

"No shit." I thought on that for a moment. "Well, Junior doesn't know what he's talking about. We bought this place for 1.4 million, but we sunk more in on top of that."

I woke up in the early morning hours, as I always did, my sheets damp. The only sound was Max, snoring softly in the bunk above me. Quietly, I dressed in the dark and, flashlight in hand, headed out the back door.

I stood on the concrete slab and looked at the charred, half-melted, half-burned stack of crap lying before me, the remnant of the garage fire waiting to be hauled to the town dump.

Barely recognizable in the tangled mess was a black, tubular frame, and tires buried to the axles. Maybe I was still half asleep or dreaming, because I thought I saw my brother, James, fishing poles in hand, sitting on the bike as he had a hundred times, motioning me to come along to do some fishing down at Echo Park. Shaking away the cobwebs, I grabbed the bike's handlebars and yanked. I pulled again and again, the spokes hung up on some piece of junk, until sweat creased my palm. A final yank and the bike was free.

The chain sagged. The tires looked like tar. The handlebar grips were gone, replaced by a residue that blackened my palms. And the next guy to try the seat would be "corn-holed" for his trouble, as Dad would say. I carried the Schwinn to the laundromat, put the kickstand down, and took to the frame with a cloth dampened with gasoline. Moving four hours north hadn't erased the pain of losing my brother, perhaps something highly flammable would.

"Sam! Let's get moving. We got a garage to build."

Dad's voice. I froze.

"Sam, where the hell are you?" He was yelling in my bedroom window.

I stood, threw the rag on one of the washing machines, and set the bike against the laundromat wall. "Yeah, coming."

CHAPTER FOUR

Locker in Name Only

Friday, May 17

A week later I found myself sitting in the principal's office, staring at the nameplate on the desk that read "Gordon Nickels." I'd been called out of class for the first time, and I was so flummoxed I still can't recall the route I had taken to get to his office. Suddenly, he entered the room. I snapped to attention. The principal went behind his desk, dressed as always in a black suit and tie, shoes and hair to match. His face was pale always, almost a match for his shirt. "Err, Mr. Robel, when was the last time you went to your locker?"

"Right before gym class."

"Which is…?"

"Third period. I go right to physics because I don't have time after I take a shower."

"Hmm, yes." Leaning forward into his walk, Mr. Nickels waved. "Follow me."

The walk to my locker didn't take long, Red Wolf is a small high school, and Mr. Nickels intended to go all academic on my ass. "You're almost a senior, Mr. Robel. What plans have you made for the future?"

"None really."

A short silence, then he said, "Do you know what you class rank is?"

I had no idea where this was going, and not a clue as to the answer. "No."

"You are sixteenth out of seventy-three. That does *not* put you in the top twenty percent. What do you think of that?"

"Not very good, I guess." A flashback to Burlington, my old high school, smashed me in the skull—the black habit, Sister Mary Hugh, her voice in my ear, "James was an excellent student. So, what is wrong with you?" My scalp was on fire.

"You guess correctly. Your class was tested at the beginning of the year." We stopped walking. Eye to eye, he said, "You should be leading your class, not dogging it in the mid-teens."

The burn went down the back of my neck. "I'm not my brother and I don't want to be."

Mr. Nickels lowered his brow. "Your brother? Who are we talking about? Joe is a sophomore. And Kevin—"

I waved my hand and looked down. "I'm not talking about Joe… or Kevin." I took a breath. "I'm sorry, Mr. Nickels. I shouldn't have said that. Forget it."

"I can't very well forget it, especially the way you said it. You weren't kidding around." He clasped his hands behind him. "Which brother, Sam?"

Except for us, the hall was empty. I swallowed. "My older brother, James. He died last year."

"I'm sorry to hear that." He paused. "Do you want to tell me about it?"

I shook my head.

"Well, that's up to you, but I can tell you this. I'm not asking you to be James. I'm asking you to be Sam."

There was silence again. It felt like I was supposed to say something, but I couldn't. I wiped a tear on my sleeve.

"Are we clear on this, Mr. Robel?"

I shrugged. "Yeah, sure."

He held my gaze for a second longer, then said, "Let's go."

We turned the corner and entered the longest hallway in the building. Mr. Cook, from maintenance, met us there; my locker was right across from the band room. I looked at the floor. My stomach dropped.

"Err, how do you explain this, Mr. Robel?"

I stepped around my jacket, splayed open across the tile, and a couple of note books crumpled on top of themselves. An old pair of basketball shoes from last season had been hung over the open door, the strings tied in knots. The Aaron Rodgers poster on the inside of the door had a jagged slash down the middle. My backpack was where I left it, hanging on the middle hook. I grabbed it and looked inside. "I didn't do this."

"These lockers have combinations," Mr. Nickels said. "Who else has yours?"

"Just me and Max Cherhasky. He would never trash my stuff."

"Hmm. Who else?"

"He's the only one." I lied. "Someone broke in."

Mr. Cook looked at the door, and then at the locking mechanism. "No sign of damage. No pry marks. Not a forced entry."

Mr. Nickels nodded. "I think you're right. Give Sam a new combination." Then he looked at me. "So, who would want to vandalize your belongings?"

I shrugged. "I don't know. There wasn't any money in there. And I don't think anything is missing."

Mr. Cook handed me a piece of paper with three numbers written on it.

"Well, clean this up." Mr. Nickels started to walk away, then turned on a dime. "And don't give that combination to anyone."

Max started to come over more often to lend a hand at the resort. He said it was because he liked Mom's cooking. But in reality I thought his home, the Cherhasky Mansion, wasn't big enough to handle his stepmother, Nadine, and him for more than three days in a row. J.R. Cherhasky was home on weekends only. He spent the rest of the week working in Chicago, at what Max could only speculate. The Wild Ass Guess Club of Walnut Creek knew exactly what was going on in the Windy City, of course, though their truth changed as often as the menu at the Front Street Grill. Whatever he did, he did it well enough to take his wife on a week-long, Fifth Avenue shopping trip twice a year. When home, J.R. acted as referee between Max and Nadine; but who was to arbitrate the father-son matches? Certainly not Nadine.

When the day's work on the garage was done, Max had taken to giving me guitar lessons, even lending me one of his old acoustics. Having held an actual guitar, my rock 'n roll dreams were one tiny step closer to reality. Could we form a band? Maybe, just maybe. I'd get Max in there with me, then a drummer... James Jr. might have been president of the Glee Club, but he'd never gotten within sniffing distance of a rock 'n roll band.

We struck the last nail on the garage on the third Friday in May. In fact, Max and I were putting on the finishing touches— toe-nailing rafters and fitting plywood for an attic floor—when Tad Simpson, the former owner of the resort, walked in and shook Dad's hand.

"Thanks for coming over, Tad," Dad said, standing below us on the concrete.

Tad's face was so deeply tanned it was hard to see his expression in anything less than full sun. "Sure, what can I do for you?"

"Let's step outside." I don't think Dad wanted us to hear the conversation, but the empty garage was like an echo chamber. I nodded at Max. Our hammer hits became few and random. A bout of polio in the 1950s had left Tad with a tilting limp that seemed to creak when he walked. Slowly, they exited. Dad said, "We had a visit today, from Shoreline Zoning."

"Really?" Tad's rolling baritone flattened every other sound in the garage. "What the hell did they want?"

"That's what I wanted to know," said Dad. "It was a guy named Blain Zambrovitz."

Max and I rapped a couple nails.

"Said he'd received some complaints about our buildings being too close to the lake." I could hear the strain in Dad's voice. "He wouldn't tell me who complained. Anyway, I told him everything is covered in the title. We're up to code except the lodge and #10, and they've been grandfathered."

"There's something not right here," Tad said. "No one else been calling? The Department of Health hasn't been out?"

I hit a few more nails. We moved closer to the door.

"No, no one." There was a pause. Then Dad said, "Last week, Junior Manticore was out here, trying to buy the place from us."

"What!" Tad's voice rumbled. "Those bloodsuckers have been trying to buy this place for years. If I'd a been down to my last nickel I wouldn't have sold to them. They make an offer?"

"Well over a million."

"The Manticores know more about this place than you do. The old man, Willard Sr., he's the brains of the operation. Junior is a just a go-fer. Steve, he's even lower 'an that, poor bastard. And," I could see Tad waving a finger, "Senior is a director at the bank."

"He's what? Damn it." Dad sighed. "They hold our mortgage and a loan."

Tad spit on the ground. "Don't like the sound a that."

CHAPTER FIVE

Nadine Spoils the Sauce

Saturday Evening, May 18

The usual landscaping crew was back together. My brothers Joe and Kevin with shovels, Max had one too, and me with a rake; all of us laying waste to ten yards of black dirt. Joe squinted into the late afternoon sun. "Let's quit. I'm sick of this." He threw the extra shovels in his wheelbarrow and went toward the garage. The mound of top soil next to the elevated pool deck was only half the size it had been at the start of the afternoon.

Max looked at his phone. "Dad is coming to get me in a few minutes. I gotta clean up. We're going out to eat."

"Good enough for me," Kevin said. He dumped the last load of dirt at my feet. "Okay, 'Sir Rake-A-Lot,' it's all yours. I'm heading in."

I spread the last bit of topsoil then joined Max in the lake for a swim. Max and I had long talks that spring about taking over Red Wolf Lake, all 6200 acres of it. It would be our endless summer. The ice had gone out barely six weeks earlier but already we had hit several of the swimming holes on the twelve-mile-long lake. Max lived on the far, south side of the West End, about four miles from Noquebay as the boat goes. Finnegan's Hole, where I'd hooked the buckle, was in the middle of The Narrows, and right in front of our place. The Narrows was generally a cruise over area. Except for Max and me earlier in the month, no one stopped there. The spot was notoriously bad for fishing. As far as I was concerned, there was no reason to go back, either. Finnegan's had served its purpose.

To change clothes, we went to a rental unit tacked onto the back of the lodge that served as sleeping quarters for me and my siblings. By the time we got back to the kitchen Max's parents, J. Roman Cherhasky and his wife, Nadine, had arrived and were talking to Mom and Dad about staying for dinner.

Max's father was over six feet tall, handsome with a full head of hair going grey at the temples. J. Roman didn't look like he was dressed for dinner, more like he was ready to sail, open collar and deck shoes.

Nadine had an aura that glistened like the one-off pop star who'd landed on her feet. She was dressed to the nines in some cowboy casual kind of way but the only thing I remember from that day were green eyes and curled, red hair that bounced if she so much as blinked. Oh yes, and the wedding ring that made her hand look like the Fourth of July.

Nadine fidgeted with her watch, but J.R. was eager to stay for some reason.

Then, direct from Chicago's Little Italy, Grandma Robel appeared, wicker basket in hand carrying two loaves of bread and a pound of Parmesan cheese. Right behind, Kevin bearing the pot of sauce. *Oh, shit* I thought. Backassward timing if there was such a thing. I've never seen anyone walk away from Grandma's tomato sauce.

A horseshoe plopped in the mud of my stomach. The Cherhaskys, one of Walnut Creek's richest men and his scandalously young wife, the very glaze on the upper crust of Red Wolf society, were going to dine with us? Having Max over was easy; he fit right in.

But his parents?

I didn't like J. Roman because I didn't like the way he treated Max, or ignored him, that's more accurate. Nadine was dressed for a night on the town. They could come to the bar anytime they wanted, but not the kitchen. That was our space. With Roman and Nadine around I was as skittish as a rat in a coffee can.

The leaf was put in the table. Joe, Kevin, and Allison moved to a card table in the living room, and supper began. Roman and Nadine sat on one side of the table, Grandma, Max, and I on the other, Mom and Dad the bookends. The flatware was mix and match, so were the plates.

The salad made the rounds, then the bread and butter. Finally, everyone filled their plates with pasta and sauce, except Nadine, who stuck to the salad and a piece of bread.

Dad stood and got a beer for Nadine. J.R. asked for a glass of water. That shocked the hell out of me. The Imperial J. Roman, he of whatever money-making machine he operated in Chicago, I expected him to ask for some fancy-ass cocktail. Word in Walnut Creek was he had mob connections, but I didn't believe it. Dad headed to the tavern for the beer.

The usual platitudes and compliments were offered even before the first bite was taken. Mom offered a recipe to Nadine but she declined, which got me an elbow in the ribs and a snort from Max. The gathering was bigger than anything J. Roman was used to, and he liked the change.

"Nothing new to me." Nadine picked up a fork and stabbed her salad. "We had more kids 'n this when I was little." She sounded like she wanted to take a chainsaw to the family tree.

Then I remembered the story Diane told me: Nadine was rags to riches, starting out by Left Foot Lake in a tar paper shack without, as she said, a pot to piss in nor a window to throw it out of.

J. Roman put a steady hand on Nadine's forearm. "Well, Sam, the whole town is talking about you and that buckle you fished out of the lake."

Max leaned over his pasta, then he turned his head toward me. "When are you going to talk to Diane? About the locker."

"Yeah, yeah." I sat back. "School's out. I guess I could drive to her place and ask. Is she living at home?"

Then Joe piped up in his sing-song voice. "Why do you want to talk to her?"

Mom passed me the butter. "Tell us. I'd like to know too. Why is Walnut Creek talking?"

Startled, I put down the butter dish. "Nothing, just stuff."

Joe bit off his spaghetti. "No, it's not."

"Shut up," I said, narrowing my eyes.

"Sam." Dad's voice turned my head.

I looked back at Nadine and Mr. Cherhasky and said, "Sorry." I took a breath. "She might know something about the… someone broke into my locker at school. She might know who." Because of my poor manners, I felt like I should say some more. "I think it has something to do with the buckle and blue fabric I snagged out of Finnegan's in May."

The beer half gone, Nadine tilted her head toward her husband and said, "Finnegan's?"

"If she knows, you should tell Mr. Nickels," Dad said.

I took a drink of milk. "It's nothing I can tell him, nothing for sure."

"Does Diane know your combination?" Mom asked.

"Why does everyone ask me that?" I pleaded.

All eyes on me, the table was silent.

"Yeah, she knows." Allison giggled.

The worst part was out, so I decided to tell the story of the weathered piece of crap, including the fact that it was no longer in my possession.

"Wait. What?" To my surprise, it was Nadine who took the keenest interest, especially in the cloth. She took another drink of beer, then her eyes were on me. "You said the fabric was blue—"

"Washed out, kinda blue." I nodded.

"That's it?"

I asked. "What do you mean?"

"Like, was there any writing on it?"

"Yeah, letters, but they didn't make any sense." I went back to the butter.

"Letters? What letters?"

My grip tightened on the knife. "Ah, well, let's see. It was 'e-r-s' and then 'N-u.'"

Nadine's fork tumbled noisily to the floor. She made no move to pick it up, so her husband got it. All at once her eyes were wide, looking at me as if I'd spoken some long-forbidden code.

My knife was shaking so I put it down. "What?"

"It's just that, well, it sounds a lot like something my friend used to wear." She sat forward. "Did you dig it up? I hope it's not hers."

I croaked, "No."

"No what?" She blurted. "It could be Jeanie, it could be a break."

I looked at Max for a little help, but it looked like he had forgotten to swallow his food.

J. Roman moved his hand to hers. "Honey, settle down. Sam doesn't know what you're talking about." He looked at me. "Maybe you just misplaced it. Lost in your backpack, maybe?"

"Then you have to find it. It could be from Jean." Nadine looked sharply at her husband. "Jean Manticore. Before, when I was a waitress, we worked together. She was my best friend, until she married Junior."

The crust of bread in J. Roman's mouth must have been pretty rough, because it went down hard. "She was your friend? You never told me."

"What was the point?" she said softly through her teeth. "Disappeared from her job six years ago and no one ever saw her again. We thought she was running away from…" She took a deep breath, looked across the table at me. "Where did you find it?"

"Like I said, on the end of my line. We were fishing over Finnegan's Hole and I snagged it."

"Finnegan's? What's that? A place on the lake?" Nadine fisted her hands. "Oh crap! You don't think… That son-of-a—."

CHAPTER SIX

Tapper Mitch

Saturday Evening, May 18

"Nadine!" Roman said.

Nadine heaved a breath. "They have everything over there. If Big Daddy Manticore wants someone to disappear, they can do it. The farm, Junior's brother with the construction company—"

"Tapper would never!" J. Roman must have known how loud his voice was, because he stopped himself, swallowed, and then continued. "Mitchell Manticore runs Square M Construction; it's legitimate, well-run. It's a legitimate business. He would never have anything to do with whatever problems his brother might have on the farm."

"Who's Tapper?" I asked.

Roman took his napkin off his lap and dabbed the corner of his mouth. "Ignore that. I'm going back, way back to my high school days. Tapper was Mitchell's nickname."

"And Big Daddy, that's the old guy," I said.

Nadine nodded and sat back in her chair.

I asked, "Where did Jean work?"

"Carter's Nuts and Candies."

Mom put a hand to her mouth. "They, the employees, they wear blue belts."

"e-r-s N-u," Grandma said.

"Sam," said my father calmly. "Where is the buckle right now?"

"I don't know!" I put my elbows on the table and wedged my head between by hands. My temples throbbed. "Like I said, I think it was stolen… from my locker."

"Do you know who stole it?" Mom asked.

"I have zero proof." I looked at Dad, then Mom. "So, no, I don't."

"You must be kidding." Nadine hit the table with her fist. The flatware rattled. Grandma winced. Roman put his arm around Nadine's shoulders.

Mom looked at Dad and said, "Jim, this is too important for the dinner table. Why don't you take Sam and Max and the Cherhaskys in the bar for some privacy?"

Dad stood up. "Good idea."

Nadine stood slowly. "I'm so sorry. I ruined your dinner." She stepped away from the table. Roman rose with her. "I'm so sorry."

"It's quiet in the bar," Dad said. "Come on." He opened the door.

Nadine was in full retreat, Roman right behind. Max and I got up and followed. Nadine and Roman sat at the bar, Dad stood behind, serving beer to Roman and Nadine. He had ice water for Max and me.

"Won't you have something, Jim?" Roman asked. "I'm buying. Least I can do."

"Maybe later."

"Then let me start." Roman took a sip of beer and lowered his brow. "Jean was married to Junior Manticore, the middle son out at Manticore Farms."

"Yes," Dad said. "I've—met—him." I shot a look at Dad. After the meeting he had with Junior a week ago, I wanted him to say more. But Dad was never one to talk family business with outsiders.

"Your bad luck." Tears traced down Nadine's face. She used a napkin to wipe away the mascara, then took a long draw on the beer. "Jean told me a month before she disappeared, Junior was beating her. And he was, I saw the bruises. She was going to divorce him. He told her 'no way, no divorce.' But she had some dirt on him. If he didn't give her the divorce, she'd use it." She looked at her husband. "You've known Mitch since high school. You know what that family is like."

"Wow," I mouthed at Max. "Who is this Mitch dude?"

Roman looked sidelong at Nadine. "The oldest of the boys. Classmate of mine in high school, but I haven't spoken to him in… many years." Roman put his arms across his chest. "It was pretty quiet at the Manticore place until this—"

"What! Quiet?" Nadine turned on her husband. "Mitch did time for killing Nora Loomis!"

Roman closed his eyes. "Now wait a minute, honey. He was young. It was an accident."

Her thumb worried at the label on her bottle. "So what? She was just as dead. Runs in the family."

Dad leaned on the bar. "That Square M Construction that Mitchell runs must be a big outfit. I see the name on projects all over, big ones."

Nadine said, "It sure is. And it gets worse. The Manticore's bought off the sheriff. They never did squat about Jean's disappearance." She finished her beer and held up the empty bottle. "I'll have another."

"Those are rumors," Roman said. It seemed every time someone threw shade at the Manticores, Roman had a response.

A puff of air escaped her lips. "Only a silly-ass lumberjack would think it was anything but fact."

"Be that as it may," Roman said. "She's still missing. Most people around here think she ran off, because of Junior." There was a silence, then he said, "And you have *no* idea where the belt buckle is?"

I hadn't been looking at J.R., but I did then, just long enough to see the aggressive glint of accusation in his eye. What did he have against me all of a sudden?

Of course, I had every reason to think Steve Manticore had the buckle, but J.R. had a reputation for a nasty disposition, and I couldn't tell whose side he was on, so I wasn't going to volunteer anything.

Dad put a fresh beer in front of Nadine.

"Most people round here think she's dead." Nadine pointed the full bottle at me. "And now we've got a lead."

"But whoever has the buckle won't be in any mood to give it back to me," I said.

Max laughed, looked down and shook his head.

"What's so funny?" Roman asked.

"Not funny," Max said. "I just thought of Sam going up and saying 'Hey, buddy, here's a pack of cigarettes, now give me the belt, give it back.' He'd laugh his ass off."

I winked at Max, because we both knew it was Steve Manticore. And we didn't want that hot-head on our backs unless we were sure. But Max's message was clear. Not even my best friend thought I could pull it off. A fall-behind, half-baked, jackpine savage had outsmarted me.

"Figure out who's got it." Nadine shook the hair off her face and looked directly at me. "Then trick him, Sam; bribe him—"

"Come on, forget it," J. Roman said skeptically. "If he *says* they don't have the buckle, then they don't. Sam's not a private investigator."

"I know that. I'm not dumb." Glassy eyed, she looked at her husband. "You and I tried P.I.s and they weren't any good." Then she looked back at me, and suddenly, it felt like I was looking at someone much younger. "Summer school project. What do they call it now? Independent Study."

CHAPTER SEVEN

The Wild Bunch

Friday, May 24

The first Friday free of school was spent working toward the Memorial Day Weekend—vacuuming the pool, hand mowing the drainage ditches, and cleaning the bait tank. After supper, I was sent out to work the tavern.

I wiped the length of the bar and washed dirty glasses. Two quarters came out of the till. I dropped them into the jukebox. The ancient Wurlitzer was about fifty years old, but electronics were like dogs—in human years it was three-hundred. I wish I still had it now, it was and is collectible. So were a lot of the old records inside, if we'd have had the sleeves. Finnegan's skull would have looked great on top of it. The 45s were nothing current, obviously, but we had a few Nirvana, Green Day, and Beyoncé disks. Dad outlawed hip hop from the get go, which was fine with me.

After that, bartending was but a small step up from hauling trash. Most nights were deadly dull, and the chatter was all the same. I didn't have what it took to be a good bartender, still don't. I didn't care if others found me interesting, and rarely addressed strangers unless they spoke to me first. One of our regulars, A.J. McTibble, was in his usual spot on the end next to the dartboard. He of the Alfred Hitchcock profile would whistle whenever the bottle wasn't at his lips.

My grandmother's Wild Bunch were up for the week. The gang of five grannies came up every year to fish, play cards, and wreak havoc in the tavern like no other group short of the deer hunters in the fall. The Wild Bunch arrived in two Buicks. Gardie was wide of girth, the sergeant-at-arms for the games. Hilda was tall and thin, sharp of tongue, and enamored with her brandy. The bartender of the group was Carolyn, who drank very little for fear of losing too much money. Grandma was the card sharp and pragmatist, keeping track of the score and the day's schedule. And finally, Doris, everyone's favorite because she always seemed to come out behind at the end of every card session. They walked in the front door and took over the porch. Carolyn was sent in to get the beer so the Sheepshead could begin. The double-hung windows between bar and porch were open. Grandma stuck her head through and said to Carolyn, "Quit flirting with the bartender. He's too young for you. And bring the beer."

Carolyn took the tray of five beers. "Put it on our tab, you know, the Wild Bunch."

The bell hanging on the door rang. Phillip Vedder and Wes Van Zandt came in, the two as opposite as they could be. Phillip was short and spoke quietly. Wes was coarse as a corncob, wide as a silo, and had a voice to knock the hair off a Holstein. They had their usual stools near the open end of the bar: the first spot, still empty, belonged to Fanny, Wes's wife. I set up Pabst for both, looked at Wes and almost asked, since he was Diane's uncle, if he expected her to come by.

"Well, that's too bad." Phil swung a leg over the barstool. "The boat'll feel empty without Buck. Never could fish a lick, but he was always good for one of those cock-a-mamie stories of his."

Smelling of cheap aftershave and expensive booze, Wes grabbed a napkin and wiped a spot of sweat off his face. "Yeah, he's in La Crosse, baby christening or some such crap."

The phone rang and I picked it up. "I'll tell him," I said, and hung up. "Sorry, A.J. It was your wife. Time to fire up the lawn mower."

"Damn it to hell, that woman." A.J. tipped his hat to the bar and waddled out the door.

While my back was turned, someone said, "Hey, Sam, pack of Kools."

I turned. "Nic, how are you?" The rumpled shirt, swimming shorts and backward baseball cap look stayed all summer, even on cool days. So did the flip-flops and the goatee.

"Good, now that I'm here." He threw a ten on the bar and put an arm around Phil Vedder. "Hey Pops."

"Nic! How's it going son? Good trip up?"

"Traffic was terrible. What's new?"

"When does work start?" Wes asked.

"Few days. Hey, Wes, haven't seen you since Labor Day last year. How are you?"

"Better than a dry martini."

Nic slapped him on the back. "Good for you, man."

I put the pack and the change on the bar. "Anything else?"

Nic extended his hand to shake. "Three months' vacation. Short of that—matches?"

I pointed at the box on the bar.

He nodded upward, then turned back to Wes. "No college. This summer, what's the word? I'm mah-trick-u-latin' at the university of Chrysler-Ford. Got a branch right in town. Mechanic. That's what a 2.1 grade point gets you in Valparaiso, Indiana. Gotta take the boat out. Later." On the way out of the bar, Nic pointed at me. "Thanks again for helping last month with the pier. That was a bear. I owe you big time."

"Anytime, Nic," I said.

I heard Wes mention his wife. "Where is Fanny anyway?"

I had no more than asked when she and Diane Warren came through the front door. Was I ready for this? A solo conversation with Diane, about Steve and the buckle, no less? I didn't want to believe she was a turncoat, but Steve got my combination from someone.

"Speak 'a the devil," Wes growled. "Just talking about you."

"That explains the glassy eyes," said Fanny as she took her seat.

I walked around the bar, grabbed an empty stool, and set it so Diane could sit next to her Aunt Fanny. Like a proper bartender,

I stood in front of her, smiled, and asked, "What you drinking?"

Diane was wearing too much eye makeup, but she smelled good. The rest—the sandals, the light blouse, the shorts—Diane in her summer clothes. How could she have a tan already? She stretched her neck. "Beer, whatever you got, except PBR."

"Oh no you don't," Fanny said. Her clothes were altogether different; a loose-fitting, lightweight sweater and blue jeans. "Your mother will have my hide if she hears you're drinkin'. A Diet Sprite for Diane. The usual for me, Sam." Fanny tapped down a cigarette she didn't light and elbowed Wes. "Pay the bartender, and get us some Beer Nuts."

"What about me?" asked Wes. "I'm hungry too."

Fanny winked at me then looked sidelong at her husband. "Fry you some bluegills if you take me and Diane fishing tomorrow."

"Sorry, can't." Wes pointed at the man seated to his right. "Fishing with Phil every Memorial Day. You know that."

Fanny slid back on her bar stool and motioned toward her niece. "What about Diane and me? We have a situation. You boys understand, don't you?"

Diane leaned into her aunt's arm and said, "I'm sure they do."

Wes' voice was a chant through a foghorn. "Save it for Sunday, girls. Poor planning on your part does not constitute an emergency on mine." Wes took a sip of his beer then pointed it at me. "Hell, you don't need me. Have Sam do it."

Why hadn't I thought of that? Take Fanny and Diane Warren fishing. I should've been right there, life jackets shish-ka-bobbed on my arm, volunteering all over myself. "Yeah, sure."

Fanny's fingernails clicked on the bottle. "Can you run our motor?"

Wes answered for me. "Of course, he can."

"Sure, I can," I echoed.

"Just don't come nowhere's close to us," Wes said. "Fanny here is like a buffalo in a boat, like to scare the fish to the other side of the West End."

Fanny opened two packages of Beer Nuts. "Okay, tomorrow,

eight a.m. at my pier. Can't wait. You bring the worms and I'll bring the bottle fish."

"Bottle bass. She means beer," said Wes. "And no-you-won't. Sam's not of age. And Diane's only eighteen, not that that's ever stopped her."

I turned to Diane. "You should be able to drink. I mean, you've graduated now. The laws around here suck." *Talk about drinking*, I thought, *and she'll have to mention Steve.*

"Wait. What? Did you mention school!" Diane's face darkened. "Only a bookworm would be thinking about school the week after it ended. I worry about you. I really do."

"I was just saying—"

"I'm not thinking about that. First chance I get, I'm blowing this one-horse town." Diane said, her eyes diamond-hard. "No idea what or where, just know there's something better than jack-pine savages and Ethyl and potholes and raccoons in the trash. That's where my head is at."

"When? Where will you go?"

"When, where doesn't matter. It's money that matters, and as soon as I get a little extra in my pocket…" She tapped her head with the soda. "We'll see."

There was an all-too-familiar ache in the back of my head reminding me of the day James left. "Why move? You've got people here who like you. You can't leave. You're the only friend I got; you and Max, and I never know what the hell about him."

"You got your own peeps." The hard expression gone from her eyes, she put down the bottle. "Don't count on no one but yourself, that's what I learned."

That hit me harder than she knew. I had come to accept we'd never walk hand in hand in the moonlight, but she just said she couldn't rely on anyone, and that had to include me.

Then Carolyn was back, beer tray in hand, tapping the bar. "We need another round." *Again?* I thought. Another distraction. When it came to talking to girls, bartending sucked.

"You girls must be thirsty." I got five more beers and set them on a tray.

"Yes, and we're going to play some pool now. How do we get the balls out?"

"I'll show you." I took two quarters from the till and walked around to the table. In went the quarters; the balls barked and rolled into the tray. After racking them I said, "Okay, you're all set."

Carolyn carried the tray to the poolroom and set it on the seat of a chair. "All right, girls, come and get it."

Shaking my head, I walked back behind the bar and watched the Wild Bunch select their cue sticks. Gardie was so wide she could barely fit between table and Wurlitzer, so she shot from the other end of the table only.

I handed Diane another soda.

She swiveled on the barstool and took some nuts from Fanny's stash. She saw Fanny talking to Wes and Phil, so she pushed her soda aside, took a draw on Fanny's beer, and licked her lips.

"Keep that up and I'll lose my job." I coughed. "Diane, can I ask you—

Doris and Grandma shrieked, then they all did, every one of the old ladies, except Hilda. She pulled back on her pool cue and slammed the butt into the jukebox. A tray flipped. Beer bottles fell like tenpins. Carolyn, in a panic, tried to right the bottles. The needle screeched across the record—the *Joyride* was over for Roxette.

CHAPTER EIGHT

Diane and Jean

Friday Evening, May 24

I grabbed a towel and raced around the end of the bar, but it was too late. Beer bottles glugged. The jukebox skipped, the needle popping at forty-five rpms. The Wild Bunch scattered like flies. Who flipped the beer tray? Who slammed the record player? Mom rushed in and saw everyone, from Diane on down, turned on their bar stools, shrieking with laughter.

I knelt in a puddle of beer, patting the carpet with a towel.

"It's our fault," Grandma said. "We spilled the beer. We set it on the chair. Isn't that dumb?" Grandma chuckled. "Then Hilda took a shot at the record player."

Dad opened the jukebox, stopped the needle, and removed the damaged record.

Mom asked, "Is everyone all right?"

"Fine as frog's hair," answered Carolyn. "But I'm moving the Wild Bunch back to the porch. We do less damage there."

Ten minutes later, I was back at Diane's side, as breathless as ever.

Diane made no attempt to cover her smile. "Hot damn, Sam, you have got the coolest grandma in the world. And this gig is sweet, I want your job."

I squeezed dry the rag just used to clean the carpet. "Really?"

"So, you were saying?" Diane asked.

"Oh, right." I put down the rag. "It's about the buckle I showed you the other day." A noncommittal shrug from her.

"Did you tell anyone I had it?"

"I don't know. Have to think. What if I did?"

My belly tightened. "A week after I showed you, Steve Manticore stopped me outside school and wanted me to hand it over."

"Did you give it to him?" she asked.

"No. But a few days later someone broke in to my locker and trashed it."

"Your locker! Why didn't you tell me?"

"I've been meaning to, when I got the chance." Her high cheekbones blushed. "Besides, it was all over school. Were you skipping classes?"

"Meh." She shrugged. "Toward the end. You ought to try it some time, Mr. Straight."

"And guess what was the *only* thing missing from my locker?"

She looked at me, eyes wide, then looked at her drink. "Why would Steve take that piece of junk?"

"Why did you tell him?"

"He's a friend of mine. We were talking. I didn't think he'd bust into your locker."

Whatever expression was on my face, she obviously read it perfectly because she went on, "Just because you don't hang with him doesn't mean no one else does. What's it to you?"

"But I mean, come on, your sister. Steve's brother had something to do with why she's not here right now. Doesn't that ever come up?"

"Steve isn't close to either of his brothers, in age or any other way. They treat him like the hired help. Do does Big Daddy. He feels like he always has to prove himself."

"Whatever. And he didn't bust in. He had my combination. Any idea how he got *that*?"

"Wait. What are you…" Diane stopped, then put her hand to her forehead. "Oh, shit, the drinking game."

"When was that?"

"Campfire, maybe a month ago. We had a few beers. The guys asked the girls how many locker combinations they knew."

"And it was Steve's idea."

41

"That shithead," she said, knowing she'd been had.

Someone down the bar needed to be served. That took a few minutes, but this time, I didn't lose my line of thought. Diane came back from the restroom.

She chewed on some Beer Nuts. "Well, now we got to find out where that belt came from, or who."

"That's a switch. You didn't think it was much when I showed it to you."

"If Manticore wants it, there must be a reason. If it's my sister's, and she was dropped into two hundred feet of water, then someone's going to pay."

"But you said she's still alive, she's on the run."

"I don't know anything for sure, Sam." Her eyes turned cold, haunted. "But I can read the writing on the wall. If the Manticores are involved with the buckle, it's a bad sign."

"I don't know, Diane. How do we get the buckle back from Steve?" I leaned forward and lowered my voice. "Listen. The Manticores are already giving us the squeeze. The old man, Big Daddy, he was out here. Poked me in the chest and threatened to throw our family on the street. They got us for the septic system in the cabins. Dad said that could run us thousands of dollars." I turned my head, looked down the bar. "I ain't gonna fuck with them."

"Sounds like they're already fucking with you," she whispered. "Believe me, sitting on your hands won't stop them. Opening an old murder case against Junior…" She sat back. "That might put them off your ass for a while, maybe forever."

I ran a hand through my hair. "It might, it just might, if we can get the buckle, belt, whatever it is, and turn it in."

"Not knowing if your sister is dead, that sucks. You have no idea."

"Diane." I crumpled the empty nut wrappers and threw them away. "The year before we moved up here, my older brother died. I know exactly how that feels."

She straightened. "Holy Jesus, Sam. I'm sorry."

I reached for the chain under my shirt and tugged.

"What's that chain about?" she asked.

"Oh." I pulled my hand away. "Nothing."

"My sister wasn't nothing, I can tell you that. When I was born, she was twelve and lucky for me, because she about raised me. Ethyl was a biotch, still is. Wasn't for Jean, I don't know where I'd be."

Then Fanny elbowed her niece, the unlit cigarette still between her fingers. "Can I interrupt the beer, sex, and money talk for a minute? Look at this, honey." She grabbed an advertising section out of the local paper, spread it out on the bar, and showed it to Diane. "We can't go fishing. Setterman's is having a Memorial Day Sale. Time to buy some shoes."

"Sam, the beer coolers are running out," Dad said.

"See that? Sale extended to Tuesday."

My heart dropped like a bottle-cap down the chute.

Diane grabbed Fanny's arm. "Can I bring Gail Bender? She wears the same size. We share shoes all the time."

Memorial Day just went to piss in a pickle jar over a stupid shoe sale.

"Sam! The beer."

CHAPTER NINE

Till It's Gone

Saturday Afternoon, May 25

The sun was out. Mower in hand, I was trimming the twenty-or-so trees in front of the five sister-cabins. I had stopped to wipe sweat from my face when I heard Diane call my name. She had returned from her shopping trip an hour earlier, successful, she said, because Fanny bought her two pair of pumps that she promised to show me some time. But first, she wanted to share with me some pictures she brought from home. I was never able to deny her anything—which I think she knew—and followed her to #5, Van Zandt's cabin.

We went inside. Fanny and Wes were already gone to an early dinner date. She grabbed three high school annuals off the metal and Formica kitchen table and we sat on a couch in the front room. Before opening the annual, she put her hand on the cover and said:

"I want to show you who she was. So you'll see why I feel the way I do. If she's not out there, living on the road in some other life… I've dreamt all kinds of things for her in the last six years. But if she's at the bottom of Finnegan's…"

I nodded. I felt like I was being allowed a glimpse of a world that no longer existed, except in Diane's mind and the pictures she was about to show me. The books were thin, embossed with *RWHS* and dated ten years ago and more.

I pointed at the most recent. "Is that the year she graduated?"

Diane said it was and showed me her class picture. Jean was

pretty, small mouth like Diane with the pouty lips; but did not have the drop-dead gorgeous eyes of the girl sitting next to me.

"Was she in any clubs or band or anything?" I asked.

"Oh yeah." Diane pointed at a majorette shot with pride, Jean standing at the head of the marching bank. "Isn't she beautiful."

I pointed at the facing page. "There she is again." It was a group shot of Homecoming.

"She was Senior Class Representative. I was only, what, six or seven then? But she let me sit next to her in the parade. It was a convertible, and we sat on the back, waving at the crowd." Diane bit her lip. "The first time I got dressed up for anything."

"Is there a picture with you in it?" I wanted to see what she looked like ten years ago.

"Of us, in the car?" She turned the page. "Right here." It was one of the parade shots. Diane was small because her car was second in line.

"You were cute already." Then I looked closer. "But where did you get that hat? It's way too big." I laughed.

She smiled. "Jean stole it from her boyfriend. She worried I was cold. I never gave it back." I asked if she still had it. She shrugged. "At home somewhere."

"Don't lose it. That's going to be, whadda-ya-call-it? An heirloom, someday."

"Get out-a-here. Really?" She went on to tell me that later that afternoon she'd come down with a sore throat and a fever. Ethyl was gone for the weekend. The baby sitter called. She was sick too. "She missed the dance, Sam." Diane sniffled. "Even though I had already stayed at home by myself lots of times. Because of me, she stayed home to watch me."

"You were only seven," I said. "And you were sick."

Diane waved me off. "Jean said I could have been seventeen, she didn't care, she wasn't going to leave her little sister if she was sick."

We looked through the other annuals, Diane telling more stories as we went through the photos. Somehow, the more I heard of her, the more beautiful she became, and the more I wondered what it must have been like for Diane to lose her.

"I can see why you want her to be out there, even if it's no-where to you." I had her Senior Class picture in front of me. "Because then there's always a chance."

Her shoulders shimmied. "Imagine losing your only sister and your mother on the same day." Her fingertip tapped the picture. "That's what it felt like."

I was reminded of what Max had told me about his mother's disappearance. Max was only four years old when she died on a camping trip. She and J.R. had gone to the National Forest up north and on the first night a man-eating black bear attacked and dragged her off. A search party found traces of Madeline's blood but nothing else.

I was telling the story, but I didn't have to. Diane knew the details of the Cherhasky disappearance as well as I did. "Sounds like they didn't look very hard," I said.

She said, "It was springtime, the blood stopped at one of the rivers. They think she was lost in one of the rapids. Never found the body."

"And you believe that?" I asked.

"Yeah." Diane slid closer. "Now, as for the new Mrs. Cher-hasky, all she had to do was fall off her heels in front of J.R. He rescued the drunken damsel, took her home, and later that night it was heels up, if you know what I mean. Let the sexting begin."

"Okay, then tell me this. Why did she go nuclear on me the other night when I told her about the buckle?" Diane wondered how I got into a conversation with "Miss Clickbait of Stephenson County." I explained the dinner, and Nadine's claim of a close connection with Jean before she married Junior Manticore. Diane said it was all true.

CHAPTER TEN

Nadine Ups the Ante

The Week of June 3

Grandma's Wild Bunch packed the Buicks, the trunks closing with a thud, then five doors in quick succession. Instead of blowing horns they left with a wave. The Wild Bunch, after terrorizing the resort for almost a week, was on its way home. I was sorry to see Grandma Robel's cronies leave. In their wake, the pace slowed so much I wondered if summer was really here. Only four of the cabins were occupied, all of them with people interested in one thing—fishing. No one at the newly-opened pool, no skiers from whom I could mooch a ride.

It started to rain. Was the drought finally over? Wednesday came with the answer. The music of the falling rain stopped. But the gloom continued. It came in a letter from a Walnut Creek sewer contractor who said it would cost $66,500 to repair the septic between #10 and #11. A collective nausea oozed through the entire family.

On Friday I was to sleep over at Max's house. Until then, there was nothing but cutting grass, reviving the Schwinn, the radio, and me.

The towering, green and white, three-story Victorian rose abruptly from a base of dense evergreens like a peak in the mountains, the roof blotting away a large wedge of the starry sky. Dad parked in front of the garage. "You sure Max is home?"

I grabbed my duffel bag. "The light's on in the kitchen; Nadine's there. See ya." Dad said I had to be home next day at two p.m. to paint the garage. I shut the door and waved as the SUV rolled away.

Max skipped down the steps of the back porch and walked toward me, holding a basketball in one hand and slapping at mosquitoes with the other. The kitchen door opened again and out bolted a black and white, shorthaired mutt that weighed all of ten pounds but acted like a pit bull. Middie was her name, and she barked her fool head off until she got a sniff of my shoe. Then her tail wagged and she started to whine. I picked her up and got a doggy facial.

Max bounced the ball. "Hey, wanna play some hoops before we go in? Or you can mow our lawn if it'd make you feel more at home. We got headlights on *our* rider."

"Ha, ha," I grabbed the basketball. "Tonight's the night. I'm gonna beat your ass."

We played three games, then went inside, had a snack in the kitchen, and went upstairs to Max's room. When I asked about Roman and Nadine, Max said they were downstairs watching TV. I couldn't believe it: a house so huge there were two other people present, and I hadn't noticed.

Keeping the volume low, we listened to music for the rest of the night. Max played along to the songs on his Stratocaster, but didn't dare plug it in, not with Nadine around. He showed me some chords on the acoustic and in ten minutes had me playing "I Should Have Known Better," an easy song by the Beatles. I thought I heard the sound of Max's parents going to bed. Soon after, Mr. Cherhasky stuck his head in the door, told us not to stay up too late, and closed the door again. About an hour later we were both yawning. The lights went out.

———————

Morning sunlight framed the window shade. I rolled off the air mattress and sat on the floor. Max had the blankets pulled tight to his chin, snug as a baby kangaroo. Something at the base of the bed moved and up popped a jet-black head, ears at attention.

"Hello Middie," I whispered.

There was a picture of a toddler and a young woman on Max's nightstand I hadn't noticed before. It was black and white and a little faded, but in a frame. I turned it around. On the back was written *Madeline and Max, age 2.* I set it down.

I turned and sat, back against the wall. Max sat up and put his feet on the floor. I said, "You got a T-shirt? Forgot mine."

He threw a shirt at me. "Let's go eat."

Middie raced ahead as we descended the stairs. She stopped and waited at the bottom of the staircase, then ran ahead again, nails clicking on the hardwood floors. The kitchen was spotless, unused. We sat on stools at the large countertop that separated the kitchen from the dining room and ate out of oversize bowls with spoons big enough to serve ice cream.

In the far recesses of the living room, Roman Cherhasky appeared, his tall, thin frame looking good in blue jeans and a sweatshirt, his face glowing with a July tan arrived a month early. With a set of binoculars, he peered through a crack in the draperies for a minute or two. Window coverings carefully replaced, he came into the kitchen. "Morning, boys." The man whose name was always on the lips of half of the residents of Walnut Creek walked past Max and me and said: "Boys, remember keep those curtains closed, right."

It was not a request.

"Morning, Dad."

Roman got the paper from the backdoor stoop and said, "Sam, you recover that buckle?"

I was startled by the question. I swallowed my cereal before answering I had not.

"You're sure?" He wrinkled his brow, and the smile looked artificial. "Getting a lot of attention around town for something you don't have, aren't you?"

"Dad, he doesn't have it, so how would he know?" Max said.

Roman cleared his throat. "Right." He put the newspaper on the table in the breakfast nook and sat down. "Just asking. What did you do last night?"

Max shrugged, "Played records."

"Any I know?"

Middie barked and rushed to the back staircase. A sandaled foot appeared first, then her legs, then the hem of a knee-length terrycloth bathrobe. Max asked for the milk. I straightened in my chair and passed the sugar by mistake.

"Morning darlin.'" White robe checked at the waist with a knot, the lapels relaxed, Nadine walked behind Roman, wrapped her arms around his neck and gave him a hug.

"Hello," answered Roman. "Sleep well?"

"Like a log." Nadine drew a bead on me. "Oh, hello." She looked at Max. "I didn't know you were having a friend over."

"This is Sam, Nadine," Max groaned. "You met him before."

"I remember. You lost that piece of Jean's belt." Her eyes widened as she tightened the belt on her bathrobe. "But, he's going to get it back." She looked at me a second longer, then said, "I'm starving."

She moved from toaster to drawer, stretching for this, bending for that. I watched, and warned myself, too. *Remember where you are, numb nuts.* I wondered what she looked like before, when she was poor. But she was too far gone from that life. The rag doll wore hand-me-downs no more.

She walked to the table and said, "Have you found out where it is?"

"Don't bother," Roman said. "I already asked. He doesn't know."

Nadine got herself seated, put down her breakfast, and picked up a *People* magazine. She shifted as if to look more directly at her husband but spoke to me. "Have you talked to your girlfriend?"

Max elbowed my arm and smiled. "Well, it's a friend of Sam's who's a girl."

"Right, and yeah, I talked to her. But she didn't know."

Nadine bent forward. "Didn't know or wouldn't say?"

I swallowed hard. "Didn't know."

Nadine sat back. "Did you tell her to find out?"

"Uh, yeah."

Nadine casually dangled the sandal from one foot. "Good. You tell me when you know."

As we got up to leave, Roman lowered his paper and said, "You boys remember my rule—the shades stay down."

Then Max asked about the boat. We planned it that way, he and I. Catch the J. man at breakfast with Nadine in the room and make a play. The whole summer hung in the balance, and we needed the Cherhasky speed boat in the lake more than anything in the world.

Roman frowned and pinched the bridge of his nose. Max was pleading a lost cause and he knew it. The excitement drained from his voice, he scrambled for another angle. "We'll do all the work *and* buy the gas."

"That thing is a mess, and besides, duty calls." Roman otherwise acted as if he hadn't heard a word Max had said. "I'd love to if I could find the time, but this meeting today, can't dump it."

"Yeah, meetings." Max's eyes were cold and hard. "Just like basketball. You didn't come to a single game last year. Not one!" Middie scampered under the table. "It's always something: meetings, traveling, parties with Nadine." The sandal stopped flipping on her foot. She put down her coffee.

Nostrils flaring, Max said, "Find the time? Everybody always says how smart you are, but you can't find twenty minutes to put a boat in the water."

Roman's eyes came off the paper. "Watch your tongue, young man. Listen, I have a job. It keeps a roof over *your* head and clothes on *your* back, and I don't hear you complaining about the stereo or the vacations or the guitar. *My boss*, I might add, scheduled the tee time three months ago. It's not up to me to break it."

Max threw a towel against the wall. "It's always someone else. It's your boss, it's the customers, it's the fuckin' man in the moon. A few minutes to put it in. We'll clean it, we'll do everything, but no, you have your… golf."

The newspaper crumpled. "That's it. Take it somewhere else. Damn ingrate. Want to play basketball? Fine, knock yourself out, but it's your life, not mine. I've got business. You may not like it, I may not like it, but that's the way it is."

I was paralyzed. Middie cowered, waiting for Max to make the next move, and so was I, except I hadn't found any cover. There was a cough—short, soft, raspy—followed by a sharp breath in through the nostrils. It was Max. I looked at him. Tears traced slowly down his face.

Fingertips pinching his nose again, Roman closed his eyes.

The silence grew like a mushroom cloud. Against all I knew, or thought I knew about the three other people in the room, it was Nadine who broke the stalemate:

"Honey." She put her hand on his. "Have them clean it up. They're seventeen. They can do it alone. You can prep for Mandelli and his cronies this morning. If the boat is ready before your golf time, then maybe you can put it in."

Max's eyes were glowing. "Yeah, yeah! Like that. And Sam has to be home by two. I could take him in the boat. Then you and Nadine don't have to drive us. We can, Dad. Just like Nadine said."

Roman picked up his paper, shook it open, and started to read. There was a pause. Then he looked at Max and me. "Well, you better get moving."

We bolted up the steps.

CHAPTER ELEVEN

Endless Summer Stop

Saturday, June 8

Max and I were pumped. The day was perfect. We raced into the shade behind the garage, hooked up the trailer hitch to the John Deere, and pulled the weather-beaten boat to the driveway.

For two hours we pored over the boat. Bucket of soapy water at my feet, suds trailing down my arm, I scrubbed the hull and deck. Max jumped inside and vacuumed the interior. The storage bins were a mess, full of rusty cans, candy wrappers, and dead flies. Splats of bird droppings peppered the seats and deck.

I asked Max why his dad was so suspicious about the buckle.

"I don't know. He thinks you're milking the story for some reason. He's a naturally suspicious guy. Like with the curtains." Max turned on the vacuum. "The first thing we gotta do is find *The Paradox*, it's a speedboat." He'd spotted it through a telescope from the window of his bedroom last summer. On board, the bikini count was three every time. If the search took all summer, then so be it. Max asked about Diane, but I hadn't seen her since Memorial Day. The last Max had heard, she and Steve were dating.

"Really! Manticore?" I threw the sponge into the bucket. "You're shittin' me." Was that her way of "taking care" of Steve? To date him? I wanted to believe she was doing it for the cause, to get the inside dope on the belt, and hoped to God I wasn't wrong.

"You guys ready for inspection?" Apparently, prepping for the meeting had taken less time than expected, because J.R. had spent the last hour with his classic 1958 Corvette, caressing the blood red finish to within an inch of its life. He walked toward the boat in sandals, shorts, and a golf shirt, a broad smile slicing his deeply tanned face. The emotional blow-up at breakfast that morning apparently all but forgotten.

"The boat," I said, "is dope."

Roman hopped into the boat and sat in the captain's chair. "Let's take a look. If the boat passes muster, we'll put 'er in right after lunch."

———————

We walked into the kitchen, Roman in front, Max and me in tow. Middie yapped like she wanted someone's leg.

Nadine was at the counter, wearing a swimsuit and a sleeveless white beach jacket barely long enough to cover her bottom. "Don't touch a thing before you wash your hands. I don't want anything from that boat in my kitchen."

She spooned store-bought macaroni salad from a plastic container into a bowl and put it on the table. I joined Max at the sink.

We stood over the food: a plateful of boiled hotdogs stuffed in buns, quarter-sliced watermelon, and a bag of chips.

We sat down to eat, all except Nadine, who stood at the counter facing us, stabbing a fork into a bowl of mixed fruit.

Roman laid down the law. "In that boat today, you keep your distance. Gets crowded on the West End, just move to the Narrows or Horseshoe Bay. And if the Shore Patrol pinches you for a violation, it's your dime. Don't come begging."

Max's mouth was buried in a crescent of melon. "I know; we're cool."

Roman put up a finger. "When you're done, the pier…"

Someone knocked on the back door. Middie again, with her bark. "That dog is half bark, half suck-up, half chickenshit." With hooded eyes, Roman turned to Nadine. "You expecting someone?"

"Like who?"

"I don't know like who. One of your friends?"

Another, more insistent knock.

Roman rubbed his brow. "Well, go and see about it, will you?

And get that dog to shut up." His hand tapped the table. "Where was I? Now, the pier."

Nadine's befuddled voice echoed from the back hall. "Wait. What? Who are you?" The response through the screen door was a low rumble. Roman continued his conversation with us, but again, Nadine's voice interrupted. "Well, I guess... I have to, don't I? I mean, I can't say no."

Roman said, "What is it, Nadine?"

From my seat at the table, I saw the backdoor open. Nadine backpedaled. My stomach tightened. Two large silhouettes followed Nadine into the kitchen.

Sitting back to the door, Roman let his hands plop onto his lap and spoke to the ceiling. "Nadine, whoever it is, just tell them 'no,' it's a Saturday, and if it's a salesman, tell him not to come back."

"We know what day it is, Mr. Cherhasky, and we're not selling anything." The deep monotone immediately drew everyone's attention. There was a black hole in the hallway, two dark figures, sunlight streaming in from behind. They entered the kitchen, both of them in white shirts, sunglasses, black ties, and expressions of stone. One wore a dark blazer; the coatless man a holstered gun. I tried to swallow the rock in my throat and looked away from the gun, as if to make it disappear.

The men scanned the kitchen for a moment. I shuffled my feet and accidentally kicked Middie, hiding already, as silent as a gerbil. Max was as stunned as I was. Nadine retreated into a corner, her expression like Halloween, a wax figure melting into the stove.

Steel in his jaw, Roman sprang to his feet. "Who the hell do you think you are? Get out of my house." His voice made me flinch, but not the men. "Nadine, call the sheriff."

"I don't think you want to do that." Crescents of sweat darkened the shirt of the coatless man as he took a position behind Nadine. The man in the blazer stepped forward.

It looked professional: line of sight, military posture. Sunglasses in the house? The Mob, it had to be the Mob. Walnut Creek had been whispering about it for years. Roman paid for the house, the cars, everything, with extortion and big-city money and then screwed the wrong guys once too often.

Yes, Nadine, the phone! Now they had come to settle the score. *Nadine! For chrissakes, the sheriff!*

"Free advice, Mr. Cherhasky," said the coated man. "We have the sheriff not a quarter-mile from where you stand. Be here in twenty seconds. You want that kind of attention in your backyard, just say the word." He reached inside his coat pocket.

Nadine gasped. Roman put up his palms and took half a step back.

"I am Special Agent Bauer; this is my partner, Agent Randall Shepard. F.B.I." Both opened I.D. wallets. "Jeremiah Roman Cherhasky, I presume."

Roman's eyes dropped to the floor. A moment later, face twisted, he rallied. "And that gives you the right to barge in to my house and scare my family half to death on a Saturday afternoon?"

Bauer ignored the question. "Mr. Cherhasky, the sheriff, yes or no?"

Roman slipped one hand into a back pocket and rubbed his face with the other. "No. No sheriff."

"Hands in front of you, sir, where I can see them." Bauer paused until Roman complied. "Very well. J. Roman Cherhasky, we have a warrant for your arrest." A tri-folded court order slid across the table. "The charge is grand larceny and interstate trafficking of stolen goods. The warrant includes a search of the premises. Agent Shepard will read you your rights."

Max's eyes were wet. He stood abruptly. "What? Interstate what? No... Dad?"

Shepard's voice snapped, "Sit down. Son... Sit!" Slowly, Max did as he was told. The agent went on. "You have the right to remain silent..."

"Roman, tell them, it's not you," sobbed Nadine. "It was all Mandelli, the oily bastard. He's the one you want. Tell them, they *made* you..."

Roman's head snapped toward his wife. "Nadine, shut up!" She shuddered and almost fell off her heels. She grabbed the sink to right herself. For the first time, I felt sorry for her. Roman's face colored from pink to blue. "Shut up! I have to think."

The seconds dragged into minutes. I remember hearing "felony" and "nineteen counts" and not much more. Bauer extracted a pair of handcuffs from a belt clip. My hands went cold. Max's were shaking.

Roman recoiled. "I'm not resisting. You don't need those. Not in front of my family, not in front of my son. Nadine, take the boys outside."

"Everyone stays put until our search is complete," Bauer said. "Get comfortable, it's going to be a while."

"Why?" Roman cried. "They're not suspects." Before he even finished the sentence, the cuffs were on. The metallic click stung like a needle in my ear.

Nadine hid behind a handful of paper towels, dabbing her eyes.

Roman spoke to his wife, but looked the other way. "That's enough. Stop your crying, for chrissakes. After I leave, call Sid Benemente at home; tell him what's going on. He'll know what to do." Finally, he looked at her. "That's it: Don't do anything else. Don't call your friends, don't use the phones. Period."

"You'll get one call after we book you," Bauer replied.

Two more agents arrived. The search started in the kitchen and took half the afternoon. Doors and drawers opened and closed in every room of the house, including the attic. Then they went through the garage. Max, Nadine, and I were detained in the dining room. We sat so long I thought my bladder would burst. Agent Shepard stood a few feet from Roman, who was in the kitchen, hands cuffed. For the first time, I saw Roman sweat. The other agents worked steadily. Several times they walked past, accordion files in hand. By the time they finished, the watermelon was wilted and the hot dogs wrinkled.

Roman was escorted down the back steps, past the gleaming boat and the red Corvette, toward a black sedan. From the back porch, Nadine, Max and I looked on in stunned silence. Roman Cherhasky folded into the back seat and disappeared down the long, winding driveway.

CHAPTER TWELVE

The Road to Cool

Friday, June 14

By the second week in June, the drought had done a number on the grass. Some weeks we didn't get the lawn tractor out at all. Sure, the shoreline was still green, but that was easily handled with the hand mowers by Kevin, me, and especially Joe, who always showed a special fondness for anything with an engine. Max hadn't been around since the arrest a week ago, so I wasted my time on the Schwinn, rubbing that charred frame back to life. I had an attraction to lost causes, but I'd avoided Diane, so gave myself credit for that much. Like the bike, she had her flaws, but she wasn't a two-wheeler, she was a Harley-Davidson, and god help the guy that tried to retune that girl. I didn't dream of texting her to tease out the business about Steve. I shared the cell with my brothers, and if she sent back an outrageous response and Joe or Kevin saw it, I'd lose phone privileges for a month. I texted Max every day, but never got a reply.

Mower in hand, I was on my way to the peninsula when I saw a car parked in front of the bar that stopped me cold. Dad came down the front steps. He obviously recognized the driver, and when I got closer, so did I. The car door opened and Willard Scott Manticore, Jr. stepped out. The window on the back door went down two inches. Again, in the back seat, Big Daddy. He didn't move.

"Hello, Junior," Dad said.

"Call me Scott." There was an envelope under his left arm.

He extended his right hand.

Dad shook. "Right, Scott. Didn't expect to see you out here again." I was looking over my father's shoulder and could see both the old man and his son.

Scott looked down and grinned. "Not at all, Mr. Robel. Business is business, as they say." He turned and glanced at the Mobile Home Park. "How's the trailer park coming along?"

"Mobile homes. Just fine. You interested in leasing a spot?"

Scott chuckled. "No. We have lake property right down the way, toward Back Bay."

A low grumble came from the back seat. It sounded like, "Get on with it."

Scott Jr. reacted like someone jabbed him in the kidney. "Right. I understand ah… circumstances have changed out here, at the resort since my last visit." He squinted at Dad, though the sun wasn't shining.

"Our cabins are full. That's changed."

Scott tipped his head. "Ah yes, well good. But no, I was referring to an unfortunate dust-up with Shoreline Zoning. Word on the street is that cost of repair is going to be considerable."

"That's confidential, and none of your business."

"As I said, Mr. Robel, we've had an interest in this property for a long time. If it's too much of a headache, we can be the aspirin, if you will."

Scott put the envelope in hand. "Now, with a major septic upgrade needed, we certainly can't match our original offer. It wouldn't be smart business. But 1 million, that's our new offer, and it's generous, considering. You need the revenue from the trailer park to make a go, but the park can't be finished because of this *new* expense you're facing." He shook his head. "Bad luck. Look around you. Resorts are going belly up all over Red Wolf. You don't want to be the last resort on the lake." Scott extended the envelop. "Here's the offer."

"Listen," Dad said, the back of his neck coloring. "I don't care what's going on anywhere else. And I don't need you to tell me my business."

The back window went completely open. "That's where you're wrong, Robel." A cane between his knees, hands propped on the handle, a surprisingly dark, waxy face leaned forward from the headrest of the back seat. "Willard Manticore, of Manticore Farms." He nodded and tapped his forehead with his cane.

I was glad for Dad between me and that old man.

"Forgive my manners, but my legs don't serve me as well as they used to. I'm a trustee at the bank." Willard coughed, or wheezed. "It's my job to keep an eye on the health of our loans. You are in violation of your mortgage agreement. It is my duty to bring it up to the board, which I will do at the next meeting." He tapped his cane on the door sill. "Junior, get in."

Willard coughed into a handkerchief. "Most people don't read the fine print on a mortgage before they sign it. I suggest you take a look at yours. One million." He sat back. "Go."

Dad watched the Cadillac drive away. "Sonofabitch," he growled. Then he glanced at me. "Better get going."

I moved on toward the peninsula.

When the trimming there was done, I pushed the mower aside and walked the gravel trail to the tip of the narrow strip of land. I sat on a shelf of grass and looked at the island a quarter-mile away. This was a trap, this spot where I sat, and I walked right in. It was too easy here, to be alone. Seconds later, I was gazing down at the pebbles in the water, and somehow, I saw the face of James, waiting in the car to drive us to the American Legion baseball game, as I'd done for so many games. I knew all the guys, most of them five years older than me, on a first-name basis. They came to calling me 'Tag,' because that's what I was, to my brother, and I loved it.

I bought in to the Noquebay escape because I thought I would get away from these visions, but I was wrong. In my mind, on a remote shore they are relentless, the visions cling and claw and rearrange themselves into patterns of stone and, once again, James was calling me.

―――――

I was taking the mower back to the garage when I heard Dad's voice calling me up to the pool. He threw chlorine in the water and rinsed the pale. "Peninsula done?" I said it was. "That's good." Dad wrapped up the hose and put it in the pool house. "Now, what's this Joe is telling me about bar time last weekend?"

I felt my forehead fold like an accordion. "What about it?"

"Don't give me that. Yes or no, did you set the bar clock ahead to get off your shift half an hour early?"

All the air in my chest was gone. Of course, I'd done it, and it worked. Except I forgot the final step—reset the clock.

I looked away. "Yeah, I did."

"When are you going to grow up? You're the oldest and still you pull these schoolboy pranks on your brothers. I thought you wanted to move here, maybe you didn't, but this place is our livelihood now, and it's too much for your mother and me. We want your help—we need your help—or the whole thing won't be worth a fiddler's fuck on a Friday night. And one other thing, you weren't the only one lost a brother. Joe, Kevin and Allison did too. They feel the loss as much as anyone. Their life is tough enough right now. You, of all people, ought to know that."

Head down, digging the toe of my tennis shoe into the concrete, my eyes burned. Somehow, the chain around my neck was suddenly ten times its normal weight. I looked up at Dad, and nodded.

Dad's shoulders lost their edge. The creases in his face mellowed. His voice was softer, too. Its tone matter of fact. "Pull that crap again and you'll be grounded, no boats, no cars, no phone. Now, go paint the garage, the side facing the lodge. Come get me when you're done."

I was never so glad to see the sun start its descent. Had we lived in the land of the midnight sun, Dad would have had me working until the cock crowed. I finished painting in time for supper.

Grime and sweat streaking my face and shirt, shoulders aching, I took a swim in the lake. The wind had died and the water settled with it. It wasn't my turn to work in the bar with Dad, so I shot some pool with Kevin and Joe and played pinball until it was time to start the fire in the pit out front of the lodge.

Nightly campfires, tended by my brothers and me, started in June and became a nightly ritual. Because parents rarely stopped, they attracted kids like mosquitoes to a yard light. I sat on one of the two picnic tables, surrounded by cabin kids, stuffing their faces full of chips and popcorn. Kevin and friends sat on the other table setting up tomorrow's walk in the woods. Allison and a couple of her friends sacrificed marshmallows in the fire and worried over the boy-band rumors. To my immediate right were Joe and Harry Cashen, who argued outboard motors—was Honda or Mercury the best?

I shook my head. I was starting to get the *monkey island* feeling, and I was the zookeeper.

"Hey, dweebo!"

I straightened.

"Ha! He looked." Max's grin was as fresh as the day we cleaned the boat. "That your new name?"

"How'd you get here?" I asked.

"Crazy Nic Vetter. He just drives up to the pier 'cuz he sees me in the yard. Says come on, let's ski. So, we did, all afternoon. We even put our boat in the water. Where were ya?"

I spread my hands like a king. "Here all day, with the share-croppers." I got up and gave him a hug. "So how is it, you know, at home?"

He had not been living the life of a hermit for the past week, as I thought. Walnut Creek was an easy walk from his home. Nadine and Roman were so distracted by legal hassles they barely noticed the nights Max stayed out late, usually to party with friends.

"What!" I pulled him away from the fire. "You went to a party? Man, I am so far out in the sticks. Where was it? Who was there? What did you do? And why didn't you answer my texts?"

"Dad confiscated my phone. He thinks the F.B.I. has all of us under surveillance. Anyway, Steve Manticore works part-time for his brothers. He has the key to one of their empty pole build-ings behind the grocery store. We give him the money. He buys the stuff."

"Drinks?" We walked farther from the fire. "Drink what?"

"Shhh! Tell the world, for chrissakes."

I lowered the volume, but the tone was the same. "Beer? Wine? What?"

"Yeah."

"Yeah?"

"Yeah."

"Yeah what?"

"Both of 'em."

"Jesus." I picked up a stone and threw it in the lake. I won-dered if Diane had been there, but didn't know how to ask.

"What did you say?" Max asked.

"Nothing."

Of course, Diane had been there, and the life of the party for sure. "And you never invited me, dipshit."

"What invited? You don't send out invitations to a beer party in a pole building. Text sure, but not to your phone and we both know why. It just happens, man. I walk into town and see who's hangin' out."

I looked toward Max. "Manticore buys the stuff?"

"Yeah. Got this new Mustang he's gonna tune bumper to bumper."

What was Max doing, hanging out with a hard-guy like Steve?

A deerfly buzzed. I waved it away. "Are Steve and Diane still dating?"

"Sticks has her hooks in him." Max kicked a stone on the shore-line. "Why do chicks go for this guy? Mr. Dark and Disturbed."

"Wait. Who's this *Sticks* chick?"

"Your backseat buddy. Everybody calls her Sticks."

I was too embarrassed to ask how she had earned yet anoth-er nickname. I'd always known that life traveled fast in Diane's world. And she was still dating the enemy.

"There's a couple," Max said. "Hacked at each other one

minute, lovey dovey the next. I thought she'd ghost him for sure, but they're still together."

"Hey, there's something else I got to tell you." I walked toward the parking lot, picked up the basketball, and tossed it to Max. "Old man Manticore, the one at the farm, he made another offer."

Max dribbled the ball slow and hard. "Big Daddy was back? When? Did he offer more?"

"Fuck no. Less. Three hundred thousand less. Few hours ago."

"And you said there was no mafia around here."

"I said your dad wasn't mafia. I don't put anything past the Manticores." Max took a shot, I got the rebound. "Diane has this theory. We get the belt back and give it to the sheriff. That will reopen the missing person case on her sister and put Junior, you know, in trouble again." I threw the ball to Max.

He nodded and shot. "But you don't even have the belt, Steve does."

"Diane is my connection. She's got reasons, I got reasons. We're a good team. I think she's going with Manticore to find out where the belt is."

"Really. You finally found enough confidence to actually talk to her by yourself."

"Who me? Come on."

"Yeah, you. You turn into an eighth grader with a capital 8 whenever she's around."

The asphalt crackled behind us. A yellow Ford Mustang, nose to the ground, a pair of black stripes wrapped around its tail, growled to a stop. I jumped back. Steve emerged and stretched, trying to turn his Johnny Depp frame into Captain America. The expression on his face matched the scowl on the front of his car, the sort of look that could get you arrested, the kind that girls seemed to love. We said hi. Steve was too busy for even a nod. The stay pins on the front of the hood—put there, supposedly, to keep it from flying off whenever the car exceeded the speed of sound—were not sitting right. He fussed until they were perfect, the muscles in his forearms flexing; the skull tattoo on his bicep clamped down on the long-stemmed rose between its teeth.

I rested my thigh on the fender and watched the riveting performance, wondering if the smell was Steve's aftershave or transmission fluid. "So, what are you doing here?"

Steve's eyes burned a hole in my cut-offs. "Hey, four-eyes, like to pay for a new paint job?"

I backed my leg away from the fender. I thought to say, "Go to hell," but I wasn't stupid. Manticore was one scary cat.

Steve wiped bug marks off the headlights. "What you two pencil-necks up to tonight?"

Max and I shrugged. Steve chuckled through his teeth. "Figures. I'm gonna hang out down by the Van Zandt pad. You in?"

"The Van Zandts in #5?" I asked. "You know them?"

"Yeah, Einstein, there any others?" Steve knocked a Marlboro out of the pack, and then rolled it back up the sleeve of his T-shirt. "Sticks is Fanny's niece."

"Yes, I know, and…" must have been written on my face because Steve added: "She's down there. Wes and Fanny are gone. We got the cabin."

My stomach flipped. Max answered for both of us:

"Cool. We'll be there. Thanks."

The cigarette twitched in Steve's lips as he spoke. "Don't thank me. Sticks put me up to it."

Chapter Thirteen
Sticks, Jim Beam, and the F.F.A.

Friday, June 14

Steve Manticore slipped back in the Mustang. The engine sprang to life; the chassis shook. The fading sunset flashed in the Mag wheels as he headed down the gravel road to #5.

Back in my room, Max borrowed a shirt, I changed, and we were off. Ten minutes later, faces aglow like the first day of second grade, we walked into the Van Zandt cabin.

Like its four sisters, #5 was a rectangular log cabin fronted by an enclosed, white porch. Inside, Fanny and Wes had done some remodeling, but not much. The walls were paneled and painted in a cream color, except the kitchen, which was frost green.

The door creaked shut behind me and a wave of acid erupted in my throat. I coughed a couple times and pounded my chest with my fist.

"Got a problem, Robel?" Steve asked.

"No, fine." I looked away from the sight that had gagged me—Steve and Diane sitting together on the couch, both of them well into their first beer.

"*All you need is beer*. Isn't that how the song goes?" Diane wore a red tube top under a button blouse. Her clothes were never quite the right size and no one ever complained. With the red lips, top, and fingernails, she sparkled like a ruby.

Diane set her cigarette in an ashtray. "Beer's in the sink. Self-serve." She had an arm around Steve, a sight so nauseating I wasn't sure I could swallow anything, but after that entrance, I needed something.

Max and I hesitated. She must have seen the wonder in our eyes because she said, "Loosen up. Wes and Fanny are gone, bar-hopping Red Wolf in the boat. And it's a big lake, so they won't be back for a *long* time."

A small boombox played country and western because that's all Steve listened to. Diane slapped a Pabst in my hand and sat at the kitchen table next to Steve. I took a chair across from her and next to Max. Bottle tipped high, I forced the bitter liquid down my gullet.

Steve shook his head. "Well, I'll be damned, knock the dust off another virgin."

Diane got up. "Maybe it's not your brand." She opened Fanny's refrigerator, and suggested, "Here, try a Hamm's. From the land of sky-blue waters. Wes loves 'em, but you gotta eat a candy bar with it to kill the sour. Or Coors."

Steve sneered, "Yeah, Sticks, give him one of those."

There it was, that name again. I didn't like it, and not just because I didn't know what it meant. It wasn't good enough, and neither were any of her former nicknames—DiDi and Jaz—the first one came and went before I knew her.

"Well, I tried." Diane closed the refrigerator door and nodded at Steve. "Ignore him." She stood next to the table. "Don't worry about it. Everybody has their own pace."

When finally I finished the first one, she asked if she could get me another?

"Yeah, I'll get my own." I pulled an iced Pabst from the kitchen sink and removed the cap with a church key. On the sly, I dumped a couple of swallows down the drain before joining the other three. My way of "catching up."

Back at the table, Diane was sideways to Steve and leaning away. "Yeah, and what about Debbie Piccolo?" she asked.

I looked at Max and pointed my beer at Diane. He shrugged.

"That wasn't nothin.' She came in for a tire rotation," Steve said. "That's what I do." He had a part-time job at the Ford garage just to get a discount on parts for his car. Why a son from the well-heeled Manticore family would need the money was beyond me, but it did go along with something else Diane had told me. Steve always got the leftovers from Big Daddy Manticore, as if there was a dog house out at the farm, and Steve its permanent resident.

"Really. And for that you talked to that skank for half an hour. I'll bet she was impressed. And all she wanted was an oil change." And Diane didn't mean 10W40.

This was starting to be fun. Halfway through my second Pabst I announced, "Gotta pee." As I rose the chair tipped and hit the floor with a thunk.

Diane giggled. "Jeeasus Sam, take it easy."

When I bent over to pick up the chair, my head rushed. "Be right back."

"Thanks for the warning," answered Steve.

Max and Diane laughed.

I rolled my eyes and looked at Steve. *Greaser.*

When I returned, Diane had the guys singing "5-1-5-0 someone call the po po" and passing a bottle of Jim Beam sour mash. Eyes glued to the yellow label, I watched as it made its way around the table, and tried to be optimistic. *If beer isn't my thing,* I thought, *maybe whiskey?*

Max took a swig. The bottle came down; his eyes snapped open. "Yeah, that's… awful!"

Oh, shit. If Max couldn't handle it, I had no chance. He set the bottle in front of me. I grabbed it by the neck and read the label.

"Hey, Baby Jane," sneered Steve. "That's how you hold your sodie pop."

Diane pointed her chin at me. "Steve thinks you're a wuss if you hold the bottle like that. Hold it down by the label."

Steve waved at the Jim Beam and me. "Either drink whiskey or pass it over."

I took a sip, a small one and glad of it. Another ounce and my ass would have melted to the chair. The bottle dropped away from my mouth. Air billowed from my lips, like I was vomiting air. "Huuuh!" Everyone laughed, even Steve. I blinked. Small as it was, I had my first laugh of the night.

I passed the bottle to Diane and noticed her eyes were the same color as the whiskey. I wondered out loud how they would know of Wes and Fanny's return.

"The searchlight mounted on the boat," Steve said. "We'll see 'em coming."

I walked to the front door. "I better look." The front door swung open and I went with it, my grip on the doorknob the only thing between me and a gravel sandwich.

"Whoa!" blurted Max. "Way ta move, Grace."

"You see that?" I looked down. "That sill jumped up and tripped me."

"It's not a sill, dip shit." Steve put out a cigarette. "A sill is on a window. That's a mantle."

"No, it's not," countered Diane. "It's a threshold."

"And how would you know? They cover that in *Cosmo*?" Steve rolled his eyes, struck a match on the side of his shoe, and lit a cigarette. "You take shop class, wood working, basic carpentry? Ask Mr. Biggins. I teach the class more 'n he does. Sticks, that smart mouth of yours ain't so smart now." This time he had her.

Diane didn't take the bait. A smile tickled the corners of her mouth. "Don't spend half the day shining doorknobs. Oh, and I forgot. You're F.F.A. It's all about the cows, man. What's that motto? 'Where men are men and the sheep are nervous.'"

Diane caught Max with a mouthful of beer on that one. He slammed his palm on the table. Pabst spewed all over the dining set. I laughed more at Max's red face than Diane's line. The fun came to a screeching halt when we noticed Diane and Steve, locked in a till-death-do-us-part stare down. Light ran from the room. Max and I were silent, our backs straight against the chairs. Steve clenched his fists; Diane didn't flinch. The stalemate continued until I said:

"When I get married, I'm going to carry my bride over the *mantle*."

Diane blurted a vicious laugh. The angry expression on

Steve's face exploded into a puzzle of surprised bits and fractured rage. My wise-ass tongue had finally gotten ahead of good sense, and it took all of two beers and a swig of Jim Beam to get me there.

Manticore's nostrils flared. "Didn't I tell you to keep your nose out of my business?"

I couldn't remember him telling me anything, but it didn't matter.

Steve stood up and knocked his chair over. "Come on, you little asshole. Right now."

"Forget it, Steve," Max said.

Steve kept coming. Diane got up behind him. I felt beer and booze rise in my gullet. This whole "hanging out" thing was supposed to be dope, cool, but if I got into a brawl in one of our cabins, with paying customers in #4 not twenty feet away, I'd be strung up like a dead buck in gun season. And not by Steve, but my father.

Snarling like a bear, Steve raised his fist.

Diane parted the drapes and said, "Hey, there's a light on the pier."

Chapter Fourteen

Blackmail

Friday, June 14

Max shot out of his chair and went to the window, striking Steve's shoulder with his as if by accident. Steve stopped, flexed his fist, then dropped his arm. He pointed his finger and said, "You're one lucky son-of-a-bitch."

"You think it's Wes?" Max asked, his voice louder than it needed to be.

Steve turned his head, then joined them at the window. I stayed put. The debate was brief. There was a kid on the pier with a flashlight. Wes and his party were nowhere to be seen, but I think Diane knew all along.

The night was a goner, that's what I thought, but for Diane, nothing new. She walked to the sink, grabbed three bottles of beer, and put on a Willie Nelson CD. Music to soothe the savage beasts.

Steve sat down, sulked, and swiped his Pabst off the table. "I oughta wrap that radio cord around your skinny neck, Robel."

"Get off it, let's be cool," Max said.

I put up my hands. "Good idea."

Diane told Max and me where to sit. I followed; so did Steve a second later.

Then it was Diane in her finest hour, going from guy to guy, lap to lap, her own little game of musical chairs, revealing some small, embarrassing secret about each and then handing him a beer. First was Max. He got the most attention, set the tone by sitting still for the whole thing, and loving it. I should have grabbed his phone for a video, but I didn't.

I was next. Her ass slid onto my lap. Determined not to enjoy myself, I flushed anyway. Seated sideways, one arm around my shoulders, her breasts were so close I could have touched them with a smile. Smelling of shampoo and beer, she flicked my nose with her finger and said, "Still working on that old bike? When you gonna take me for a spin?"

The whole Schwinn revival had taken a back seat, and I said so. Then Max reminded me that I'd just gotten new handlebars and a seat.

"And you won't take me for a ride?" Diane asked. "Huh. That's a first." She moved on to Steve. To everyone's surprise, he went along. The stop there was the shortest; and though not very long or convincing, he got the kiss.

The sound of young voices coming from near the lake startled everyone. I called all quiet, rushed to the front window and peaked through the curtain. I told the others my kid sister and her ditzy friends from #2 were messing around by the pier.

Max joined me at the window. "Kids nowadays. What the hell are they doing out at this hour?"

Diane laughed a little too loud.

"Shhh." I turned off the lights. "We gotta be cool 'til they leave."

By the time Allison's gang turned in for the night, the alcohol was gone. Steve walked out the door to his car and said he was going on a beer run. "Who wants to go?"

"Shot gun," called Max as he bolted for the Mustang.

Still pissed at Steve and Diane, feeling nauseous from the Jim Beam, and too drunk to remember the reason I wanted to see Diane in the first place, I decided to walk home.

"Suit yourself, leaker." Resting an arm on the top of his car door, Steve looked at Diane. "You comin'?"

"No. I'm gonna clean up. Fanny'll be back soon."

Steve slammed the door and turned the key. "All show and no go, that chick." Gravel stung my ankles as Steve peeled out and drove away.

Her body outlined by light from behind, Diane leaned against the doorjamb of the cabin and watched me wobble into the moonless night.

I waved and said goodbye to Diane. The road slanted toward the lake and was lit only by curtain-filtered light from the one of the cabins. I stumbled into the pump house sitting in front of #3. I held on to the wooden frame. "Ya, you see that? Damn thing jumped right in front a me."

"That's what you said about the threshold." She walked toward me. "Why you in such a hurry?"

"Patty's over." I felt I was made of wax. "And, I'm fa . . . good."

"*Patty* never got here, Gumby." Diane put her hands around my arm and directed me down the road. "Three beers, for God's sake. You're lit up like Lambeau field." With a tug and a push, she had me back on the road and straightened my shirt. "You can't go home like this."

"Can't stay here." Her oddly determined expression didn't change, so I went on. "You're with Steve—"

"You don't know anything about me and Steve."

The heat in my head went down a notch. I mumbled about "knowing something."

"Nothing, smart ass." She spun me around and we headed back to #5. "You need a cup of coffee."

"Don't like cawffee."

"Did I ask? Come on."

She slipped close to me and pressed her breast into my arm. I protested for all I was worth, which wasn't much with beer blitzing my brain, a breast pushing against my arm, and her voice in my ear. I melted.

Diane dimmed the room, leaving the pole lamp next to Wes' chair as the only light. She set a tea kettle to boil, put a coffee cup in front of me, and dropped in a teaspoonful of instant coffee.

The teapot whistled. She got up and poured the boiling water in my cup. "Don't burn yourself." The pot went back on the stove. She turned down the boombox.

"Can't drink it back," I said. "Err, black."

"Milk's in the frig."

I got the carton and went about fifty-fifty coffee to milk.

She shook her head. "You're not going to like that."

Poking my own chest. "I know what I like."

She waved the back of her hand.

I took a sip of the bitter brew. "Thanks."

"I'd say the coffee and you deserve each other."

"Did I do something wrong?" I figured I had the high ground here, she was the one dating the enemy.

She grabbed her beer and took a drink. "You've had an interesting night; had your fun with Steve and me—" I made some kind of ha-ha-ha reply and she went on. "Enough of the easy living. Let's get to business. What's new on your end?"

"My end a what?"

"Bar talk, you ditz. Memorial Day weekend, remember? Jean and the belt buckle and the asshole Junior."

"Yeah, yeah, sha…sure." I took another drink of coffee and told her the Manticores lowered the offer on the resort. "It's getting worse, just like I said it would." I looked into the coffee cup. "What did we do to them? They always wanted the place, yeah, fine, but they never har… harass… bothered Tad Simpson like this."

"Tad never had a big loan with the bank." Diane got up for another beer. "Willard couldn't squeeze the Simpson-family jewels. The real question is, what does Steve want with the buckle. It's useless to him."

"I think he's looking to get in goo… good with his old man, maybe even his brothers. He tells them the story, shows them the piece, they're forever in his debt." I sat back and belched. "Sorry. Turns out, that belt has been nothing but trouble. Now, if Steve's smart, he's destroyed the damn thing, and my family is up to its ass in alligators."

"Hmm." Fresh beer in hand, Diane sat down. "If that's true, why are they still putting the squeeze on you guys?"

I put my palms on the tabletop and bent toward Diane. "Most of Walnut Creek knows about the buckle; and if anyone thinks it belongs to anyone besides your sister, I haven't met them yet." As soon as the words left my mouth, I felt like an ass.

Diane looked away. Her eyes misted.

"Diane, I'm... Beer brains. What do I know?"

A strange intensity returned to Diane's eyes. She pulled her chair closer to the table. "No. Now it makes sense." She shook her head. "That stupid bastard."

"Who? What do you mean."

"You're giving Steve too much credit."

She drained her beer, threw the bottle in the trash, and got another from the frig. Watching her move from chair to sink, I suddenly realized, for the first time, I was alone talking with this enchanting creature.

"Your version, it's pretty good." She came back to her seat. "Cheers!" We tapped bottle to coffee cup. "Right up to the most important part. Then it's all wrong."

"What? Even the part about the Manticores squeezing us?"

"No, that's probably right. They do that to anyone and everyone, just for shits and grins." Fingertips tapping the bottle, she threw back her hair. "What you don't get, what you will never understand, is Steve." She tipped the bottle toward me. "First of all, there's no love lost."

"What?" I ask quickly. "Between yu...you and him?"

"Try to focus, Sam. Between Steve and the rest of the family. He's been the odd man out like forever. Everyone at school knows it. Hell, all of Walnut Creek knows it, but worst of all, Steve knows it. He's heard the rumors. The Wild Ass Guess Society loves to bring down the Manticores. Makes the WAGS feel good. Steve always gets the worst of it."

"Why? What did he do?"

"Nothing. It's what his mother did. Found an alternate sperm donor for her last kid. Can you blame her? You've met Big Daddy. He's a pig. Makes my skin crawl."

"No shit. Who's the father?"

"I don't know. I'm not sure if Steve knows. The WAGS have their favorite suspect, an orthopedic surgeon in town. Deborah

Manticore worked at his office back in the day…"

The twisted family story reminded me Steve was supposed to return with more beer. "Shouldn't we be watching for the Mustang? He's been gone awhile."

Diane slowly shook her head. "He won't be back. Probably ran into some friends. He's bitching about me right now, guaranteed."

That made me smile for the first time in centuries.

Her fingertips tapped the bottle again. "He works for them, on the farm or over at the mansion on the lake. Makes good money, they even let him use that fancy boathouse as a mechanic's garage to make a little on the side."

"So, what's his beef?"

"Who the hell knows? Who can figure out families? Anyway, Steve's master plan isn't the goody-two-shoes arrangement you dreamt up."

"You mean he still has the belt?"

She was smiling so wide she could barely take a draw on the beer. "I think he does."

"What's he going to do? Go to the cops?"

A frown, equally intense, replaced the smile. "Oh, no, no, no, no, no. Where's your imagination?" She set down the beer. "He hasn't come right out and said so, but it all fits. Off-handed comments about coming into some cash, getting even with the Old Man, he's got the goods to do it, and on and on. Never put it together until you gave me the final piece. He's blackmailing his own family, except I'll bet Big Daddy thinks it's your family, with the buckle discovered in May, and all of Walnut Creek knows you found it."

I was stunned silent. Was it the beer? Fatigue? The very idea of someone blackmailing their own family was preposterous, and then again so crazy it just might work. But was Steve, of all people, bright enough, did he have the inventiveness necessary to put something like this together? I couldn't have done it. Of all the people I knew, Max maybe. "Do you really think so? Steve took the buckle—"

"Yes."

"To blackmail his own family."

"Yes."

"But Big Daddy thinks we're doing it, so to retaliate he's putting the squeeze on the resort, and the only way out is to get the buckle back."

As if punctuating each word, she stroked the air with her finger. "Yes. Yes. Yes."

"Do you know where he's keeping it? The belt?"

Her eyes brightened. "Finally, asking the right questions." Her lips became a straight line as her thumbnail dug at the label on the bottle. "No, I used every trick in the book, couldn't get that out of him. But I'll give you a guess."

I leaned forward. "Where?"

"I think it's cooled off." Diane took the rubber band out of her hair. "Don't need this anymore." She tossed her head and ran her fingers through her hair. She looked back at me and said, "I'm sorry, what was the question?"

It felt like I had Dave Grohl pounding his drums inside my chest. "Did you know your eyes are the same color as Jim Beam?"

She smiled, showing off her smile, really. "I'm pretty sure that wasn't the question."

"What?" I had almost forgotten. "I mean where? Where is the belt bu... buckle?"

"Steve loves to be the clever one, but..." She got up and walked away from me and dropped the beer bottle in the trash. Then the dish cloth was in her hands. She rinsed it out, bought it to the table, and wiped down the top.

This sudden spurt of energy put me off balance. A whirlpool formed in my belly. She swept back and forth before me, arms, fingernails, shoulders. "Clever one, but?"

"Oh, yeah. 'Right under their noses,' that's what he said. 'In a place they'll never look.' Yeah, it's all clicking." She took the cloth to the sink, rinsed, and hung it to dry. "In my book, there can be one place. Somewhere in the garage, the one for his weekend work. The one connected to the boathouse out at the lake."

I sat up straight. The blackmail story would explain a lot of strange coincidences, weird behavior, not all of it mine, I had to remind her. Her theory was better than anything I had cooked up, and I told her so. "But I gotta know why you're dating Steve. It's an act, right? You don't belong with him. You're so fascinating…"

She stood behind my chair, ran her fingers through my hair and said, "And how do you think I found out about Steve and the belt? The local gossip pages? I had to get close to him, drunk, and alone. So, be careful out there, Sam bone, because so far as I know, there are three people who know about Steve's plan, and two of them are in this room."

I felt lightheaded. My eyes went to the saucer and cup, my finger and thumb flicking at the base.

"So what's your next move, Sam?"

Move? Certainly not away from her hands. "Can't let it go on like this. Manticores thinking wrong, doing us wrong. Steve thinking he's king shit. I have to get the buckle."

"And then what?"

"Give it to the police." I blinked a couple times. "Are the lights flickering?" I urped something bitter. "No… I—"

She tilted my head back towards her. Her brunette hair enveloped me. Her chin bumped my nose and then there was only her mouth. Her lips pressed on mine, her tongue searching for mine. I lost track of where her's started, and mine ended. She moaned softly.

I smelled hops and yeast and nicotine on her breath. Something irresistible rose in me. Slowly, she moved to my side, and I…

I broke free, stumbled over a chair on the way to the bathroom, and fell to my knees. In the closet-sized room, I wretched.

Chapter Fifteen

The Missing Three Percent

Monday, June 17

The wind was beating the tavern window like a bass drum. Waves ripped into the shore. Fountains of cold spray hit the lodge. Churning black water. Churning black clouds creased with shards of lightning.

I leaned against the cool glass, sure I was looking at the only excitement a mundane Monday afternoon would have to offer. An after-drunk slump, that's what it was. A four-day hangover. And as bad as the night ended, it could have been worse. Steve had me in his sights until Diane faked a pier arrival and Max knocked him off the punch. Diane, what about her? The girl had put her hands in my hair and gave me a kiss. Then I puked. I should have stuck to talking. She left with Fanny on Saturday morning and went back home. I hoped we were still friends. I heard from an acquaintance she was seen with Steve over the weekend. She hadn't missed a beat.

The storm rolled on and I wondered: what next that was worth the wait, that three percent of life that makes the other ninety-seven percent worthwhile?

Max was gone, too. I hadn't seen him since the party either. He had called once (the cell phone was not bugged) but there was no way he could come to Noquebay. He'd been grounded. Last Friday night, he got home well after midnight, and his father was there to greet him. Max staggered into an argument that might have registered on the seismograph all the way down in Madison. The taillights of Manticore's Mustang had barely faded from view when the sentence was handed down: one week, no friends over, no trips into town. But for the first time, Roman Cherhasky had taken notice of his son. Not the type of notice Max wanted, but attention it was, the kind Dad laid on me when I screwed up. Just before Max hung up, the call got stranger still. He was grounded, yeah, but he and J.R. had played golf and gone to a movie. My hope was the good vibes between Max and his dad would translate into a shortened sentence because the information Diane had dropped on me about the buckle was growing stale. I needed to make a move. The tavern was empty. I picked up the cell phone and dialed Max.

Knowing Dad would be coming by to put me to work, I went right to the point. "I think Diane's right about all of it. She can read a guy like an open book."

"She's got you figured out," replied Max. I could feel the snarky grin right through the phone. "That don't mean she's got all of us whipped."

"Yeah, yeah. But Steve, he's the guy always trying to sound smarter than he is. I can see him hiding the buckle in the Old Man's garage and blackmailing him with it at the same time."

We didn't have to worry about where Diane stood on this either. She had made a copy of the key to the service door of the Manticore garage that she got off of Steve's keyring. Even with the key, there were a lot of unknowns, so I told Max we needed to case the joint and soon, that Wednesday would be best, with the final date for the job in two weeks, when the moon would be full. Coming in by water was the safest, but Max didn't want his boat anywhere near the Manticore pier, not with all the trouble happening at his house.

I hadn't thought of that. "Okay, right. Let me think about it. But you've got the fastest boat of all time. The FBOAT." He laughed at that. "You, me, with a key, this will be one sweet operation, man. And quick, too." Trying to hang some FOMO on him there.

"Until someone sees you."

"I've got us ski masks just in case. Gloves. Flashlights. Extra clothing, got it all bagged up for the job. But this week, all we're doing is looking. All you gotta do is get away from the house. Tell your dad we need help over here putting in the Mobile Home Park, which is always true. Maybe that'll be enough to get you clear."

"It just might. So, you and Diane, you're partners, that's it."

"Yeah, sure. Just like I said." A boat laboring through the whitecaps caught my eye. The vintage, wood-hulled ChrisCraft that Dad sold to a vacationer the fall before was caught in the storm. Dad called my name from the other side of the bar.

"Out here, Dad" I replied. "Dad's coming, gotta go. You wanna do it, I know you do. Think about it. Bye." I hung up and called out:

"Who's in #9 this week? They the ones who bought that old boat? That's them out there."

"Whadda ya mean 'out there?'" Dad grabbed the binoculars from off the sill. "Jeasus Katie Key-rist. Yeah, that's Lloyd Stoker all right. We were just talking about the weather yesterday." The brown hull lumbered ponderously between the waves. "He'll need help tying up if he makes it to the pier. Last time I saw him working on that thing the engine was running rougher than a three-day beard. In the meantime,"—he nodded toward the tavern—"looks like you have work to do."

The J-shaped bar was thirteen stools long, anchored on one end to the wall and on the other by a two-gallon jar of pickled eggs. There was room for two-dozen patrons if half of them didn't mind standing, three dozen if they didn't mind being familiar. I walked behind the bar and checked the candy boxes on the top shelf and the beer bays under the bar. The freezer needed ice cream, and the refrigerator was low on soda.

The suppertime storm was mostly wind and thunder, not enough rain to revive the brittle-brown lawns nor the most optimistic farmer. As soon as the clouds parted, the people emerged from their cabins.

I grabbed a bar rag. The place was starting to hum: beer glasses clinking, billiard balls cracking, voices with a sound all their own. Someone had put quarters in the Wurlitzer and played nothing but B sides. Two familiar faces were next to the pickled eggs. Wes and Fanny Van Zandt were getting an early start. They came in so often it was assumed the two bar stools and renting #5 were a package deal. Fanny's tobacco laugh reminded me of Diane.

"Two bottles of Pabst, Sam, when you get a chance," bellowed Wes, whose baritone always rattled the glasses. Fanny asked for a pack of cigarettes. He coughed. "Thought you were cutting back."

"Tried." Fanny checked her rouge with a compact. "But if I don't light up, my car won't start." She looked sidelong at her husband. "Who are you to talk? Mister 'I'm-giving-up-on-the-beer' man."

A vaguely familiar face appeared out of nowhere and slid between Fanny and Wes. Nic Vedder had been in over Memorial Day for a few minutes, but he'd put on some weight since then.

"How you been?" Wes asked. "Ain't seen hide nor hair of ya since Memorial Day."

"Can we buy you a beer?" Fanny asked.

"Love to, but not right now. I have work to do at the cabin before I report." He looked at me. "Pack of Kools, Sam, and change for the laundromat."

"On me." Wes pointed at the smokes and held up two fingers. "Yeah, we heard. Joined the Army. When do you go?"

"I leave in about a month." Nic looked past the bar to the lake. "It'll be a while before I'll be back, so keep a spot for me." He held up the Kool cigarettes. "Thanks, Wes. Adios."

"Stop by our place before you leave," Fanny said.

"I will," Nic replied, and he was gone.

Nic was about the same age James was when we lost him. I tightened my shirt collar to cover the chain around my neck, the tags attached making it feel suddenly like a millstone. The bell rang on the pizza oven. The pie wasn't done. I slammed the rack back home. The red pepper shaker tumbled off the table and dropped to the floor.

"Sam, are you all right?" Fanny asked.

"Yeah, fine." I retreated to the register to ring up the sale. An unfamiliar voice from the other side of the egg jar asked for some change. "Be right there."

Three dead soldiers went into the empties case. I went in search of Miss Pool Change. She was leaning on the end of the bar, facing the jukebox, calling across the room to a friend.

"Need change?" She didn't hear me, so I took a beat. She was blond and thin. No, thin was a pencil. She was standing still, but her lines moved, flowed from one delightful curve to another. The slender arm perched on the bar was tanned, the fingernails painted. She looked about my age though the scent of her perfume said she was older.

I touched her arm. "Can I help you?"

She spun around, a bit surprised. Her lips moved. I can say now with confidence she was talking, though I don't remember a word. She smiled and everything else disappeared.

Except the missing three percent.

CHAPTER SIXTEEN

Fanny Calls the Shots

Monday, June 17

Her voice was lost in space, as if the words were bouncing off a satellite and seconds later arriving in my ear. No, that wasn't it. I was on the stage at MTV *Spring Break*, that's what it felt like, music playing and all the cameras on her, and me, too.

The dream dissolved. The cacophony returned. My throat fluttered. "You want change?"

She nodded. Hair brushed across her cheek. Short hair, off the shoulder.

"And I'd like that back when you're done with it." She glanced down at her arm and my hand, still holding on.

"Hey kid! How 'bout a beer down here?"

Hardly believing the hand was mine, I recoiled. "Huh, sorry." She waved three singles, folded between her fingers. I opened the register. "All quarters?"

"Yes… No, wait, I'll have a diet cola." A girlfriend called from the poolroom. She answered, "Be right there." I handed her twelve quarters. She creased the corner of her mouth and showed me the coins. "You didn't take out for the cola."

"I didn't? Huh." Suddenly, I could hardly count. Fingertips brushing across her palm, my stomach jumped as I plucked away the quarters.

She gave me a look, friendly and… what else? I didn't know. Deep? Yeah, deep, deeper than Finnegan's, deeper than the ocean for all I knew.

"Thanks," she said.

"Ah, okay... yeah." I watched her weave through the crowd, and then disappear behind a knot of people. I looked down at my shirt, the one with the old ice cream stain on the collar.

"Still waitin' on that beer."

"And where's my pizza?"

I craned my neck to get another look at her. She and her friend were talking and scattering balls around the pool table. Then someone played a slow country western song, and there it was—in Noquebay Bar on Red Wolf Lake in the middle of nowhere. The most beautiful sight in the world: a girl swaying to the music.

Miss Pool Change wore a halter-top tied above a tanned belly. Her shoulders were wide for a thin girl, and she had a dimple in her chin. As if an anvil was tethered to my chin, my gaze was pulled downward, past the white short shorts to her legs. Beach legs, the likes of which Noquebay had not seen since, well, since Diane was here.

Whirring from the pizza timer.

"Hey! Is this a tavern or a church?"

The bar was a disaster. Customers neglected, bottles sitting like tenpins, the pizza oven two behind, and I didn't care. My focus was on reeling in the blond. But how? Another request for change was out. Even from behind the bar it was obvious: the girls didn't know a cue ball from a baseball. A dollar fifty would last all night.

The crust browned; pepperoni curled at the edge.

Fanny peeked around the pickled eggs. "A penny for your thoughts."

I heard some words.

Fanny tried again. "All right, I'll go a nickel, but that's my final offer."

When I realized she was talking to me, I tried to change the subject to the weather, or fishing—anything but the girl.

She asked for another beer. "Take your time. You're awfully busy. Anyone can see that. Not all of it bartending, I'll wager."

I spread my arms. "Fanny, you know I love working here."

"Love it like a root canal." She looked toward the poolroom. "Do you know who she is?"

"Who who is?"

Fanny's throaty laugh would have taken me aback had I not heard it so often. "Don't play dumb with me. The blond that melted the buckle off your belt, that's who. And before you answer, keep in mind I've been sitting ringside for the entire match."

"Hell if I know."

Fanny waved her beer. "Didn't you hear? The other girl called her Erin. They've been in the cabin by the lake for—"

"Number 10! She's in #10?"

Dad joined me behind the bar. "Hello Fanny, hi Son. How's it going?" One look at the bar gave him the answer. His next look could've split me the long way. "You've got a whole case of dead ones sitting on the bar. Christ all fishhooks, Sam, it's a holy mess, and you're not that busy."

"Oh, he's been busy," cooed Fanny. "Busy all right."

I scrambled down the bar, grabbing crumpled cellophane and empty beer bottles as I went.

Dad checked the beer bays. "We're down a case of Hamm's and two down on Pabst. What you been doin' out here? Get some beer and fill these coolers."

I walked past the pizza oven and smelled disaster. I yanked out the tray. The cheese and crust were black. There was no way I could serve it. Dad wasn't looking so I tossed the charred pie into the trash, put in a fresh pizza, and went for the beer.

The door to the walk-in beer cooler slammed behind me. Three cases of beer in hand, I was about to reenter the bar when Diane walked in the porch door. I had nowhere to put the beer, so all I could do was say hi.

"Hey, Sam bone," she said. "Thought I'd find you here. Working? We have a spot for you in the boat." She pointed at the dock in front of the tavern. Max stood up and waved; so did a handful of friends from Walnut Creek. A few of them called my name. I swore under my breath. My FOMO was off the charts.

"Look at the bright side." Diane squeezed my arm. "Lifting beer cases will get you in shape for football." Then she reached in her pocket, pulled out a key, and held it up. "Here it is." She tucked it in my back pocket. "As promised. Manticore garage. For when we get the buckle back." She was already halfway out the door. "Gotta go." She waved, went down the steps, and ran to the boat at the end of the pier. I watched every step.

The beer was getting heavy, my arms about to fall off. I put down the cases and then transferred the bottles from case to cooler.

Fanny hadn't moved. "What's your plan, honey?"

I looked up and shrugged.

"Oh, come on. You're just dyin' to go over and talk to that girl. How you gonna do it?"

"No, Fanny, no plan. Even if I had one, so what? I'm stuck back here."

"Stuck, schmuck. You've got to follow up, it's elementary. How's she going to know if she made an impression?" Fanny crossed her legs. "A girl's got to have more to think about than change for a dollar."

I kicked an empty case aside and started on another. "What reason would I have to go over there?"

Fanny's hand plunked down on the bar. "We've already covered that, to talk to her. If I didn't know better, I'd say you lost your nerve. And all it took was a single look from a girl who hasn't even filled out yet. Now listen, I've invested too much in this little soap opera to watch it fizzle. As entertainment, it isn't Broadway, but it makes for a pretty good Monday night." She took a sip of beer. "Play the jukebox, right next to the pool table. Right in her backyard, if you know what I mean. Think you can handle it?"

Handle it? I bristled. Of course, I could handle it.... Maybe.

She pushed a couple coins across the bar, her blood red nails glowing against the dark wood. "Here. Play something I like, none of that nails-on-the-chalkboard hip-hop. Merle Haggard, Waylon Jennings. You know."

I looked at Dad.

"I'll cover for you. Go!"

And go I did. Standing in front of the Wurlitzer, I studied the titles as if I'd never seen them before. My tongue was flypaper stuck to the roof of my mouth. Somewhere behind me, Erin and her friend chatted away. I tried to eavesdrop, but that was impossible with Allison and a clique of screeching girls chanting from near the bowling machine:

If your nose is kinda runny and you wanna kiss your honey
You might think it's funny but it's snot!

The quarter clunked. I punched A-16.

"Hey! Can we pick one?" A female voice, but not the one I was hoping for. The screeching girls were bearing down on me like the Light Brigade, Allison at the lead. Before I could say no, Allison wedged herself next to the jukebox. "What did you play?"

"Nosy people don't live long." I pushed C17. "Besides, its Fanny's money, and she don't like boy bands."

"Oh, come on," bleated Allison. "She won't care."

I'd lost track of Erin. The plan was falling apart. "Pick something good and I'll think about it."

"Deal!" Allison planted an elbow in my chest. The next moments I don't so much remember but relive as often as sanity and life will allow. I stumbled backward and ran into the back end of a cue stick. My hand went out reflexively for something to hold on to. What I found was Erin's derriere.

As if doused with ice water, Erin straightened from over the cue stick and cried out. Billiard balls scattered across the table. The guilty arm splatted against my chest, I leaned away and said, "Sorry! Didn't mean to, I mean, my sister pushed me and…"

Laughter from the other girl sounded across the pool table.

Erin turned, saw my open-mouthed horror, and shrugged. "Well, never mind. You probably helped my shot." A ball dropped into a pocket. "See, I made one."

I peeked over her shoulder. "How do you know it was one of yours?"

"What do you mean? They're all mine. Which one was it?" On the other side of the table, the brunette said it was the nine ball. Erin shrugged. "Yea for me!"

There they were again: perfect teeth, perfectly stunning.

The brunette smirked. "Except you were aiming at the red one."

"Then it's slop," I said. "Are you playing slop counts?"

Erin wrinkled her nose. "What is that? It sounds like a pig."

"No, no." I shook my head. "When a ball goes in and you didn't aim at it, it's called slop. Some people count it anyway and you haven't lost your turn. Step right up and hit that paddy-whacker again."

"But it only went in because you grabbed her butt," argued the brunette.

"Grabbed? I didn't."

"Did so." She looked Mediterranean, with dark skin and black olive eyes.

The dread of bumping into Erin had been replaced by irritation with her friend. But, in retrospect, the aggression was easier to handle than rejection, so in a backassward way, she was helping. "It was a tap. Call it a tap."

"Tap!" Now Erin was bothered. "What are you doing over here, anyway?"

"Here? I live here, I'm the bartender."

"No, I mean over here, by us. This isn't the bar."

I shrugged. "Playing songs."

"You're not old enough."

"Anyone can play the jukebox."

"Not old enough to *tend bar*," Erin said.

"Well, that's what I'm doin.'"

"Don't look like it."

"Well, not," I stuttered and looked away. "Are you playing eight-ball?"

"What's that?" asked Erin.

"Thought you'd never ask." I grabbed a cue from the rack. "Name is Sam."

"I'm Erin; this is my sister, Linda."

Allison weaved through the crowd and tugged on my sleeve. "Dad said get back to work."

My chest sank. "Sorry, gotta go." The cue clicked back in the rack.

Now Dad was calling. Erin rounded her eyes. "Whoa. Are you in trouble?"

"No. I don't know, maybe." I exhaled. "Why don't you come back tomorrow? I won't have to work and we can shoot pool."

Erin leaned on the cue like a shepherd's staff and gave her hips a little swivel. A flush went up my neck. She said, "Okay."

I looked to Linda. Her expression was stony, and focused on Erin. The time to leave had come. "Cool, gotta split. See ya tomorrow."

The bar greeted me with smelly ashtrays and a sink full of dirty glasses.

Fanny looked down at me, hunched over the power brush, and tapped her fingernails on the bar. "My, my, amazing what you can still get for fifty cents. Correct me if I'm wrong, but so far I've heard only two of my songs." From the poolroom, Allison and her friends, in full throat, rattled the windows singing an old pop jingle.

I shook my head. "Sorry, owe you."

"Just keeping an eye on my investment," Fanny replied. "Have you set another date? If you like her, do it now. These chances aren't like the mailman, they don't come every day."

CHAPTER SEVENTEEN

Unusual Ink

Tuesday, June 18

With morning came a white-blue haze hovering over Red Wolf Lake, its surface dead calm in the heat. On the pier in front of #9, Lloyd Stoker was tinkering again, this time with the electrical system on the old in-line four that was supposed to power his ChrisCraft. Pounding through yesterday's storm left water in the bilge and the engine without a spark.

I spent the morning with Joe and Kevin, ankle deep in the lake, pitching weeds out of the water. The gobs of kelp, peppered with dead snails and bloated fish, collected in piles onshore. We worked mostly in silence until Joe noticed Lloyd hadn't taken "Noquebay Resort" off the back of the ChrisCraft. Kevin leaned on his pitchfork and said Dad had asked him to remove the name when he sold it to him last year. "But Lloyd said he plum forgot."

I almost missed Kevin's last comment because my attention was snatched by a rather pale, elongated piece of shoreline trash. Whatever it was had been ensnared in a tangle of weeds, was only as wide as a pencil, and about an inch long. But it didn't fit, didn't look like any of the other rubble we were used to seeing. I used a tine of my pitchfork to free the whitish twig from the weedy nest, bent over and picked it up. It wasn't a match, but the resemblance was close enough to leave no doubt: I'd found my second human finger bone.

The weeds dried over lunch hour and were hauled away in the rusting 1971 Chevy pickup. The final run ended at two-thirty p.m., the engine bellowing through a corroded muffler, water dripping off the back bumper.

Joe hit the brakes as we idled past the mailboxes. I felt sticky and grubby, so I jumped off the tailgate and walked up to the pool. While dropping my shoes next to the fence, someone called my name. I turned and stepped to the edge of the water. Erin and Linda were in the middle of the deep end, surrounded by a handful of kids chanting "Mar-co Po-lo, Mar-co Po-lo."

A little overnight snooping in the resort register had revealed a lot: #10 tenants Sheila and Will Eklund were from Skokie, Illinois, and had two daughters, no sons, no pets. This was their first visit to Noquebay.

Erin walked toward me, the water receding as she got closer. I couldn't let her get close; not with dried sweat on my face, dirt all over, and a smell on me like a dump, so I jumped in. When I surfaced a few feet from her, she said:

"Hey Sam. Done working?"

"Yeah, fun's over." I pulled myself out of the water, sat on the edge of the pool, and thought, *thank god for chlorinated water.* "How are the Eklund girls today?"

"We're fine," said Linda in a coarse monotone. "We were just leaving."

"How do you know my last name?" Erin asked. "I didn't tell you."

She caught me off guard with that one. "Ah, you must have, or maybe Mom told me."

"Yeah, right. What else did your mother tell you?"

Even dripping wet, that made me blush. "You're from Illinois, but that was easy. I could tell by how you talk," I deadpanned. "You both have accents."

"Oh, I'm sure," Erin declared.

"See? No one from Wisconsin would ever say that. Illinois all the way."

Erin teased water from her hair. "Is that some kind of line?" Linda mentioned the time. Erin frowned. "What's with the shirt?"

I tugged at the t-shirt, clinging to me. "Nothing. I wear it all the time." I tugged once more, to make sure the chain beneath was not visible.

Linda pulled herself out of the pool and stood over both of us. "Erin, you coming?"

Erin rolled her eyes. "We have to get going. We gonna play pool tonight?"

Linda shot a look at her sister. "We're going out for dinner. Remember?"

"Oh yeah." Erin approached the edge of the pool. "We'll be home around eight. How about after that?"

"After eight. I'll be playing pinball or out by the fire." Erin swung her legs. I grabbed my glasses. They grabbed their towels, slipped into sandals, but only Erin waved goodbye.

––––––––

At 7:15 p.m., in front of the bedroom mirror, the vigil began. The old me had to go. If I was going to impress Erin, like a lizard or snake I had to molt. But how was I supposed to know what would impress a girl from the big city? I headed to the bar porch for a game of pinball, just to settle my nerves. Alas, I was wound so tight even the loosest machine tilted me out.

The second game went much better. I even earned a free ball. That was good. I didn't want to look too much like the dog at the door, waiting for master to return. Another quarter went in. By the time the Eklund car finally appeared at eight-forty p.m., my deodorant had failed twice, and I was on my third shirt. I slapped the flippers.

"So, how you doing?" Suddenly there she was, two steps away.

Had the door opened? I didn't hear it. My new-Sam reply was, "I'm ready to for whatever."

She pointed at the machine. "No, I mean how are you doing?"

I took a couple seconds. "Not my best machine. How about your sister, she coming?" Linda's absence was a big relief. A full day spent thinking about Erin meant I had no time to figure out what to do if Linda started again with the F.B.I. routine.

Erin cozied up to the machine and gave a small wave. "Already in bed, said she was tired. There's more to it…" She leaned over the machine and looked up at me, a wisp of wine on her breath. "You promised a game of pool."

Suddenly, my throat was sawdust. I took her inside, put two quarters in the pool table, and asked Erin to rack while I got the sodas.

We played eight-ball. But first, her cue needed chalk. When I took hold of her stick my hand touched hers. She glanced up as if it was planned. I wished I was that clever. I pointed at the table. "Ladies first." She bent over the stick and took aim.

"Hold it," I said. She straightened, a little peeved, with a 'now what' look on her face. "Powder." I got the bottle off the window sill and held it ready. "Your hands, you forgot the powder."

"Since when is pool so complicated?"

I held her right hand in my left. A streak of heat went up my arm. "You have long fingers."

Again, her eyes, watching. "Not as long as yours."

"Well, almost. Hold up, palm to palm." We did. "They are, they're as long as mine." I tapped the powder.

"Are not." She clapped away the excess powder.

We knocked around the balls until finally the "8" fell. I set another rack. I'd been watching her from the left. When I stood on her right, I saw a tattoo on her shoulder, and got a sudden coldness in my chest. I looked away and coughed.

Another man slapped a quarter on the edge of the table.

"Are you okay?" Erin asked. "Do you need a drink?"

I waved. "No, I'm fine." It was only a glance, but the tattoo looked like the one on Steve Manticore. I didn't know what to do with my eyes.

She looked at me for a moment, a blank expression on her face. "Is something wrong? Do you know that guy with the quarter?"

"No, it's nothing. Sorry." I clicked my stick in the rack. Of course, it was something, but how was I going to ask her about it? I barely knew her, and it really wasn't any of my business. But for this evening to go any further, I needed to see if she really did have a skull with a rose between its teeth tattooed on her shoulder.

Pool was not her game, and I needed a change so we moved to a small table on the front porch. Outside, the campfire blushed the night. She watched a contentious game of "kick the can," Joe the ringleader, as always. I watched her. Her shoulders were the color of cinnamon. The delicate gold chain around her neck stirred visions of city lights, high heels, short skirts, and fast cars. She killed me with her smile, which was good in a couple of ways. I needed something else to focus on while I figured out how to ask about the tattoo.

Erin sat back in her chair. A fresh bottle of diet cola sat in front of her. The dimple in her chin looked cute. "I've been thinking about last night." I raised my eyebrows in a "me, too" way. "You put the jukebox in a very interesting place. Makes me wonder, you know, well, it's a perfect excuse for say a bartender to leave his post but act like he's still working."

"I came over to play some songs."

"Yeah, right." She moved the straw in her soda up and down.

"I do it every time I bartend."

"Oh," she said, visibly deflated.

What a dumb thing to say. "And talk to you."

She smirked. "Too late."

My fingers tapped again. "I don't know, it just happened."

"The jukebox just happened. The grab just happened." She bent the straw, put the tip between her lips, and took a sip. "You leave a lot to chance, don't you?"

I was dying in little pieces. "The grab, I mean *tap*. You believe me, right? And Linda, she, she wouldn't let up."

She fiddled with her bracelet. "What do you do for excitement around here?"

Erin dropped the question lightly but it hit me like a mid-July storm. Girls with tattoos probably lived a life beyond anything I had ever imagined. I had an answer, but it would never do: *I talk to pretty, big-city girls on the bar porch, that's what I do.* "Excitement?" I asked. "I don't go into Walnut Creek much, except to visit Max. He's my best friend. That's hell and gone from here."

She wrinkled her chin. "What else?" Her foot started tapping.

The ever-dangerous pause. In the last six months, something interesting must have happened. "Last May, I was fishing in real deep water, right out there." I pointed toward the darkness of Red Wolf Lake. "And snagged a piece of a belt with a buckle. About this big."

"Welp. Okay. Is it valuable or something?"

"Maybe. The last person wearing it was reported missing six years ago, might have been murdered by her husband—"

"What?" She grabbed the edge of the table. "And he dumped her in the lake!"

I put my finger to my lips. "Shhh. Not so loud." I leaned in closer. "The killer's brother busted into my locker and stole it, but I know where he's hiding it. Next week, Max and I are gonna get it back."

"Why doesn't the other guy give it to the police?"

"And turn in his own brother? Believe it or not, if that's all there was to it, the cops would have the buckle right now, but they don't. My friends and I, we're busting our heads over that one."

She narrowed her eyes. "You mean he'd bust his own brother?"

"Steve? Oh yeah. Long story. He's the black sheep of the family over there and he knows it. Diane and I, we think —"

"Wait. What? Who's Diane?"

"Just a friend." Sensing I'd gained a square inch of high ground, I paused. "Anyway, we think he's trying to blackmail his own father, who he obviously hates. They're very rich. Own the mansion east of here. In fact, that's where the buckle is right now."

"That's so screwed up." Her eyes now on mine, her feet quiet, she grabbed my hand. "No, that's b.s. You're going to break-in to a mansion?"

The tattoo came into view. She had hold of my hand. It was getting hard to think. "Not the mansion; the boathouse. Night raid, got it all," I tapped my temple. "right here."

She let go my hand. "Holy shit. That is so bad."

"Really? You think so?" I didn't think she'd take the plan seriously.

"Just the two of you?"

I nodded, though I hardly had the right. Max had agreed to nothing, and neither had Diane. And she'd make three. By then, disbelief was again in Erin's eyes, so I said, "I'll show you something, but you have to swear not to tell anyone, not even your parents. No one."

"What is it?"

I reached in my pocket and came up with my hand in a fist, which I extended toward her, palm up. I opened my hand. She saw the bone but didn't understand what it was. As she looked at me, a couple of vertical lines formed between her eyebrows.

"Yeah, so what is it?"

"A finger bone, from a human. I found it on shore, right over there, just today."

She sat up straight, looked at me, then the bone again, and said, "How do you know it's human?"

"Looked it up. Google. I got two now, both out of the lake." I put the bone back in my pocket. I think the buckle and the bones came for the same place."

At midnight, I excused myself and went to the bathroom. On my return, I found Erin standing by the window looking across the lake.

"Dad's fixing to close up."

"Yeah, I should go." Erin sighed. The lake was dark. "Where's the moon?"

"Not around this week." She was about to say something when I asked, "Can I walk you back? Can't be too careful." *Even girls with tattoos*, I thought. "Really, you're not in Skokie anymore. Raccoons, skunks, bears, they're outside your door."

"And what would *you* do if we ran into a bear?"

"Run like hell."

"You can't outrun a bear."

"Don't have to, just have to run faster than you."

An old joke, but one that had apparently not made it to the big city, because she laughed.

Should I take her hand? Grab hold those long, lovely fingers? If she was crazy enough to inject ink under her skin, I was crazy enough to grab her hand. My second bumbling attempt got her wrist. I slid my hand into hers, and there we were, her fingers locked in mine.

We started back to her cabin. The yard light next to the pool faded behind us.

"I have to tell you why my sister was so weird." Erin took a breath and said, "My boyfriend is coming tomorrow."

"Boyfriend?" I stopped and stared at her. "Like, you're dating a guy boyfriend?"

Erin looked down, and then met my gaze. "Well yeah, I guess."

"Ya guess you're dating?"

She looked at me and bit her lip. "It isn't all my fault. You only bumped into me last night, and I just wanted to play pool, and now we're holding hands, I didn't do that."

No, and I never thought, or didn't want to ask if she was dating. I wasn't seeing anyone so I'd assumed she wasn't either. Wishful thinking of course, I can see that now. But in the moment, if it occurred to me there might be someone back in the big city, I crushed the thought.

She pursed her lips and looked away. "The plan is John will stay over tomorrow night. He has to go back Thursday, and I'm going with him."

A groan stuck in my ear before I realized it was me who uttered it. "Gone. In another day?" Couple of nights on vacation with nothing to do. Well, why not? Just a game of pool.

I sighed. We walked.

"What are you thinking?" she asked.

"Nothing. Not thinking nuthin.'" But I was. Another night with the current prettiest girl of all time, the PGOAT, was going to end in embarrassment. A light, southern breeze curled around us. We stopped.

Erin's voice was a half whisper. "Are you mad?"

"Trying to be." My voice was too loud for the night. "It's not chiseled in stone, you don't have to go back."

She put two fingers on my lips, looked warily at the cabin, and puckered her lips to say "shhh."

Mistaking this for an invitation, I lowered my lips to hers. My heart felt weak. Her hand went firmly to my chest—not a green light, barely a yellow. Erin's eyes were already open when I opened mine. Her pupils were dark and wide, pushing the blue into a thin rim.

She whispered "Good night," slipped her hand from mine, and snuck in the back door of the cabin.

CHAPTER EIGHTEEN

Misadventures

Wednesday Morning, June 19

The runabout sprinted past the lodge; its engine's roar split the peaceful morning. Not an unusual sight—except the boat had no visible driver and was headed straight for the neck of the peninsula. Without missing a beat, the speedboat sliced through bull rushes, rammed the shore, and came to rest high and dry, engine bellowing, the prop churning nothing but air. Another fifty feet north and it would have hit #10. Fifty feet south, and it would have hit Kevin and me as we trimmed the shoreline. Still not a soul in sight, we dropped our scythes and ran toward the vessel. Inside the boat, empty beer bottles scattered forward and aft came gradually in to view. A man and a woman, obviously shaken, scraped their bones off the floor.

Kevin leaned over the dash and turned off the engine. "Holy cow! You all right?"

"Huh? No." The man was wearing a swimming suit that might have fit him in high school. The hair on his head was thinning, graying on his chest. "We… we're fine." I wanted to ask how they could have missed seeing the peninsula, but I could see the man was in no mood for explanations.

The woman looked stunned. She was considerably younger than her companion and had lost control of her clothing. She wiped her mouth on the back of her hand, smearing lipstick towards her ear, then tried to sit up. She leaned against the far gunwale, lined by custom-made life-jackets, each with a Square

M Construction logo on the breast.

I backed away. "I'll go for help."

"No!" yelled the man. I flinched. "I mean, don't bother, we're all right." He pointed at the woman's blouse. Half his index finger was gone. "Wanna fix that?"

I side-eyed the girl. *Was that a nipple?*

Kevin ducked for a look under the bow. "The hull looks okay, no holes, some scratches."

I stepped to the back of the boat. "Tapper's Toy" was scripted on the stern. "The prop is mangled, and the motor smells hot."

"Yeah, thanks," groaned the man in a mocking tone. He put on a red baseball cap inscribed with CCT. He finally looked me in the face, then at the lodge. "Hey is this Noquebay? Then you must be a Robel."

"Yeah, I'm Sam, this is Kevin."

"Well, Sam, Sam Robel if you know what's good for you, keep your nose clean." He glowered at me for an uncomfortably-long second, then at the motor. "Only thing we need is a push. Come on, show off your muscles for your girlfriend over there."

Kevin and I turned toward #10. Erin had exited the porch door. Kevin whistled and said, "Here we go."

My heart leapt, and then I flushed. The way I had fallen for her in a single night—it was scary. Scary as hell. But god, she could put one foot in front of the other. We pushed. The engine sputtered. The boat sped away, the man behind the wheel, the girl in a seat in the back.

"Keep your nose clean. What the hell does that mean?" Kevin asked. He looked at me then walked back to his work.

Erin approached. I held my ground, but if I'm recalling it correctly it was because my legs wouldn't move. I said hi.

She pushed her hair behind an ear. "Hi. A couple from the resort?"

"No." I snorted. "And I doubt that was his wife."

"His daughter, then?"

"Yeah, right, his daughter." For just a second, *I* was the wise one, and it felt good.

"You don't think," Erin's eyes, so innocent and blue, grew wider. She looked for the boat, but it was long gone. I mentioned I hadn't met the driver before, but that he had threatened me, or I thought he had.

I wanted to forget about him and think about her, which was easy. Too easy in fact and she was so close. I took a breath. Was this a second chance? A shot at redemption? Only the most inexperienced, hotheaded, boy-moron would blow a chance to make time by questioning her motives. So that's exactly what I did. "What you doing here? Where's your Ill-annoy boy?"

Her hand dropped. "John, his name is John, and he won't be here till after lunch, *and* he's from Chi-ca-go."

I scowled. "You keep saying Chicago, you're from Skokie. Not the same. I looked it up."

"*He's* from Chicago. I know where I live." Her eyes narrowed, innocent no longer. "Mom was right, should've stayed put."

"Maybe you shouldn't have taken my hand."

"Maybe you shouldn't have *grabbed* my hand." The color drained from her face. "Boat crashed into the shore. Thought I'd take a look. Not here for the company, that's for sure."

"Well the show's over, you missed it."

"Fine! Go chop your weeds. I'm leaving."

"I know. You told me."

I felt blood rising in my neck and anger too, and not with Erin, but myself. She'd taken a handful of steps when my eyes wandered back. I melted.

I caught up and spun her by the arm. "Wait, don't go. That was dumb. I'm still mad from last night." I let go. "Sorry." I took a breath. "Gonna take a break. Want to come? Sit on the swings, over there."

No was written all over her face. But I talked fast, called it penance for Tuesday night and said after all, she was still free until lunch anyway.

She shook her head, but not in a bad way. "Okay, for a bit." Then she pointed behind me. "Did you drop something?"

Back where the boat had been there was a matchbook on the ground. I retrieved it and brought it back to show it to her. "It must have flown out of the boat. Look, the same letters on the front as on the hat that guy was wearing, CCT." I slipped my thumb under the flap and opened it up. Half the matches were gone. Then I saw something that made my throat go numb.

Erin looked at me. "What's the matter? What does it say?"

"Nothing." I closed the matchbook. "It's a…a dirty joke. Awful." I put it in my pocket. "Come on."

The seats on the swing set were whitewashed pine, the chains rusty and stiff from lack of use. We sat side by side and looked across Lennon's Bight. Water lapped lazily on the beach, a couple of seagulls circled overhead. We talked about music, school, and which teachers we hated. Drivel mostly, until Erin asked me what I was going to do after high school. Outside of college, I didn't have much to say, so she told me her plans.

She shook her head. "School is not where it's at for me. One more year, and that's it. I want to get married, have some kids."

Why was she bringing this up now? Keep her out of John's car, that's what I was all about. To hell with future plans, which, now that I heard them, were kind of a drag anyway. "You're really looking ahead. I hardly know what's happening next weekend."

"Yes, you do." Her lazy gaze was now intent. "Next week you and your friend have that crazy idea to get the belt back. Have you talked to him about it?"

"Mission: Jeanie Blue?" I had given it a name. "No, but I'm seeing him tonight. Why?"

"It's like nothing I ever heard of," she said. "How are you going to do it?"

"You're awful curious." I looked at her. "I don't know if I should tell you. And besides, you'll be leaving tomorrow, so—"

"So, your secret is safe with me."

"Maybe." I squinted at her. "First, you have to promise not to breathe a word to anyone, not your parents, your sister, not Father O'Brien in the confessional."

She nodded. "Yeah, so…"

"Okay, the Manticore place is maybe a mile that way." I pointed left, in front of her. "And Max's place is way the hell at the other end of the lake, southwest by five miles or so. The Manticore's have a boathouse, huge, with a garage attached to the back. I have a key—"

"Wait. What? How'd you get a key?"

"A girl I know, she owed me."

"Diane? Owed you for what?"

"Never mind." She raised her eyebrows. I said, "You want to hear the rest of Mission: Jeanie Blue or not?" She couldn't believe the place would be empty in the middle of summer. There were public wetlands right next door that were perfect cover for the nighttime approach.

Her father called her for lunch, but she ignored him, impatient to hear more of the plan. He called again.

"Coming!" She stomped her foot. "They don't like that I'm out here."

I suppressed a grin. "Come on, I'll walk you back."

Erin walked backwards, half-a-step in front of me, trying to slow the pace. She pushed lightly on my stomach and said, "Quick, tell me the rest."

"No time. I've barely told you half." I didn't have to fake regret at her leaving. This was fun all over again. She grabbed my upper arms with both hands and squeezed. She was desperate to know the end game. We stopped next to the back door. I said, "Too risky. Only way for you to know that, you'd have to come along; you know, a partner in crime." I sighed dramatically. "Can't happen, of course, since… well."

Erin's smile ran away. She opened the door, walked in, and looked back through the screen. "That's a dirty trick, Sam Robel."

––––––––––––

To this day, I don't know how Max escaped his father's grounding sentence, but it obviously had gone the way of the rotary phone. Already Monday night I'd seen him driving the boat, waiting at the pier while Diane delivered the Manticore key to me in the tavern. That was the night I met Erin, so in retrospect missing out on the boat party was a wash. Now, Erin's boyfriend had arrived, so I was ready to check in with Max again, try to restart our Endless Summer, and more importantly, case the Manticore property. He picked me up in the boat at seven. Dad had me on a curfew of ten p.m.

I wasn't sure what to expect when Max and I walked through the Cherhasky's back door. Middie raced from the other side of the house, barking at me like I was a Zombie Flesh Eater until she got a sniff of my shoe. Then she was all wagging tail and prancing paws until I picked her up. The kitchen was spotless, waiting for a call from the Parade of Homes. There was the smell of wax and wood, but of baking cookies and spaghetti sauce, not a whiff.

Max's father was in the study, the door cracked open but saying "Do Not Disturb" at the same time. We walked by. Max pointed his thumb toward the office and shook his head.

I followed Max up the stairs. Middie raced ahead, her nails clicking on the old hardwood.

"Where's Nadine?" I asked in a stage whisper.

Max shrugged, saying nothing. We entered his bedroom, which smelled of old socks and Old Spice. He grabbed his Stratocaster, told me to throw the clothes on the floor and sit on the bed and started playing an old blues song "Born Under a Bad Sign." The mournful riff, the lines seemed to fit. The guitar wasn't plugged in. In fact, the amplifier was at the end of Max's bed, shoved against the wall and covered by piles of paperbacks, a stack of CDs in front. He was more reserved, not so irreverent, but one does not look upon the arrest of a parent and come out clean, not even Max. His voice was muted, too.

He stopped singing. "So, have you talked to Sticks?"

"Diane? Not since Monday. And don't call her that."

"Why not? She likes it. Who wouldn't?" Max silenced the strings and looked at me. "You don't know what it means."

I went back to the CDs.

"Just what I thought," Max said. "It means legs. She's got them up to her neck."

My spine shrank into the wall. "Who doesn't know that?"

"The other thing about her, I've never seen her drunk. Steve says she never pukes, cast iron stomach."

"Manticore sucks. Why do you hang out with that dick-wad anyway?"

Max shrugged. "I don't know. Just to piss off my dad. You ought to cut him some slack."

"Who? Manticore? What for?"

"His dad used to beat him like a bass drum. Still treats him like he's the hired help."

I stopped with the CDs. "Why didn't his mom do something?"

"You're kidding, right? He probably beats her, too."

I read a CD cover and told him about the boat that ran into the peninsula, the name on the back and the custom-made life-jackets for Square M.

"Was Mitch Manticore driving, or… not driving?"

I waved the CD. "How do I know. Never saw him before."

"Was he missing a finger on one of his hands? I forget which one."

"Yes, yes he was."

Max hit a power chord, E major I think.

"Ol' Tapper was out with a sweetie, tied down the steering wheel, and just ran out of water," I said. "Kind of a jerk. Wouldn't want to work for him. How does a guy go from prison to running a big construction company in twenty years? I'd like to see Steve do some time."

The pick dangled on Max's lips like it was a cigarette. "Don't worry, you won't see him around Noquebay. Diane broke up with him."

"Good. Which reminds me, we should do a practice run of Mission: Jeanie Blue."

"What? Now we're calling it Mission: Jeanie Blue?"

I got off the floor and sat on the edge of the amplifier. Having given the presentation to Erin earlier in the day, I had it down pat, even the section I had left unsaid. "We should do it tonight. It's deadsville over there, and we'll find a place to hide your boat in the Back Bay."

CHAPTER NINETEEN

Scouting Party

Wednesday Evening, June 19

Max guided the boat away from the pier and headed out of the West End toward the sparsely-populated Back Bay on the other side of the lake, which was only busy during spring fishing and autumn duck hunting season. Much of the land here was state and county owned, primarily wooded and wetlands.

The bow of the boat hit bull rushes first. Max slowed to a crawl and tilted up the motor. Within another minute we were out of sight of Red Wolf Lake, surrounded by marsh grass, pussy willows, and the county forest. We found a piece of land to bring the boat ashore. Max turned off the engine and tipped it out of the water.

I jumped over the gunwale, and pushed the boat, stern first, into the soft bank. Max handed me the anchor and we tied down the boat. I grabbed a bunch of white cloth strips from the glove compartment. Max pulled the key and we headed for the woods, in search of a deer trail headed west.

I tied a cloth strip on a trailside branch. "How far to the mansion do you think?"

"Mile, maybe less." He looked at his wristwatch. "I should time this."

The CCT matchbook felt like a hand grenade in my pocket. CCT was J.R. Cherhasky's trucking company. A matchbook in a boat could be a coincidence, the message written inside was not. I wanted to ask Max about the connection between his dad and Mitch Manticore, but every time there was a break in the conversation the coward in me won out.

"Did you hear about Nic Vedder?" I groaned. "He's going in the Army. He's gotta report in a few weeks."

"Report—damn." Max swung at a low-hanging branch.

"Sucks, man." I slipped a hand into my pocket. A vague taste of bile rose in my throat. "Hey, almost forgot. Look what I found." I flipped the matchbook in my fingers, then opened the top. "CCT, is that your dad's company?"

Max took a quick look, then grabbed a couple limbs and bound them together with a single tie. "Since when do you smoke?"

"I don't."

"Where'd you find it?"

"Found it on… in Walnut Creek." Why did I lie?

He kicked a tree branch off the trail. "Yeah, Cherhasky Capital and Transport. So what?"

"So nuthin.'" But what was Mitchell "Tapper" Manticore doing with a brand new CCT cap on his head and CCT matchbooks flying out of his boat? In my head, that sounded like an accusation. Before I implicated J. Roman Cherhasky in some wild-ass conspiracy theory, I needed time to think.

I pocketed the match book. "This'll be more up your alley. Monday, I met this girl, Erin, and…"

Max stopped cold. "Erin? Time out. Who is this chick and why haven't I met her?" He pointed at me. "Wait a minute. She's one of them, isn't she? One of the girls from *The Paradox*?" He poked me.

"Whoa. No boat. She's in a cabin. Just met her two days ago." I laughed. "You can't believe it. She's, she's, she dresses like a city girl and all that, and acts it too. But, for some reason, I like it, and I didn't think I would, but I do. She's not stuck up, that's why. Come on, we have to keep walking."

"So, what are you doing over here if you've got super chick waiting at the resort?"

I threw up my hands. "Because the second half of the story sucks. She's got this boyfriend, works in her uncle's machine shop. Erin says he'll be front office, five years tops. Soon as she graduates, wants to get married."

Max tied a cloth strip. "Dangerous vibe, don't knock her up."

I shoved him in the shoulder. "Fat chance with her boyfriend around." I looked up at the sky. "She looks a little like Miley Cyrus in short hair. She has a scar on her chin she got from diving."

"The singer? That Miley Cyrus?" Max, laughing. "Except for the scar."

"Oh, she's got a dimple in her chin."

"And the tattoo."

I rubbed my neck

"Got it bad, don't you?"

"Ah, shut up." I grabbed a small limb from the trail bed and smacked it against a tree trunk.

I placed another tie; we had done so many, we would never lose the trail, full moon, new moon or shoot the moon. We moved on. "Which reminds me, now that I'm single again, why don't you come over tomorrow. Bring the guitars."

"Sounds good. I'll come in the boat." He ran his hand through his hair. "Listen, man, I got to tell you something, and you're not going to like it."

I stopped walking. By the look on his face, I thought something awful happened. "What? They put your dad in the slammer? You're moving?" Max shook his head. "What then?"

"It's about Diane…and me." He squinted one eye. "We went out last night."

"Went out? Like on a date?"

"Yeah, a date."

I braced my forehead with my hand. "Max, you can't…" I paced across the trail then back again. "This… this is bad."

"I'm sorry, dude," Max said. "I know how you feel about her. But, now you've got Erin, right?

"No, Erin's leaving." I looked up at him. "And no, It's not that. I mean, me? Date Diane? I wish. But," I shook my head. "…forget it."

"Then what's the problem?" asked Max. "I like her, she likes me."

"We need her for the mission, that's the problem. When we do this, she'll have to be with Steve, even if it's only as a spy. What if there's security at the garage and we set it off? Steve is the go-fer over there. They would send him to check it out. If word gets out you two are dating, that's a problem."

"If you really think that'll happen, then we shouldn't go at all."

"I think it could happen, but I'm still going. I don't have a choice. If you decide not to go, your dad's thing and all, we're cool."

Max closed his eyes and tilted his head back. Then he looked at me. "All right, let's go. We'll figure out Diane later."

"Figure her out?" I laughed. "Yeah, right. You're in up to your eyeballs and you don't even know it."

The tavern was quiet when I checked in. Mom, Allison and Grandma Robel were on the porch, playing canasta. Dad had turned the volume down on the jukebox and was playing bar dice with A.J. McTibble. "Hi, son. Home a little early. Everything all right?"

I mumbled something that had nothing to do with spying on our filthy-rich neighbors.

I walked past the bar and asked if the Eklunds had come in. Dad saved the boxcars and shook again. "Haven't seen them. Don't forget, you're on duty with me tomorrow night."

"I know. Going out by the fire."

The treetops on the far shore were outlined by the last glow of dusk. The smell of melting chocolate and burned marshmallow flavored the air. Around the campfire, the picnic tables were full, so I stood next to the pit.

Joe threw an empty soda can into the flames and asked, "Going to see Erin?"

I put my hands in my back pockets. "Nope. Mr. Ill-annoy is taking her home tomorrow."

Kevin spit into the fire. "Don't look now, but here they come."

Everyone looked toward the road except for me. I ducked behind Joe and begged the rest of them to stop their gawking.

My eyes tracked Erin and John as if they were nuclear warheads honing in on the lodge. Arm in arm, they entered the front door.

Joe dabbed under his eye, like dear, old Aunt Millicent. "They look sooo happy."

"Ha ha." I emerged from hiding and rubbed my neck. "I need a spy to go inside and check them out." I held up my palms to Joe and Kevin. "Don't even say it. She knows both of you."

"I'll do it," said a voice from the far side of the fire. Allison, a graham cracker in each hand, was constructing her third s'more. She was no stranger to Erin, but only thirteen years old so no one would suspect her, and devious enough for undercover work. Perfect.

I held out my hand. "Here's some money; play the jukebox, make it look good. Then come back and tell me what they're doing."

Night settled in and stifled the fire. In ones and twos, the kids drifted off, leaving me to wait and listen to the music emanating through the tavern windows. Ten minutes, twenty minutes, forty-five minutes later, Erin and John exited the bar. Allison and one of her friends strolled out behind them, but had enough savvy not to come directly to the fire pit. When the couple was well down the road and into the shadows, the girls skittered over to me.

I tilted my head. "What took you so long?"

"I had to hear my songs," replied Allison.

"Okay, okay, cough up the goods."

She put a finger in front of her ear. "He's got sideburns, long ones, down to here."

"And his watch is really cool," added the friend.

"Sheeze." My foot pawed the grass. "What else? What does he look like?"

"He's cute," said Allison, confident she had given me a pearl. "But he got mustard on his mustache, and then he licked it off."

"Ooo, yucky!" said the friend, who wrinkled her face like an old apple.

"Yeah, great." I looked toward the distant cabin. Sitting on the pier, silhouetted against the glow from the cabin, were two shadows. In the lakeside cabin, a light burned on the front porch. The rest of the scene was darkness. A voice crept into my ear. Allison said she had to go in. "Okay, g'night."

The jukebox went silent. The lights clicked off. The lodge went to sleep. Water lapped against the boats, frogs croaked; the halting call of a loon sounded in the distance. The sweet scent of s'mores gave way to ashes and dying embers. I took off my glasses. The night became a blur. At that moment, for all I could see, the shadows on the pier could have been in Chicago.

The shadows walked off the pier and melted into the darkness of the cabin. Ten minutes later the porch light went out. I was still watching.

CHAPTER TWENTY

The Set-Up

Thursday Morning, June 20

I awoke the next morning with a headache and a vague rec-
ollection of a bad dream. Through the years nightmares and
migraines have gone hand in hand. This dream was something
about John-John, Erin's chosen one, driving the boat into the
shore, the engine roaring ceaselessly, and Erin, sitting in the
boat, wiping lipstick across her cheek.

After rising and dressing, I went straight to the kitchen for
a breakfast of O.J. and two Excedrin tablets. No deodorant, hair
uncombed, I went to the tavern and found Mom, fresh and crisp
as a September apple, working on a pile of receipts, a tri-folded
letter with the bank's letterhead sitting nearby.

She appraised me with a single glance. "Sam, for the love
of Pete, look at your clothes. You ought to fire that shirt." She
stood and zipped the bank satchel and, just as quickly, folded the
letter back into its envelope.

The letter looked suspicious. "What's that about?"

"The bank. It's nothing." She reopened the satchel and put
the letter in. "Are you feeling all right?"

I croaked something about nightmares and got to work re-
stocking the back bar. While retrieving a case of beer from the
cooler, I peeked toward Erin's cabin. John's Subaru was gone.
Erin hadn't wasted any time. "Mom, did you see a car leave from
#10, a blue one?"

"About an hour ago."

"Anyone with?" The question stuck in my throat.

"In the car? Two, Sam, sorry." She closed the cash register. "When you're done, go out to the laundromat and get the linen ready for Saturday."

———————

Thursday mornings in the laundromat were quiet; just the Schwinn, two washers, a commercial dryer, and a folding table to keep me company. I stacked clean pillowcases and sheets on the shelves, and then shut the door. A glint of chrome caught my eye.

The bike, wedged behind the washer, hadn't moved since I last worked on it a week earlier. I had found a new seat; the tires were still a problem. I picked up a box cutter, the tool I used to strip rubber off the rims fused by the fire, and looked at the Schwinn. Somehow, the need to rejuvenate the charred remnant of Burlington had disappeared. Max had offered a set of wheels from an old bike of his. Time to give him a call. I threw down the blade and went in the house.

The rest of the family was already seated for lunch. I walked in the kitchen and joined them. Dad buttered a slice of bread and asked, "Where's Joe? Time to eat. He ain't here, it's tough titty."

"Down by the cabins, mowing," Mom said. "He'll be here."

Dad pointed at my shirt. "Don't come to the table looking like that. Go change your shirt."

I pushed the chair back, and got up. I stopped a second to make sure I'd heard correctly, but no one stopped me. There had never been a dress code at the lunch table. Swim suits in summer, no problem. Okay, no muddy boots, but I was far short of that. A minute later, I retook my seat.

Mom said my shirt was a big improvement, that you never know who might notice. I wondered out loud who would care, threw a piece of pizza on my plate, and was about to take a seat when Dad asked me to check on the second pizza.

"Did the timer ring?" I asked. "I didn't hear it."

"Check it anyway," insisted Dad. "Weren't you the one that

said you're the 'Aaron Rogers of the pizza oven?'" Allison giggled. Dad flipped his thumb toward the tavern door.

A mouthful of cheese and pepperoni bloating my face, I opened the door and headed toward the vacant tavern. The buzzing pizza timer was the only sound. I met Joe coming down the hall, a sly, sarcastic smile on his face, but for once nothing to say. We moved on, in opposite directions.

While rounding the end of the bar I looked up and froze. Was the migraine causing a hallucination? Blinking once, twice, did not make the vision go away. Sitting on the bartender's stool, turning back and forth and biting her lower lip, was Erin Eklund. The flinty clump of pizza chaffed like an old corncob on the way down. "Erin, I thought—"

That big-city look again. "Sometimes you think too much."

"John-John's car?"

"One 'John' will do. He left this morning; my sister went, too." She slid off the stool and walked toward me. The pizza bell rang. "Now, stop thinking about them and start thinking about me. I've got two days left, and if I get bored, it's your fault." She looked past my shoulder. "Speaking of sisters, I think yours is hungry."

I turned and saw Allison, spying from the hallway. "Allison! Get lost."

Kevin's hand grabbed Allison by the shoulder and dragged her back down the hall.

I shook my head. "But... you're still here." I couldn't help it. I stared out the front window, searching for the Subaru.

"For God's sake." She grabbed my chin. "Now, what about this afternoon?"

"Okay, yeah, sorry. I'm free after two."

"Cool, let's lie out in the sun. I haven't done that yet."

Then I smelled burned crust. I turned back to the oven and pulled out the tray. The pizza was black.

"Man-o-man, my family'll have a fit."

"It's not so bad." She pointed at the pizza. "I like black olives."

"Those *were* mushrooms. Sheez, I've never done this. Usually, I'm a really good pizza maker. Now I've burned two in the last three days." I put the pizza on the cardboard. "Want to join us?"

"Gee, thanks, but I don't think so. By the way," She looked me up and down. "Is this a new style, the hair?"

I blushed, ran a hand through the tangled mess. "No, I gotta fix it."

She gave me a peck on the cheek. "See you at two, right?" She smiled and was gone.

The pizza plopped in the middle of the table. Catcalls, whistles, and groans filled the air.

"I'm not eating this." Kevin peeked at the underside. "It's black as a crow."

"No one else wants it, slide it over here," Dad said.

Mom looked at me. "Maybe you should make another one."

Kevin popped out of his seat. "OMG, not him."

At that point, there was nothing that could spoil my mood. "Nice set-up, Dad."

Dad lifted an eyebrow, smiled, and kept eating. "Just remember, you're on duty tonight."

I had totally forgotten. "Joe, you gotta trade with me."

"Me? No way." Joe cut the black off his pizza. "Me and Harry and a kid from the cabins, we got plans."

What kind of luck? I deflated and crashed—the Hindenburg without the flames, and me captain of the ship.

CHAPTER TWENTY-ONE

Chained

Thursday Afternoon, June 20

I heard once you can tell a man's profession by his hands. My first experience with this, and therefore the one that stays with me, was Will Eklund's handshake. I would know it later as a plumber's grip. Somewhat against type, his smile was dry.

Mrs. Eklund put her grip to a different use. Chopping carrots with a blade as big as a machete, she looked up for a second and said hi, her smile as clipped as a Beverly Hills poodle, then started a toneless, dissecting barrage. How do you like school? (That is, how are your grades, and do you have a brain?) Are you in the band or play sports? (Or, should I say, lumberjacking?) What church do you go to? (Heathens and social lepers need not apply.) Before we left for the sun, Sheila's dark eyes softened a little, and she invited me for ice cream and cake in honor of Erin's birthday.

"Birthday? You didn't tell me. How many candles?"

Erin bounced a little bounce on her toes. "Seventeen."

We set her portable speaker next to the soda, spread the towels on the dock, and found just enough room for strangers to lie side by side. The sun was high, the breeze light, and the water calm. Erin rolled on her side and propped herself on an elbow. The two-piece suit fit her perfectly, and was different from the one she'd worn at the pool. I don't know why I hadn't noticed earlier, I should have because it was obvious, she had the muscle tone of an athlete, especially in her shoulders, which had more definition than a dictionary.

"How do you get in such good shape?" I asked.

"A pickup line? Really. I'm already here… with you."

But I was serious. I couldn't believe she was born with what I was seeing, though I didn't say it that way. And I was right, she'd been swimming competitively for three years. Her high school had a swim team on which she did the backstroke in the two-hundred medley relay and the one-hundred individual. Her relay team got to sectionals in the State Tournament last year.

She looked up and squinted. "Sun is too much. I'm parched. Aren't you going to take your shirt off?"

I faked a frown. "Nah, I leave it on."

"Why, you got a birthmark or something?"

"No…." The chain dangled from my neck, but I went with the same bullshit answer as always. "Working on my farmer's tan."

"Sure you are." She slid forward and grabbed a soda, her belly at about the level of my eyes. The nearness, the boldness of it, surprised me. But if this was what big-city girls were all about, I would have to get used to it.

She slid back again. "So, what's happening tonight?"

I turned on my side, my pose a mirror image of hers. I wore the reflecting sunglasses; the ones Max had given me. Without prescription lenses, I could see about two feet, but we were close so it didn't matter. "Ahh, about tonight. I gotta work."

"Aw, really? Can't you get out of it? Just this once?"

"I tried, believe me. But Joe wouldn't trade. Something about the new moon and his friends. I might get out early."

She rolled on her belly and propped herself on her elbows. "What about after that?"

My stomach tightened. Her ass was right there. Her voice and smile, the bikini, how could all this *fantastic* come in one package? The pier levitated and like a magic carpet, we were flying. Or at least I was. "I have… haven't thought about it."

"I have."

I was glad for the mirrors hiding my eyes, because I'm sure they were wider than Red Wolf Lake. "What's your idea?"

"The weather's good, the wind hasn't been blowing. That's good if you're in a boat, right?"

"…Right."

"When is your friend coming over? I want to meet him."

"Max? He's coming later today. We're going to play guitar. Why?"

"He's got the boat, and you said we need him."

"*We* need him? For what?" I tried to get a read on her. What was she getting at?

"Yeah, and his boat." She was on her side again, facing me.

I shrugged. "You want to learn to waterski?"

"Yes, I do, but not tonight. Your guess is cold, very cold."

"Ah… Sunset cruise on the lake?" She said I was getting warmer. I tried to think, but there was nothing there. "I give."

"You need a third person for Mission: Jeanie Blue." She opened her hands. "Here she is."

"You!"

"Tonight would be perfect."

I looked at her over the top of my sunglasses. "For the raid?"

She poked her finger in to my chest with each word. "For-the-raid." She took my sunglasses and put them on. "I've been thinking about it ever since we talked on the porch. You couldn't pick a better person than me."

I might have heard half of what she said. "Tonight?" I shook my head. "I never… for one thing, there's no moon." I searched for the slightest break in her gaze, a twitch of her lip, anything that would say she was putting me on. "Wait a minute, you're kidding, I get it. Okay, you got me."

She tightened her jaw. "No, I'm not. You can't predict the weather. Next week it could be crap. And you're better off without a moon. Not exactly legal, this raid of yours, now is it?"

I wondered, *Is this her real reason for staying?* "And you figured, 'hey, the weather's good, let's break into someone's garage.'"

She pushed herself upright, bent her knees and sat on her feet.

ROLLING IN THE DEEP

"What do you think I am? Some kind of juvenile delinquent?" She slapped me on the butt. "There's more to it than that, if I can believe you. Is it true? The story about the murdered girl and the body in Finnegan's Hole?"

I sat on the edge of the pier and put my feet in the water. "I've heard the same story from three different people, so I believe it."

"That's it then, we're doing it for her, for Jean."

I picked at the edge of the pier. "Jean Manticore, you remember her name."

"When I go back to school next fall, I want to tell everyone at Morton East I did more than hang out and go to parties."

I wondered, *Could this be my Bonnie Parker?* If I was going to be Clyde Barrow, I needed one. Max had Diane, so why not me? I looked at her tattoo and took my glasses back. "Not good enough. What happened to Miss get-out-of-school-and-get-married? She would never go on a night raid with a couple of guys she hardly knows."

She put on her own sunglasses. "You first. Why are you really doing Mission: Jeannie Blue? You never met Jean so she can't mean anything to you. Why is getting the buckle worth breaking and entering?"

There was a high arching sky overhead and miles of open water in two directions and still I was cornered. The story was so ingrained in my brain by then, I could recite it even to a girl in a bikini. The buckle, the Jean Manticore rumor, Steve and blackmail, Diane and her connection.

"So, I know Diane's reason. What's yours?"

"Helping a friend, that's not enough?"

"If you're tearing off a felony? No."

"Smart ass." I kicked the water. "The Manticores think my family is blackmailing them with the buckle. It's a long story." But she sat and listened attentively to every detail. When I finished she added:

"And the Manticores will have a new problem with this murder investigation."

"Exactly."

She put her hand on my shoulder. "Well, that's your jam."

Her touch sent a rush of heat through me. "Right. And yours? I don't buy the 'What I did on summer vacation' story."

She switched to sitting pretzel-style. "Kinda lame, huh."

"Kinda. And remember, I've got to convince Max about this."

She took a breath. "I was in seventh grade. My best friend, we were connected at the hip. We dressed alike, sleepovers, the whole bit. We were like twins. Her mom was divorced, which was bad enough because her father basically left both of them high and dry. And looking back, her mom was no bargain either, fragile in so many ways. Took up with guy after guy. For one reason or another, they all left her. Then one day, her luck ran out."

I leaned back on my hands. "Her luck? Sounds like all she had was bad luck."

She looked directly at me. "Her luck went from bad to worse." A deep sigh. "This is pretty dark. Sure you want to hear it?"

I nodded.

"She started dating a real creep, a knuckle-dragger. I still have nightmares about the jack-ass. After I met him, all the sleepovers were at my house." She wiped a tear from under her sunglasses.

"Are you all right. You don't have to tell me if you don't want to."

"I'm okay. I want to tell you. This whole Jean Manticore thing has brought it out." She reset her glasses. "Anyway, one day, it was a Monday, I remember because she was absent from school, and I thought nothing of it. She was sick or something. When I got home, I called her to see how she was, and she wasn't there. Her mom answers, crying, said she never came home from the store Sunday morning. It was only three blocks away and she walked there all the time. Almost two nights and she hadn't been home. Her mother hadn't even called the cops. Nothing!"

I pulled my feet out of the water, grabbed the towel, and handed it to her, because there were more tears. Pretzel-sitting right in front of her, my voice as soft as lake water, I asked, "Did they find her?"

She shook her head. "I never saw her again."

121

"And you think it was the boyfriend."

She throttled the towel. "I know it was. The police think he offered her a ride home from the store. She probably got in without a fight. No witnesses. No leads."

There was a silence that was not at all awkward. "I'm sorry. What was your friend's name?"

She lifted her head, and said as clear as Northern air, "Jeanie Bloom."

"Jean." My stomach dropped for a couple reasons. Sure, the first names were the same, but also because now it was clear, she was still here because of the Mission, not for me. "I just got a shiver. I think your reason is as good as mine." I pursed my lips. "I know how you feel. Really." Without thinking, I reached under my shirt and twirled the chain around my finger.

She nodded sideways, saw my fingers, tangled. I could tell by her expression, she didn't believe I could understand how she felt about death and loss. I pulled off my shirt. "Mine wasn't a friend. Not exactly." The chain around my neck carried two, small metal plates. I took it off and handed it to her.

She took the chain in her palm, spread the plates to read, then looked at me and said, "Oh my god, Sam. These are dog tags. Who is James Arthur Robel, Jr.? How did you get them?"

Something inside of me collapsed. Besides my family, no one else had seen the tags. Grief squeezed my throat, tears wetted my glasses. I held the shirt against my chest and croaked, "Brother. Afghanistan, October, 2011."

"That's why you didn't take off your shirt."

I nodded, took off my glasses, and blotted my eye with a palm. "And now you know, the other reason. I can't stand to look at them for more than a minute, so I keep them covered."

"Because you get sad."

"Yeah, and angry too. I feel like my chest will explode or something."

She took my shirt and wiped away a tear. "What are you angry about? The Army? The war?"

"Oh, sure, all of that. But mostly him." I pointed at the tags.

"James, sonofabitch, he didn't have to go. But off he goes to enlist. He left us." I took a deep breath. "I'm sorry. I shouldn't be unloading all of this on you, on your vacation."

"It's all right." She handed me the shirt. "Really." She paused a bit. Neither of us said a word. Then she reached for my hand, put the tags in my palm, closed my fingers around and said, "He must have been quite a guy. To miss him so much."

I nodded again and put the chain on. "Yup." I reached to put on the shirt.

She stopped my hand. "You shouldn't cover them."

"It's embarrassing. I can't have them in plain sight. I mean, look at me."

"Why? Because you miss your brother? Guys are such... they don't understand this stuff."

"Okay. Just for now, while you're here. I'll probably burn like a lobster." I took a deep breath. "What was with the 'graduate and get married' line anyway?"

She threw the towel at me. "Sad, I know, but it was just a line."

I went back to dangling my feet in the water. "It was just a line? Pretty weak for a city girl and possible partner-in-crime."

"Is that so. A little line like that and you're ready to dump me?" She crawled behind me and put a choke hold around my neck. "Drowning is too good for you. I think strangulaaaaaa—"

I leaned forward. We both got wet.

Chapter Twenty-Two

No Kind of Second Date

Thursday Evening, June 20

Long nights start before the sun goes down. I set a bottle of soda in front of Erin, looked across the churning crowd, and swore under my breath. So many demanding voices, a mob jostling for a spot at the bar; squeezing my girl into an ever-shrinking space. She was pretty, so pretty, glowing really, but out of place; like a rose in a trashcan. I set up the beer as fast as I could. When I wasn't at the other end of the bar, I was bent over the sink washing glasses. There was no time for talking, barely enough for a smile. If it got any busier, she may up and leave. And that was only the beginning of my problems. First, in the next couple hours I had to get Max and Diane onboard with the drastically changed timetable for Mission: Jeannie Blue. Second, I needed to introduce them to Erin and make them see she was a good fit for our team.

Then it hit me: the safest place for Erin was *behind* the bar, with me. I grabbed her forearm, got close, and said, "Wanna learn how to tend bar?"

"What? Now?"

"Yeah, it's easy, and I need help."

She looked down the bar, then back at me, and bounced off the stool. It took her about ten seconds to get familiar with the back bar. She started working the pizza oven, washing glasses, and retrieving ice cream. On her way to the freezer someone asked her for two Hamm's.

I directed her to the middle bay and told her what to charge.

"Candy bars are a dollar fifty, so is all the ice cream and soda, pickled eggs, too. Oh, and anything in a bag is a dollar. Beers are three bucks. And you don't have to ring the amount, just hit any button to open the drawer. Like this." The swan-neck plunger on the vintage cash register rang the bell. "There, you're a bartender."

It was no one's idea of an awesome second date, but it was not bad. When she needed help, she touched me at first on the wrist, the next time on the arm, and later on the shoulder. While she was talking to a customer, I stepped behind her and whispered in her ear, "hey PBOAT." Prettiest bartender of all time. As if it were all part of the job. I got my first close look at the tattoo. It was a memorial to Jeanie Bloom with her name and a rose. Not even close to a skull.

The first rush was over. Erin was killin' it behind the bar. She texted friends in Chicago about what she was doing but they didn't believe her, so I took a picture of her behind the bar, serving a beer to A.J. Mc Tibble and sent it off. The pizza oven was quiet, the jukebox playing. A lake breeze blew through the screens.

The front door opened. "Hey, Robel!" Max elbowed through the crowd and up to the bar wearing a baseball jersey and jeans. He opened his arms like he owned the place. "You working again?" He looked around. "Lotta thirsty customers. Hey, can I crash by you tonight?"

I waved. "Huh, yeah. Mom'll say okay." Erin tapped me on the shoulder and asked me to move. I was blocking the beer cooler. "Oh, wait. Max, this is Erin."

Max's smile could have sold toothpaste. "Oh, Miley."

I regretted the Miley Cyrus bit, as I knew I would. "No, her name is Erin."

She side-eyed me. "Who's Miley?"

"No one. Inside joke," I said, and then quickly added, "Not about you."

Max motioned us closer. "You two, come down to Fanny's later." He looked down at Wes and Fanny, seated in their usual spots. "They're gonna be, you know, gone."

The door opened again. A girl with long, brunette hair, dark eyes, and long legs approached behind Max. My scalp tingled.

Diane said, "Hi Sam. Who's this? Another of your cousins, come to help?"

Erin nudged me and asked, "Miley?"

I grinned at Diane's remark and said, "No, no," Then I looked at Erin. "No . . . NO!"

"This is Erin," interjected Max. "Erin, Diane Warren." He pursed his lips, eyes wide, seeing the tension and loving it.

Both girls said hi. Erin said something and slipped a hand into the crook of my arm. I tilted my head toward her. "What's that?"

"For that guy over there. I need a Coors. Where are they?"

I opened the bay and handed the can to Erin.

Diane looked at Max. "Did you ask him?" Max nodded. She leaned across the bar. "Well? You coming to the party?"

A day earlier I would've jumped at the chance to attend another party in #5, but not now. I had to tell Max and Diane they wouldn't be, either. Mission: Jeanie Blue had been moved up by a week. "Not this time."

"Ah, come on, ya neek," Max said. "Are you working on that stupid bike again?"

"I wonder about you, Sam, I really do," Diane said.

I flushed. "Hey, keep it down. I've got to talk to both of you right now. It's about the job. I think tonight is perfect."

"Tonight!" Diane said. "What happened to—"

I interrupted. "Not here. Meet me by the back porch in five. Really. Go."

Max looked at Diane then shrugged. "Let's hear him out." They left together through the front door.

I turned toward Erin. "I'll be a minute in the back. I have to see if Max and Diane can do the mission tonight. You know why. I'll get Fanny and Joe to cover for me."

She nodded. "Don't be long."

"I won't." I tapped Fanny's hand and asked her to help Erin bartend while I was gone. She got off her stool and came behind the bar, as she had done many times before. I found Joe in the kitchen, reading a magazine. I asked him to do me the favor.

Joe closed the magazine. "Erin is bartending?" He slowly rose from his seat.

"Yeah. Fanny is too."

He started toward the bar. "Okay. Take your time."

As I passed my parents' bedroom I saw the letter from the bank sitting on the chest of drawers. Pausing a moment to look around, I took the two steps into the room, snatched the letter, then went out the foyer to the back porch where I found Max and Diane. The bedrooms were deserted so I waved them into my room. Max had brought along the guitars, but the plan to play had been scotched.

"So, what's this all about?" Diane asked. "The plan was next week, when there's moonlight. Why the sudden change?"

There were several reasons, some better than others. I started with darkness, always a better cover than moonlight for the kind of work we had in mind. There was also the weather, unpredictable as Erin had said, although I didn't bring her name into the discussion at that point. "Conditions can't be any better than tonight."

"Not so," Max replied. "Wes and Fanny are going to be cruising the lake. What if we run into them?"

"Fanny's going to find out about a change in weather in a few minutes, from me." They'd be staying home, so the party in #5 was off.

"What are you talking about? It's blue sky out there," Max said.

I said, "The bartender, me, is going to tell her a lie. Storms moving in. And you know Fanny, if there is any chance of rain, she won't even get on the pier." I paused. "There's one other thing. Obviously, Erin didn't go home." I tapped the envelope on my palm. "She wants to go on the raid. She wants to go along."

"You told her about the mission?" Diane asked.

"I think that's why she stayed."

Max paced away, gazed out the window, then looked back. "First of all, you've known her what, two days?"

"Three."

He ran both hands through his hair. "Why would we trust her? Why should we take her?"

"She told me today. She lost her best friend in seventh grade, picked up off the street and killed by her mother's degenerate boyfriend; the girl was never seen again. Her name was Jean. Erin thinks if she helps put Junior Manticore behind bars, she's helping her friend." I took the letter out of the envelope and started reading.

Diane said, "That's pretty heavy. She told you that?"

"I don't know, man. She's just your girlfriend. Why should I—"

"If we're talking about hooking up, let's not forget the Steve factor here." I lowered my voice. "Now that you two are together, how long before he figures that out? In another week, our plan to have Diane in his hip pocket for at least the night of the raid goes out the window." I shrugged. "It's a small town. He might already know." I went back to the letter.

"He's got a point," Diane said.

Max looked over my shoulder. "What's this?"

"Shit." I nodded. "Here's another reason." Max leaned into me. "We got this letter yesterday, from the bank. Those bastards have called our loan."

"What!" Diane said.

"Yeah." I gave him the letter. "If we don't pay, they are going to foreclose our ass."

He scanned the letter. "How can they do that?"

"I don't know. Something about the septic not up to code." I slammed the bedpost. "You know all this is a set-up by Manticore."

"So, now we're on the clock," Diane said. "That's the real reason to flip on this."

"That bastard." I took the letter from Max and put it back in the envelope.

"We don't have a bike for her," Max said.

"I've got an old twenty-inch bike with a banana seat. Did you bring the wheels for my Schwinn?"

"They've been in my boat for a week. If push comes to shove, can she run and swim?"

"Three years on the varsity swim team. If push comes to shove, we'll be sucking her exhaust. Where did you park the boat?"

Max's boat was docked at #9's pier. He would put the new wheels on my old Schwinn while I finished my shift behind the bar. We parted ways in the foyer: Diane and Max out the back door, me to the bar.

Joe was clearly enjoying his time with Erin, and disappointed with my return.

Dad came in at seven p.m. The bar settled down.

Fanny brushed an auburn curl away from her face. "Look at my wonderful husband, Sam. Keeping an eye on Erin so you won't have to."

I opened the cash box. "Can I play you something? Got a quarter with your name on it."

She took a drink of beer. "Last time we did that I had boy bands all night long."

I asked, "Are you and Wes going to tour the lake tonight? My weather app says you better be careful if you are." I ducked a little to get a look out the back window of the bar. "Clouding up already."

"Is it supposed to rain?" Fanny tugged on her husband's sleeve. "Wes, it's clouding up, I think it's going to rain. I'm not getting in no boat if the weather's gonna be nasty."

CHAPTER TWENTY-THREE
Mission: Jeanie Blue

Thursday Evening, June 20

Erin and I escaped bar duty a little after nine p.m. Exiting the front door, we walked to the garage where I retrieved my newly revived Schwinn and a banana-seat Huffy wonder from my father's adolescence. I stood them by the garage and asked Erin to watch them for a couple minutes while I ran in the house. "Then we're off. Anyone asks, we're going for a bike ride."

I ran inside, ripped off the khaki shorts and put on two pairs of jean shorts and a couple of old, dark t-shirts. I stepped into a tattered pair of tennis shoes and grabbed another pair to take along.

Back outside, I found Kevin talking to Erin. She said, "Your brother thinks we're going to need bug spray."

In less than an hour, we'd be traipsing through a wetland in the middle of July. Kevin was absolutely right. I stepped into the garage and grabbed a can of repellant and the extra bag of clothes I had stashed there.

Erin and I got on the bikes and peddled past the pool then took a left onto the road leading to the Vedder place. Max had moved his boat to their pier. They weren't due up until tomorrow, so there was more privacy. We went down the driveway, past the cabin to the pier where Max was waiting, arms crossed, his backside resting against the captain's chair of the boat.

Erin hopped off the Schwinn and handed it to Max.

"Ok, junior, you're next." He extended a hand and the banana was onboard, too. "What's with all the long-sleeve shirts?"

I threw him the bag of clothes and said they were for afterward. I pulled a t-shirt out of the bag and handed it to Erin. "You can't wear that nice blouse where we're going."

Erin took the shirt and eyed it up and down. "Really?"

I said, "Don't give it the stink eye. It's clean." I said the white cover-up she was wearing was too easy to spot at night and would get filthy anyways.

"Don't worry," Max said. "He has an endless supply of wearable crap."

She flicked her hand, grabbed the bottom of her top, and began pulling it over her head.

Max and I cried, "Whoa!"

"We can turn, you know," I said.

Her arms dropped. "I have a swimming suit on." Max and I were still stunned. "Underneath." The blouse came off, the shirt went on.

The same was true of her white short shorts. They had to go. I gave her a pair of my cut-offs. Even the smaller pair was way too big but they covered her suit well enough.

"Enough wardrobe. We gotta move," Max said. "It's almost dark." Max's phone chimed. He took it off the dash and looked at the text. "It's from Diane. She's having a beer with Steve at Tonto's. She'll text me if there's any change." He threw the phone back on the dash.

I gave him the thumbs up but worried about "borrowing" Nic's bike for the night, but not for long. Max would use it and we'd have it back in less than an hour. I had the banana seat and Erin the Schwinn. Max started the engine. I released the lines and the mission was in motion. Max put the throttle down.

Traffic was light on the Narrows of Red Wolf Lake and very quiet on the Back Bay. As we approached the marsh, finding the channel became really tough. Erin and I got in the bow and shot our flashlights forward. Nothing was in the right place. Landmarks did not look the same as in daylight. Greens became black and the water reflected whatever the sky sent its way. Soon, shadows stretched into night and the going got tougher yet.

We'd been idling into the marsh for three minutes when I turned and hoarse-whispered to Max, "We've gone far enough, don't you think?"

"Hell if I know. Shine your light down, how deep are we?"

I looked over the gunwale and said we were close enough. Max killed the engine. I tossed the flashlight to him, jumped into the lake, then pushed the boat, stern first, until the shoreline stopped me. Erin exchanged her sandals for a pair of my old tennis shoes. We moored the boat. The mosquitos moved in on the back of the ripe tangy smell of the swamp. Max slapped his neck and legs. I grabbed the spray. We bombed up.

Bikes unloaded, flashlights in hand, we walked in search of the trail we'd marked the night before. It was soon clear that our docking point was not the same as yesterday. Just ahead, Max found an unmarked trail, but it was going in the right direction. We got on the bikes. Max took the lead, Erin next, and I was third.

Max soon picked up the markers. Ten minutes later, we arrived at the fence. The Manticore property was spitting distance away. Scaling the fence had looked like trouble during the day, near-impossible at night. We hid the bikes in a knot of underbrush and started toward the lake, using the fence line as a guide. The end post was sunk off shore in two feet of water, forcing us to wade around the end and then scale the rocky waterline.

Crouching low, I scanned the property: the mansion was a couple hundred feet off the lake, the boathouse on the far side of the triple-wide lot, the big garage attached to the back of the boathouse. "I don't see any signs of life. Do you?"

"Nothing," croaked Max, crouched next to me.

"This is a beautiful place, and nobody lives here?" Erin asked.

"Nope." I pointed at the boathouse. "It's *that* thing I can't figure. Three times bigger than anything on the lake."

"Okay, Captain Nemo," Max said. "Now what?"

"Follow the shoreline."

The Manticores had reinforced the shore with rocks of all sizes, some as big as basketballs, others as small as a grapefruit. Stumbling across the embankment was harder than we thought, so when we arrived at the boathouse, all of us were winded. We crept around the lake side of the boathouse, past the two iron runners that ramped up from the water to the inside berth where the boat was kept in dry-dock. Two vertical doors were the only opening facing the water, and they looked older than the rest of the building.

We stopped on the east side of the boathouse and huddled there, out of sight of the mansion. I was shivering, even though it was warm. I thought looking at Max and Erin would calm me down. That was a mistake. Max's face was as taut as a snare drum, his eyes burning bright in the moonless night.

Erin was different. Watching every angle, her eyes flicked from lake to land, land to sky, and showed none of the panic that had to be growing in her chest. It struck me right there—James Jr. would never, in any conceivable universe, have taken his date, or any girl, and put her in a spot like this. Ever. And this was my way to somehow live up to his Eagle-Scout National-Honor-Society legacy:

Criminal trespass, breaking and entering, petty theft. Beautiful.

"Which door is it?" asked Max.

I reached in to the front pocket of my shorts and palmed the brass knock-off from the hardware store. "Service door, next to the big one. Come on." I waved them away from the lake toward the garage.

The more I saw of the building, the stranger it became. The front section was large enough for two twenty-two-foot boats— not surprising given the size of the mansion. But on the back, they had attached a garage, the very place where Steve did his mechanic's work, that was big enough for three cars, a shop, and then some.

The service door was right where Diane said it would be. "All right, we go in, get the belt buckle, get out."

"What's that humming?" Erin asked.

I turned my ear to the door. "Sounds like it's coming from inside."

Max tapped my shoulder. "Sam, key."

I put the key in the lock and tried to turn it. I shook my hand,

I rattled the key. I went right, left, right again. "Damn, Diane!" I punched the door.

"Are you kidding?" Max said. "Wrong key?"

I stepped aside. "You try it."

He took my place, but had the same result. I pocketed the key. "Now what?"

"Now we leave," Max said.

"Maybe there's a door like this on the other side," Erin said. "Or a window."

I went around the corner and checked the side windows. "Locked, and I'm not breaking windows. This is the only door. The garage doors are out, but the bay doors on the front look old. If I can sneak under by the ramp, I can open the garage from the inside."

"What are bay doors?" asked Erin.

"The big, tall ones by the lake," I said. "When they launch the boat, they open like a garden gate. Then they push the boat down the rollers on those rails we stepped over a minute ago."

"Not worth it," Max said.

"I think it is," Erin said. "From the water, the last place they'd expect a break-in."

"Right." I said. "Max, if you watch for cars, Erin and I will take one shot at it. We have Diane keeping an eye on Steve." Max was not convinced, I could see it in his face. "Listen man. Hang with me. I got to get this damn buckle. If the bank gets our place, we're out on our ass. It all started with the buckle, and that's the only way it's going to end."

Max looked down the driveway and sighed. "Okay." He held up a finger. "One shot, and make it quick."

I waved Erin forward. "Come on."

Facing each other, we seated ourselves on the iron ramps. I lifted a hand off the metal and showed it to Erin. "Look at the rust. This would have been on your shorts."

Her hand was the same. She looked up at the twin doors rising above us and said the building looked a little like a horse barn, right down to the hinges on the sides of the doors and the old-fashioned sliding bolt and a latch with a padlock.

I handed her the flashlight. The plan was for me to jump in the water and try to slip between the lower wooden edge of the door and the concrete floor of the house. She would stay on the ramp, pull on the lower edge of the door, which was well above the waterline.

One hand on the rail, I slid into the water, and immediately a strong current pulled on my legs, as if the bottom of the lake had dropped to hell and was taking me with it. "Holy shit!" I grabbed onto the ramp, pulled up my feet and looked down.

"What's the matter?"

"I don't know. It's weird, there's some kind of undertow here." I looked side to side. "Maybe because of the drop-off."

Fist on hip, Erin said, "Thought you said you can swim?"

"I can. I'm telling you, this is… it's beyond crazy."

"Okay, forget it. Slip under the doors."

The floor of the boathouse was eighteen inches above the waterline. I used the rail to get under the lower edge of the wooden doors. There was a metal edge just inside that marked the top of the concrete floor. The space Erin made could handle my arm and shoulder. My head was next.

"Okay, pull on the door, Erin. Pull!"

"I am."

I felt the door give. Using the back of my head as a wedge, I wiggled in.

"My arms," she wheezed.

"A little longer," I grunted.

The door tightened. I felt a searing pain in my left ear. My left arm was inside the house, my right dangled. My head was being squeezed in a door and concrete waffle iron.

"Sam," Erin cried in a hoarse whisper. "Are you all right?"

My breaths came deep and fast. "The door—it's—a vise." I pushed away with my shoulder. I felt Erin pulling again. I grunted and shifted. My ear was caught on something sharp. Pain creased through my scalp. "Pull, Erin. Pull!"

Tears spilled down my cheeks. Something warm coursed

along my jaw. I tasted blood.

"Sam! Hold on."

A second later the doors creaked, the hardware screeched, and the pressure in my skull disappeared. My head dropped free.

Again in the water, I groped for the rail to keep from being sucked down by the current. Gasping for air, I pulled myself up to the rail. "Well... that ain't... gonna work."

Hand still on the door handle, the other with a flashlight, Max stood on the rail opposite Erin. "How many times have I told you not to stick your head in cracks?" He clicked on the light. "Your ear's bleeding."

"Does it hurt?" Erin asked.

I shrugged. "No gouges?" I turned my head side to side.

She turned on the light. "No, but you have a cut." Then she said. "We've got it backwards."

"Backwards?" I asked.

"I'm a lot thinner, you're a lot stronger. I should be crawling, you pulling."

This girl was unbelievable. I was ready to call the whole thing off and she was looking ahead to the next move. Before "No" left my mouth, she was in the lake.

"Wow. You're right about the current. I've been in rivers and it's nothing like this."

Max hopped off the rail onto the shore. "Make it fast."

"All right. Hang on." I moved to a spot where I could raise my foot and push off the shore to gain leverage. "What the hell? This is not shoreline." I searched around with my foot. "There's a cement wall below the boathouse."

"Can you push off it?" Max asked.

"Yeah, sure, but—"

"Then do it."

Erin slipped under the lower edge of the door. I flexed my leg, hooked my hands under the door, and pulled away. "Okay Erin, now."

She came out of the water as smooth as a dolphin. In seconds, her shoulders were inside.

"Watch your head," I said. "There's a boat motor right above you."

She slipped in up to her hips and stopped. She kicked her legs but still lost momentum. I tried to grab one foot to give her a leg up, but it didn't work.

"I'm stuck," she said.

"I know." I pulled harder but the door wouldn't give another inch.

"It's the shorts," she said. "They're snagged."

I had the sense that she was doing something with her hands. Then I heard the zipper.

"Take them off," she said.

I was a private first class seeing his first action. I froze.

Then it was an order. "Sam, pull them off."

My first effort was pretty weak—they gave hardly at all. Then I tugged harder. Erin drew her legs through and she was in. I let go the door and, my breath as short as the cut-offs in my hand, threw the jeans on shore, where they landed next to Max's feet.

Inside the boathouse, I heard doors open and close. I got out of the water. A second later, Erin stuck her head around the corner and said:

"Come on. Wait till you see this."

We followed her in the service door to the garage. Once inside, the mechanical hum we'd heard earlier became louder and closer.

Erin pointed at a second door to the left of the boathouse. "It's coming from in there."

There was a dusty set of left-handed golf clubs set in front of the door. I noticed because I'd never seen a set before. Moving the clubs aside, I put my hand on the doorknob and looked at Erin. "Did you try it?"

She shook her head.

I turned the knob. The door opened into a square, windowless room that housed a huge electric motor connected to industrial-sized pipes. I turned on the light. "What the hell…"

I circled the machine. A large switch box on the wall had two buttons, one red, one green. A couple of snorkeling masks hung on a nail with two heavy-duty flashlights next to them.

"Max, what is this?"

"Damned if I know."

I stood back from the plumbing. "You don't think…" I looked at Erin. The shirt I'd given her sagged with wet and was blotched with grease. Blood trickled from a scrape on her thigh. Her blonde hair was a tangled mess, and there were rust streaks on her face and arm. I'd never seen a more kissable girl in all my life. I said, "Could this be sucking water out of the lake?"

Her chin dropped. "Can they do that? Is it legal?"

"Not even a little bit," Max said.

She stepped back. "What would they use it for?"

"The Manticores are farmers." Max's voice was a growl. "Huge fields of corn. Miles and miles of irrigation lines. Think of a lawn sprinkler that can do eighty acres an hour."

"We're in a drought," I said. "Their well has probably dried up like everyone else."

The pump turned off. I startled, so did Max and Erin. I tried to see if we had tripped something. The switch box's green button still glowed. "I think it's okay. Turned itself off." I stepped around Erin, grabbed a mask and flashlight, and headed out the service door.

"Where you going?" Max asked

"Quick look, while it's off." I put the mask on my forehead and dangled the flashlight around my neck. "I want to see if I'm right. This is what she knew. Jean Manticore. This is why they killed her."

Erin took the other mask and light. "I'm going, too."

I turned toward her. "It's not worth it. I'm only looking for a second."

"So, it'll be two seconds, and if you get in trouble, I can pull you out."

I smirked. "Because you know how to swim."

"Right."

"Let's go." Stepping carefully, we walked to the lake. Lights on, we put on the masks, and dove in.

I scanned the wall below the waterline. The concrete extend-ed wider than the house. In the middle of the wall was an iron grid, clearly the end of a water intake pipe. Erin had her light on it immediately, but she was too close. I grabbed her by the shoulder to move away. The opening had to be twenty inches across. The volume of water the pump could suck out of Red Wolf Lake in one night, let alone a growing season, could cover hundreds of acres.

I grasped her arm and motioned to the surface. Suddenly, the pump cycled on. Instantly, the terrible, irresistible current was back. It pulled me hard, but Erin was much closer. She had no chance.

The suck plastered her leg against the grate. Eyes wide with terror, she was all elbows and arms. I thought my skin would come right off my bones. I clutched, she pushed. I grabbed, she pried. Nothing gave way. Panic roaring in my ears, I wrapped my arm around her waist, propped myself between her and the wall, and tried to wrestle her away from the mechanical mon-ster. It was no good.

Struggling, clawing my way up the wall, I breached the sur-face and yelled, "Max, turn off the pump. Erin's stuck. Turn off the pump! Max!"

CHAPTER TWENTY-FOUR
Race Through the Wetlands

Thursday Night, June 20

The switch box chinked. I went back under. The suction stopped. Erin drifted away from the grid, motionless. I put one hand under each of her arms and hoisted her up. She popped out of the lake like she weighed nothing at all. I sat her down on the rocky shore to the right of the rails. Choking and coughing, she ripped off the snorkel and gasped her first breath.

Legs shaking, I climbed onto the rocky shore, put a hand on her shoulder, and waited for her to regain her strength.

Max jogged from the back of the garage. "What the hell happened?"

"That damn pump caught us. Erin was stuck on the intake." I gasped another breath. "You saved us, man. Thanks." I crouched next to Erin. "Are you all right?"

"Yeah, I'm... I'm... I think so." She took a deep breath, then flexed her leg, hash-marked from the intake grid.

I slipped the light strap off my arm and handed it to Max, then my snorkel and Erin's, too. The breeze was warm, the sky starting to clear.

"You were right," Max said. "Damn Manticores, they're using the lake as their own watering hole." He nodded at Erin. "Where's your light?"

"Bottom of the lake, and I'm not going after it."

"I'll put these back." Max turned to leave.

"Better turn on the pump," I said. "Before someone notices.

Nothing from Diane, Right? No texts."

Suddenly, Max was looking down, grasping at the pockets of his jeans. "Oh shit, no. I left my phone on the boat."

"Okay, we get the key and bust it out of here." I sat down next to Erin. "How's your breathing?" The pump kicked on. At the same time, I heard a car click into park and an engine turn off. The sound of a car door slamming came from the driveway. I hadn't seen headlights. I turned. A slim figure marched around the corner.

I sprang to my feet. "Diane, what's going on?"

"I just left Steve. He got a call. The remote alarm went off on the pump, whatever that means. He's on his way to Manticore's to get some tools. Better get your collective asses out of here."

Max came out the service door. Erin got up and stood next to me.

Diane gave Max a kiss on the cheek and said, "Why didn't you answer my text?" He explained the forgotten phone. Then she looked at Erin and me. The corner of her mouth hooked sideways. "What the hell happened? You look like a couple a drowned rats."

"Tell you later." I pointed my chin toward her car. "How'd you get here?"

Diane's eyes were back on Max. "Steve's car, one of his old ones. He's on his bike." Then she looked at me. "Did you get it? Where's the buckle?"

"Getting it right now," I said, "Then we're out of here."

She grabbed Max's arm. "You've got about two minutes." She jogged back to the car and climbed in.

"Thanks," Max said.

She turned the car and left on County GG, headlights off.

I looked at Erin and Max. "I've got to go through the tool chest. Thirty seconds."

Max handed me my flashlight. "I'll close the doors."

Erin and I went in the service door, turned on the garage light and headed straight for the floor-standing, twelve-drawer tool chest. I tugged on the top tray, then the second, and the third. They were all locked. My fist came down on the top. I saw the keyhole. In my pocket, I had but one key. I took it out, shoved it in, and it turned like it was factory direct. "Thank you, Diane."

We pulled drawers, two sets of hands searched frantically, pushing wrenches aside, lifting ratchets and hammers. Panic grew as we opened the seventh drawer. Max joined us.

"Time to go. Now."

"Just a couple more."

Max went to the window. "Headlights coming down GG."

"Get out the ski masks." I opened drawer eight and put on my mask, which was soaking wet. So did Max.

"I bought a nylon," Erin said.

"Even better." My hand felt something foreign. I pushed in to the deep corner of the drawer and pulled out a buckle connected to light blue fabric. "Yes!"

"I don't want to put it on," Erin said. "It's too tight."

I put the belt buckle in my pocket. "Give me the nylon." I handed her my ski mask. We pulled them over our heads and followed Max out the door.

"Hit lights, shut the door," Max cried. "And run."

The headlights turned in: a pick-up truck and a motorcycle. We sprinted across the open yard toward the far fence line— Max in the lead, then Erin and me.

The driver of the truck popped out of the cab and yelled, "Hey, stop right there." Then, "Steve, stop 'em."

The motor cycle revved. We approached the end of the fence and swung around.

Max and Erin ran to the trail and yanked the bikes free of the bushes.

"Sam," Max cried. "Let's go."

"No names, man. You two go. Get the boat ready." I picked up a tree limb from off the ground. "I'm going to wait for dip wad. He's not coming around this fence," I said, wishing I had a bigger piece of wood.

Max got on his bike. "All right. Hurry."

Erin hesitated.

I waved. "Go on, I'll be right there."

On my old Schwinn, she followed Max's light into the woods.

In seconds, Steve's cycle was at the fence. The engine quit. I heard footsteps heading toward the end post. His right hand appeared. I smacked it with the limb. He cried out. His left hand still clinging to the other side of the fence, he wrapped his right leg around the base of the end pole. I wound up and broke the limb over his ankle. The howl echoed off the trees. He fell backwards into Red Wolf Lake.

I heaved my banana bike upright, stepped into the pedals and pumped. The bike was smaller than Max and Erin's, so I wasn't going to make up any ground, but I could out run a one-legged Steve.

He must have figured the same because I heard the motorcycle and Steve heading for the County GG. There was a fence line along the road he'd have to go around to get access to the public forest I was riding through. The gate was more than a quarter mile down the road. Once around the fence, he'd have to double back, come toward the lake, find the right trail, and finally, start his pursuit.

No doubt I had the energy to beat him to the boat. The trail was the problem—the faster I went, the stranger it looked. I missed several white ties because I was too hot-wired to notice them. I didn't have much time, and Steve had plenty of gasoline.

When the sound of the bike got further away, I breathed a little easier. I found the nylon stocking hotter than any ski mask. Sweat stung my eyes and blurred by vision. The trail became a guess, the beam from my flashlight a smear. I hit the brake, pulled off the stocking, and used my shirt as a sweat towel. From the suzz of Steve's bike, I knew he had found the trail head. The nylon went on again. I got back on the bike.

Then, the cloth markers vanished. With each turn in the trail, my chest tightened a little more. The engine came closer. Coming up was a point where the trail took a sharp turn inland. I put down my feet and flashed the light. No white cloth anywhere.

Cupping my hands around my mouth, I yelled toward the channel. "Hey, man, I'm lost. Where are you?"

The bike blared on. Max's reply came from behind me. Steve had cut me off. I threw my bike into the underbrush, jumped in after it, and waited for Steve to zoom by.

Seconds later, his headlight appeared, vibrating with the uneven ground. I shrank low. Steve decelerated for the curve, coasted through the hairpin, and hit the throttle. I sprang from my hiding place, slid the nylon off my head, and I tied one end, chest high, to a sapling on one side of the trail. Then I stretched the stocking to its tightest degree and tied the other end in the same fashion to a tree limb on the opposite side.

I mounted the bike and found a trail going toward the channel. I was two hundred feet away from the water when I heard Steve's bike, closing on me again. With still half the distance to go I heard him decelerate for the curve, then punch the throttle. Suddenly, the bike screeched and the engine died. My heart dropped into my guts. I stopped my bike, listening for signs of life. Moments later, Steve was swearing a blue streak that would've made my father blush.

I pumped a fist and yelled, "Almost there."

As I approached the channel, I saw Max and Erin in the water, pushing the boat away from shore.

The motorcycle came back to life. I pedaled the last thirty feet, hopped off the bike, and threw it into a bed of pussy willows. "Get in the boat. I'll push."

Slogging through two feet of water, I caught up and helped Erin push it to the channel.

"Deep enough. Erin, get in." Steve was fifty yards away. "Start it up." The hydraulic hummed. The outboard cranked, lake water gurgled next to my thigh.

CHAPTER TWENTY-FIVE

Soaking Up the Spoils

Thursday Evening, June 20

Max said. "Time to blow this pop stand."

I plopped over the gunwale, smashed into the wheels of the Schwinn, and curled next to Erin. "Go, go, no lights."

Max ducked behind the dash and put down the throttle. The outboard roared, the boat planed off, and the high-pitched whine of Steve's cycle faded. Staying low, I looked back over the transom into the single beam that Steve was using to scan, back and forth. I sat back and looked at Erin, seated like me on the floor, behind the back seats, both of us biting our lips.

"We did it," I whispered.

"What?"

I pulled off her ski mask. "We did it. Mission: Accomplished, girl." I tossed the mask to the wind.

Max's head was on a swivel. "We're not home yet."

"No worries. This is the fastest boat of all time."

Erin said, "FBOAT!" She whacked me on the shoulder. "Hey. Where's my nylon?"

"Tied to a couple trees back in the swamp." I raised my eyebrows. "You wanna go back and get it?"

"Hell no! But now I have a set of panty hose at home with only one leg."

We all laughed.

In less than a minute, we were on the open water heading straight down the throat of the Back Bay.

I handed Erin a long-sleeve shirt and put one on myself. She took off the wet, soiled pull-over, put on the shirt, and then her white shorts too, over her suit.

I looked at the Manticore Mansion to the northeast, fading in our wake. The place was lit up like a department store. "Something's going on by the boathouse. Shit." I looked forward toward Noquebay and sat down in a passenger seat. "They're gonna launch the boat. Did you see the engine on that thing? Bet it can fly. Get us to Vedders. We'll shut it down and scurry into the night like the vermin we are."

"How far is home?" Erin asked.

"We have to go around the peninsula, so five minutes, docked and dead at the pier."

"They're going to be on our ass by then." Max said.

"Their running lights are on," I said. "They're after us."

Max bumped the throttle. "Damn. You got the belt buckle?"

I reached in my back pocket and unfolded the light-blue piece of material attached to a buckle. "Hell right I do."

Max kept the motor at full throttle for a quarter mile past the peninsula, abruptly stopped, and turned as sharply as he could. He then followed his own wake back to a point in front of Nic's pier and did a slow left turn into shore.

Once we got close to the dock, Erin and I jumped into the water and guided the boat to a spot right behind the Vedder runabout. We removed all evidence of the mission from the boat, especially the bikes, and bolted. At the back of the Vedder garage, we stashed the bikes. Erin hoarse whispered, "Sam, look at that boat. It's putting a spotlight on the piers at the resort."

Max and I sidled next to the garage. I tugged on Erin's arm to join us.

"Holy crap, they're stopping at #9's pier. Dad isn't going to like that."

"Nah. He'll think they're customers, coming in for a drink," Max said. "You're being paranoid. But I think we should get out of here."

"So do I," Erin said. "But don't run. Walk like we belong here, because we do. Well, at least you guys do, sort of."

We snickered under our breath.

Taking the back road, we headed toward the resort. It was midnight. The operation had taken three hours. We turned onto Lake Road and back to the lodge. A car came up behind us and stopped. The vehicle was one of Steve's second-hand hot rods, the one Diane had driven to warn us. My brain automatically put Steve behind the wheel, but I was wrong.

Diane rolled down the driver's-side window. "Thought I might find you here." Her eyes were on Max. "What's your excuse this time?" She held up her phone.

Max looked at his phone. "Oh, sorry. I didn't hear it over the engine."

"Driving with your headlights now?" I pointed and smiled. "Kinda old-school for you."

She looked at me for half a second. "You've got blood all over the side of your face." Then she looked back to Max. "Wondered if you need a ride home. You won't be going out in the boat again tonight, I'm guessing."

"You guessed right." He bent low to look inside. "You don't have Steve hiding anywhere, do you? Don't think he'd appreciate—"

"He's right over there in the boat, or inside the bar asking about you guys." Diane flicked her head. "Let's go before he starts looking for me."

"See you tomorrow, man," Max said.

"Tomorrow." I raised my hand. He grabbed it and we shoulder bumped. "We killed it tonight." He walked around the front of the car and got in. Diane backed into Lewis Road, pulled out and left.

I watched the cars taillights. Erin put her fingers on the dried blood and said, "She's right. You can't go home looking like this."

I looked back at her, the rust stains on her hands, face, and arms; the parallel lines on her leg that marked her from the intake port. "You're no better." I paused. "Come on. I have an idea."

We walked briskly through the middle of the resort to the

fish cleaning shack. I slipped inside, came back out, and showed Erin my palm. "Soap."

We headed for the peninsula, passing her cabin on the way. She trotted over to a clothes line strung between a couple trees, and grabbed two beach towels. We found the gravel trail that followed the spine of the peninsula almost to its tip. The old sneakers dropped off my feet. I stepped into four inches of water. The stars were out, not a cloud to be seen. Erin sat down and undid her laces. I threw off my shirt, splashed my legs, and soaped them up.

Her shorts came off, then the long sleeve shirt, until all she had on was her two-piece suit. "How's the water?"

I looked toward the Back Bay. "A lot friendlier than it was over there." My legs fully soaped, I walked into deeper water. Then I washed my arms. "Here you go." I tossed the bar to Erin. Then I heard Max's voice, whispering in my ear, telling me to give her a hand, 'those marks on your legs might be hard to get.' But the vision of me soaping those thighs was as close as I was going to get. "I still need a dose for my hair, when you're done."

"Have you ever done this before?" she asked. "Taken a bath in the lake?"

"Sure." She looked at me sideways and *threw* the soap at me, overhand, a fastball. I cowered and held my hands up in surrender. "By myself."

My hair lathered, I took off my glasses, went under for a few seconds, and came up shaking my head like a dog.

"You still have blood on your face," she said.

"You still have rust on your cheek."

I traced a lathered finger across the left side of her face. She rubbed the spot with her fingers. "All gone?"

"No." I stepped closer, rubbed my thumb across her cheek again, the soap just enough to make it slick. "You missed a spot."

She tilted her head up. "I don't think I missed anything." Her arms went around my neck.

I slipped my other hand behind her back. "Oh, but —" I kissed her. All at once, everything glowed. I didn't have to open my eyes to see, she had blown the stars right out of the sky. I didn't have to look to know, I could feel them falling like rain all around us. She broke the kiss and asked:

"How is it now?"

I looked only in her eyes. "Perfect." I paused a second. "You were the secret sauce tonight." She smiled. "Without you, we wouldn't have gotten the belt. I'll never forget—" We kissed again. "And the sight of your pretty little ass slipping under the boathouse door. That was so bad!"

She slapped my face but not hard. "Boys are all the same."

I busied myself with the bloodied ear, soaped it up, then went half way under again. "Check it for me."

She came to my side and took hold of my chin. "Turn this way. There's still some in there. Give me the soap."

She lathered her right hand and rubbed behind my ear. That was no problem. But when she started on the inside, I pulled away. "Watch out for the cut. I don't want to bleed again."

"Man up, will you." She grabbed my shoulders and stood me straight.

"Almost gone." She cupped water in her hand and washed away the suds. "One more spot."

I should have stopped her right there, but how was I to know? And besides, she was too quick. She slipped her soapy-slick pinky finger in my ear and wiggled. My neck cringed. I stepped sideways, my foot hit a rock, and I fell in the water.

I recovered quickly. Erin had both hands over her mouth. Stifling a laugh, she uttered a so-insincere, "Sor—rry."

"I'll bet. I should dunk you for that." In a second, I was next to her, my arms had her wrapped in a clutch.

She folded her arms between us and said, "No, please. I'm too cold. I'm sorry, really." She shivered.

"Come on, let's get out."

We walked to shore and grabbed the towels. After three hours, it felt good to be finally dry. There was a ledge of grass, pushed up by the spring ice flow, that made for a perfect perch. I wrapped the towel around my shoulders and watched Erin dry her hair.

She joined me on the ledge, snuggled under my arm, and took a deep breath. Looking south across the Narrows of Red Wolf Lake, there was nothing gazing in on us except the Milky Way.

Then I remembered. Looking closely at her mouth I asked, "Are you wearing lipstick?"

She jerked her head backward. "Lipstick? Yeah, I was at the bar, but it's gotta be gone by now. Why?"

I moved my chin back and forth. "Check my lips. See any on me?"

She frowned. "No. Why? Would that be a problem?"

"No. Just the opposite. I've waited for my first lipstick for seventeen years."

She laughed, tapped my chest with her hand and said, "Maybe your luck will change tomorrow."

"Yeah, maybe."

"What time is it?" she asked.

"The time I always get in trouble with my parents." I put my arm around her and drew her near. "When Max left, it was around midnight."

"Oh man. How am I gonna explain this one?" she asked.

"Tell them the truth."

She looked up at me. "What! Are you crazy?"

"No. Tell them you rode across the lake with two guys you barely know, broke in to a boathouse, got stuck to an intake pipe and almost drowned, stole a valuable piece of evidence in an un-solved murder, and then came back and made out with the bar-tender on the peninsula."

The longer I went on, the harder she laughed.

"They'll never believe it," she said.

"Exactly. Tell them a truth they won't believe."

"No, they'd believe the first part." She nudged my chin with her forehead. "But kiss and swim with a *bartender*? Never."

I pulled the towels tight. "Never? Not even the one that al-most got you killed?"

"Not in a million years."

She pushed me on my back, and kissed me. Again.

CHAPTER TWENTY-SIX

And Then You What?

Friday Morning, June 21

Morning came. Sunlight framed the window shade. The room glowed, my head ached. I dressed and went to the kitchen. I was about to get milk from the refrigerator when Dad's voice broke the kitchen calm:

"Sam, what time you get in last night?"

He had walked in from the bar; Lloyd Stoker was with him. I steeled myself for the interrogation and peeked around the refrigerator door. "Ah, about eleven-thirty." My parents always added an hour to whatever time I gave, so I went along by giving an answer that much earlier. Dad also wanted to know what happened to Max, and why he hadn't slept over as planned. I made up a story that had him heading home in the boat after dark, and made a mental note to clear it with Max. It must have been a lame excuse for an excuse because neither Dad nor Mr. Stoker looked convinced. Dad gave me extra work to do at the pool to make the point.

"Come on, Lloyd," Dad said. "I think I got a piece of hose out in the garage might fit your fuel pump."

My work day started with cleaning the bar. While I worked I wondered, how much did my parents really know about last night? And what about Will and Sheila Eklund? Were they awake when Erin rolled in? And if so, how hacked would they be about the late hour? I hauled out the vacuum and pumped it back and forth across the floor until my arm felt like lead.

The bar was clean so I headed out to the pool. Down by #10, all was quiet. It was half-past ten; there ought to be some movement: Mrs. Eklund in the kitchen window, swinging a meat cleaver looking for the simp who had tried to defile her daughter. Or Mr. Eklund, on the porch, with a shotgun. I jumped the cyclone fence and readied the pump for vacuuming. The filter basket was full of sopped leaves and twigs, which went over the fence. I leaned over the pump and hit the switch.

"Hello."

I looked up. Standing in the pool house doorway, backlit by the morning sun was a shape I knew well. "Where'd you come from?"

"Nice to see you, too."

I felt buoyant again. One look at her and everything—the fear and the worry—evaporated like pool spray on summer concrete. "No, I mean, didn't see you coming."

"I'm sure." She stepped closer. "Whatcha doing now?"

I shrugged. "Busy work." Still not sure what to expect from her, I picked my words carefully. It wasn't a morning after, not really. But for me, the closest thing so far. She turned toward the pool. I saw no lines of worry or annoyance, her expression much like the day we sat on the swings. Even her clothes were cool: shorts and an oversize sweater, on backward and inside out. She said, "You look dragged out."

"Didn't sleep much." I stood up.

Her eyes widened. I put up a hand. "When I got home, I mean. That first forty-five minutes, I still can't believe it. Was there a sleeping potion in those beach towels or what?"

She pushed the hair from out of her eyes and said, "Yeah, I'm sure that's it. With everything that went down, it had to be the towels."

"Did you get in trouble?" I asked.

She smiled. "No! Mom and Dad think, you know, this is the backwoods, not Chicago. What kind of trouble can I get into? *Really!*" We both laughed at that one. "Then what? You're not going to be working all day, are you?"

"Dad's suspicious. Cleaning the pool is part of the penance. Got the ditches to mow after lunch, but that's an hour, two at the most." I got a glimpse of her blue eyes, the slender legs below the hem of the sweater. My knees felt like sand. "Are you feeling all right, from the grate, I mean."

She showed me an odd-looking bruise on her thigh, which gave me a shiver because it reminded me of how close we came to losing her. Max had saved her, really. I asked her to reserve time for me later, after work; but no more midnight raids. She feigned disappointment, and then asked about the buckle. I told her going to the police wasn't as easy as it sounded. My parents would have to be involved, and explaining how it came to be in my possession again would be difficult. And that was nothing compared to the blackmail theory, if I brought it up at all. I rubbed my face. "If I say the buckle turned up in my school backpack, does that sound believable?"

"No, but maybe that's because I know it's b.s." Erin sat down on an upside-down ten-gallon pail. "Okay, let's say they believe you. What if this Manticore guy comes along and says you stole it?"

I told her when it came to the Manticores, Steve was the least of my worries. Willard Jr. probably killed Jean. His brother, Mitchell, had done time for what I didn't know. Willard Sr. thought he could own anyone or anything. She followed me along as I vacuumed the pool. I'd been looking for someone to confide in about my suspicions regarding Max's dad and his connection to the Manticores. At one time it would have been Diane, but not now, not since she hooked up with Max. Erin was my best option. I told her about my misgivings and that I didn't know how to tell Max, or even whether I should.

This worried Erin more than I expected. She took my arm and said a lot depended on how much proof I had, especially since it seemed to her Max hated the Manticores. I reminded her that she was witness to some of the evidence two days earlier when the boat went aground: the CCT hat on the dash, and the matchbook. "Remember I said there was a joke inside." I shook my head. "There was a date, and it said 'load #68-M47. Light 3 bundles Call J.R.' J.R. is Max's dad."

She didn't know about the F.B.I. investigation into Cherhasky Capital and Transport and the possible connection to the Chicago mob. Or that Square M, the Manticore construction company run by Mitchell, probably installed all the irrigation equipment, the pump, and retaining wall we discovered the night before. So, I told her.

"Wow, the stuff you got going on up here, Sam. I can't believe it. Puts Chicago to shame." Still, Erin remained skeptical. "Maybe you shouldn't tell him. Unless you have more proof. He won't believe it anyway. And then all you have are hard feelings."

I went to backwash the filter. She worried the Manticores would report the break-in. I didn't think so. With an illegal pump sucking water out of Red Wolf, they wouldn't invite law enforcement over for a look. She appeared visibly relieved and said she wanted to go fishing later. She obviously noticed my lukewarm response, because she added:

"I'll bring my lipstick."

"Like I said, I am a fishing fanatic." I stood up. "Wait a minute, you're going to *wear* the lipstick, right?"

"Oh, no. Lipstick before five o'clock? That would be so uncool. But you could, you know, pull it off…." She giggled.

"Smart ass." I laughed too. "How 'bout two o'clock, your pier." I scanned the area. We were alone, or alone enough. "Come here," I whispered.

She raised her chin and narrowed her eyes. "Why?"

I grasped her hand, tugged her off the pail and away from the door, and then put my hands on her hips. She smelled like shampoo. "Kiss in the morning. Fishing in the afternoon."

———

A minute after Erin left, Max appeared, standing in the door exactly as Erin had done, hair like quills, sandals on his feet, and a shirt that looked like he had slept in it.

"Sorry I missed that," Max said.

"Hey, how did you get here?"

"Nic called. The Vedders came up this morning and saw my boat at their pier. He came over and got me. Miley, she was here a pretty long time, you hound dog, you."

I ignored the Miley Cyrus thing, hoping it would die of neglect. I grabbed the pole and resumed vacuuming. "So, are you as beat-up this morning as I am? Guess I'm not used to a life of crime."

"You're not kidding. I could barely get out of bed. But last night, we was dope, man." Max laughed. "Maybe you're a little sore from something else, something I wasn't—"

"All right, I get it." I paused and then said, "The greatest minute of my life, last night, and it didn't happen on Manticore property."

Max grabbed the vacuum pole. "Okay, stop! Are you saying you and Erin…you went…?"

"All the way?" I pulled his hand off the pole. "She let me untie the top of her suit."

"The top of her suit?" he cried.

"I'm telling you, the second that top gave way, was the greatest thrill of my life. I just about lost it."

"That was your first?" Max turned briefly. "You coulda just gone out with Holly Rush. Everybody does their first bra with her. Heck, she'll even give you an instruction sheet."

"Holly Rush never heard of me." I snorted. "Get a load of this, we fell asleep for almost an hour out on the peninsula."

He blurted a laugh. "You what? Both of you?"

"We were bonked, and cold from being in the water. And the beach towels were so warm, man, and so was she. I couldn't help it."

Max looked down and shook his head. "Moving right along. What the hell are we going to do about that damn farm, sucking the lake dry? I couldn't sleep last night thinking about it."

I moved down the pool. "I don't know. We can't barge into the cop shop and tell them. First thing they'll do is lock us up."

Max had been thinking on it, and thought an anonymous letter to the county sheriff and the F.B.I. was a good start. We both remembered Nadine's warning about the local cops, so we settled on the newspaper as our backup. They'd get a letter in two weeks if the cops were a dead end.

Max looked across the resort. "Anything I can do?"

"Yeah. How about finishing the pool? Then I can mow the ditches."

"Somewhere to go?" Max asked, though I could see he knew very well.

"Erin, two o'clock, fishing."

"Chicks love to go fishing. Can't blame you. She showed some swag last night." Max grabbed the vacuum pole. "Horny monkey, go. And don't worry, I'll get the penicillin."

CHAPTER TWENTY-SEVEN

Second Catch of the Week

Friday Afternoon, June 21

When I think of fishing, there are few images that come to mind faster or more often than these: A screen door slams. Erin's sandals flopping, her hair tossed by the breeze. The hem of her yellow sun dress foams around her thighs. This is fishing?

My toes curled over the edge of #10's pier. I took the cooler from her and said, "You are the hottest fisherman of all time."

Her smile was a flower blooming. "Yeah, the HFOAT." She wrapped my chain around her finger. "And you, no shirt."

The high sun peeked into a coffee can full of worms. White oars and grey hull shimmered. The cooler went in the boat. I pointed at the seat in the stern. "That's your spot." I untied the ropes and we pushed away. After rowing a short distance, I nodded toward Lennon's Bight on the far side of the peninsula. "See that swim raft over there? Belongs to the Vedders, but we can use it anytime we want. Good place to fish."

"And if the cops show up, looking for us…"

"It's the last place they'll look. Or we could paddle to the Back Bay, hide in the marsh, and live there forever."

She shook her head. "Ground's too mushy. I couldn't wear my heels."

A breeze walked by and pushed the sundress off her right thigh. The oars stopped in the water when I saw the bruises, like hashmarks up the side of her leg. "Holy crap, Erin. Your leg." I looked at her, then back at the bruises.

She extended her leg and rolled it inward, to show the extent of the discoloration. "I know. I woke up this morning with a toothache in my thigh like I'd been kicked by a horse." She turned sideways on the seat and only then could I see there were three bruises, parallel, as if someone had put her on a grill. "Good thing I have this dress to cover them up."

"Yeah, don't know how you'd explain them. Do they hurt?"

"Not as bad. I took some Tylenol."

The lake was mid-summer, mid-week, mid-day quiet. The raft had a wood deck held afloat by four empty oil drums. I shipped the oars and tied the anchor rope to a cleat on the raft. Poles, bait, handbag, and cooler in hand, we hopped onto the weathered boards and spread out a beach towel on which to sit.

The air was warm, the sky unmarked by even a wisp of white. Lennon's Bight was really a bay, so the water was placid and clear. Erin sat. I baited a hook, tossed the line into the lake, and handed her the pole. The water beneath us was only chest deep, so we had little chance of catching more than a small sunfish, but there was no reason to tell her that.

I glanced at the Vedder cabin. For the first time in weeks, there were two cars parked in front of the garage—Phillip's black Cadillac and Nic's Chevy. I tossed a line in the same direction as Erin's and sat down next to her. Our feet dangled in the warm water. She opened the cooler and handed me a soda. The breeze played with the dress, offering an occasional glimpse of the bruised thigh beneath.

She flicked the dog tags dangling from my neck. "Tell me about him."

After tugging on the chain earlier, I suppose I should've been ready for this, but I wasn't. I looked at the end of my fishing pole, and waved the tip at a dragonfly. "My big brother, he was four years older than me but he never pushed me around. Didn't let his friends do it either, in fact, I was his tag-a-long, to baseball especially."

"Was he a good athlete?"

"Yes and no. Always punched above his weight, I think is

the saying, but that's the way he did everything." I spit in the lake. "Could have done college. Had a scholarship in his pocket the day he signed up." Hearing the exasperation in my voice, I stopped. "Sorry, scaring the fish."

"No, go ahead."

"Never got through his first week in Afghanistan. Sniper." I scratched at the weathered boards. "Back home, James was everywhere. I was… See, I'm not captain of the football team, not going to be valedictorian—"

"Wait a minute. Not smart? Who put Mission: Jeanie Blue together?"

I waved her off. "That's another thing. The worst my brother ever did was sneak kids into a drive-in. Last night, he was rolling in his grave."

"Okay, that's James." She looked to shore for a moment. "I've only known you for four days. Max has known you a lot longer. You know what he told me? When we were in the boat waiting for you, Steve was on the motorcycle and we knew he was going to catch you. I said, 'we should go help.'" She rapped me on the shoulder. "You know what he said? Max laughed and said, 'Just watch. Sam'll fix his ass. Just wish I was there to see it.' And you did, with *my* nylon."

"He said that?" I blushed. "That neek, wait till I see him."

I showed her how to cock the rod, push the button, and throw the line. She set the pole on the raft, pulled the sundress off her shoulders, and pulled a bottle of tanning lotion out of her bag. Her hand, the fingers glistening, slid across her thighs, then her arms and shoulders. She handed me the bottle. "Can you do my back?"

I was so anxious, I dropped the bottle. I slid behind her, dribbled some lotion in my palm, and rubbed her shoulders.

She exhaled softly. "What about tonight?"

"I don't know. Most families stay for one week in the cabins, so Friday nights are the craziest of the week. Every kid will be out for one last run of the place before they go home."

I negotiated the suit ties as best I could. "What are your folks gonna do?"

She leaned forward, watching a school of minnows darting about the tanks. Their plans were to go out for a fish boil at eight-thirty. I wanted her to blow it off, maybe fake a stomach-ache and stay home. She straightened, and I thought I'd gone too low on her back with the lotion. "Sorry."

She tapped the water with the tip of her pole. "Not a stom-achache, but, well, you know girls, we have an excuse anytime we need it."

"You do?"

"Come on, Sam. Something guys don't have, something once a month."

"Oh… You use that?"

"You kidding? Works every time. I'll fake cramps and stay home. Then, after dark, you come down."

It was perfect. Erin and me alone: suddenly it felt like the raft was in a grade 4 Wolf River rapids. I didn't have to bartend. The sun would be setting. Erin took the lotion from me.

"Sam… Sam? You're gonna bring some protection, right? Tonight?"

"What? Like… mosquito spray?" I asked, not following.

She laughed. "No, there are screens on the windows. You know. You don't expect me to have one? It's up to the guy."

Finally, I got it. Good thing I was sitting down. She was talking about a condom. Had a trap door opened in the middle of the raft and sucked me to Hong Kong, I wouldn't have been as shocked.

Her head turned another click in my direction. "You've got one, right?"

Got one? I'd seen a picture of one. And there was a place for-ty miles away that sold them. Was there a chance in hell I'd have the swag to buy one from the local druggist, who knew me and my family on sight? The answer was an easy no. It was beyond belief, but I had found something worse than puking my Pabst.

"Sure, I got one."

She looked back at the bobber riding the ripples, lips pursed, her dimples like divots.

My fishing rod, which had been as still as a stump, jerked sideways. "Oh, hey, watch out for the pole. That's Kevin's favorite. He'll kill me if I lose it."

"I didn't touch it."

"You must have, 'cuz…" My bobber went under. The rod skittered across the boards and into the lake. I lunged but missed. The reel skimmed across the water's surface, then sank. "Oh shit!" I grabbed the glasses off my face, dove into the lake, and swam toward the pole's last known position. I pulled up and yelled, "Do you see it? Which way? Which way?"

Now Erin was standing, looping arms through the straps of her dress. "I don't know. Oh, wait." She pointed, "Over there."

I thrashed about with my free hand, grabbing at anything I could find.

"No! There." Feet prancing, arm pumping, she pointed. "Farther over. That way, go that way."

I spun around. The bobber surfaced and the fish jumped. "A bass! Now I've got you." I went under, eyes open, and saw the rod resting on the sandy bottom a few yards away. With a final lunge, I grabbed the pole and stood up. "Yes!" I coughed and spit and put on my glasses. Water deep to my armpits, I raised the pole, put the rod on my shoulder, like a Marine and his M-1, and walked back to the raft, the fish zigzagging for all it was worth. I held the pole up to Erin. "Here, hold it while I climb."

"Wait. What! No, I don't know how."

"Just for a second. This is a big one." She took the pole. I started up the ladder.

"Oh God!" She battled the fish with both hands. "He's really strong. Oh, look out."

I was a step short of the deck. The fish veered and yanked the line. *Whack!* The pole creased my temple. My glasses went flying. Arms flailing like a windmill, I lost my balance. She offered her hand. I grabbed her arm, but it was too late. Both of us toppled into the lake—me backside first, Erin with a belly flop next to me. The rod flew from her hand.

I righted myself and opened my eyes. All was a blur. Erin

laughed between gasps so I figured she was all right. Once more I dove. The black horn rims were easy to spot on the sun-dappled sand. A few steps away, sundress billowing, Erin pursued the pole. "It's right here." She went under for a second and came up, pole in hand. She walked toward me, water running off her like a shower. "Take it, take it."

I whooped, "Thought you said you couldn't fish." I looked at her, trying not to laugh, but I couldn't help it. "Your dress, is it ruined?"

"No, it's just water." She climbed up the ladder. I followed.

She peeled off the dress and wrung it out. "Oh, Sam. I'm sorry. Is your head okay?"

I sat down on the raft. "You kidding? Christ on crutches, couldn't be better." I trolled in the line. "It's a bass, foot and half long if it's an inch. Fight like a banshee. I won't mind cleaning this one." My hands tensed. "Okay, you ornery bastard. I'm going nuclear on your ass!"

The pole bent into a horseshoe.

The fish jumped.

The line snapped.

CHAPTER TWENTY-EIGHT

Smoke on the Water

Friday Evening, June 21

After supper Max and I finally found the time to play some guitar, although it was mostly him strumming and me watching, trying to pick up the chords. We were in the laundromat. Kevin had a set of secondhand drums there so he joined us for a jam session we were sure would go down in Rock History next to the first meeting of John, Paul and George.

After an hour we broke it off, which agitated Kevin to no end. He stayed behind and took out his frustration on the skins. Max and I had dates. Diane was coming over to Fanny and Wes' cabin. Diane and Max were hoping the old folks would get the bar hopping itch again and leave the cabin to them.

"If you get lucky, you mean," I said.

"You should talk." Max rapped me on the shoulder. "How you gonna beat last night?"

I had asked myself that very question. I knew I could mess up the date in any of a dozen different ways. I walked off toward #9's pier. "See you later."

"Later." Max continued down the road to the cabins.

I felt for the foil packet in my pocket, a habit I'd fallen into since a visit to Nic Vedder just before supper. I could think of no other condom sources, so I rapped on his back door. We sat and talked and drank, him beer, me soda. I was beating around the bush until he brought up Erin. Turned out he'd been watching us earlier when we were on his swim raft. He swore me to secrecy, then took a Trojan out of his wallet and handed it to me. "For helping with the pier last spring." A better percentage on a job done I could not have imagined.

Lloyd Stoker was on #9's pier, loading fishing supplies into his boat, so I could talk to him and watch #10, Erin's cabin, at the same time. The engine was inboard, placed amid-ship, a plywood cowling bolted down around it. The "Noquebay Resort" placard was still on the transom. I wondered if Lloyd would ever do as he promised and have it removed.

"Good night for fishing," I said.

Lloyd looked up from the back seat. "Hope so. We haven't been out all day. The kids are itching to get a line in the water. Dad and I are too, for that matter." Lloyd turned the key and the engine backfired. The kids on the end of the pier jumped.

"Hello!" I retreated a step, and then hid a grin. "Did you blow the bilge? Might be some fumes hanging around." I offered a bad gas pump as an explanation for the motor's problem. Where motors were concerned, I didn't know an alternator from an ax handle, but I had to have some excuse for standing there.

"It was running fine yesterday. I think we'll be good."

An elderly, barrel-chested man dressed in bib overalls and a flannel shirt came toward the dock, wheezing like a broken bellows and waddling like he had a horseshoe under each foot. He held a floatation cushion in one hand, a cigarette in the other.

Lloyd looked up. "Hi, Dad."

I helped the old geezer into the boat.

There seemed to be no end to the amount of tinkering Lloyd could endure without getting bored. Such was not the case for me, and since there was still no sign of movement by #10, I decided to leave. "Well, gotta go. Good luck."

The sun melted into the western horizon. The weather was beautiful, so everyone was outside. For a Friday evening, the bar was slow. I sat on the bartender's stool, chin propped on my hand, and watched Joe and Harry Cashen, a friend from the cabins, play pool.

A.J. McTibble was in his usual spot, espousing blue-collar wisdom in barroom slang with an Irish accent that was belly-laugh funny. But after hearing it for the umpteenth time, I could listen to every other sentence and not miss a thing.

"Good Christ, my wife and her laundry, goes through more water than a brewery." Old A.J. ran a finger under his collar, and I imagined that if it were a little tighter, the Noquebay barfly couldn't talk so much. "Earth to Sam, Earth to Sam."

I blinked. "Yeah, brewery water, that's a good one."

"This gin palace still serve food?" asked A.J. "I said I'll have a brat and chips."

It wasn't my turn to work, but I put in the order. Then I went to the Wurlitzer, cranked the volume. Pearl Jam rattled the ashtrays. I sat down on Fanny's stool.

THA-BOOMMM.

The concussion about knocked me off my perch.

Harry looked up over his cue stick. "What the hell, was that thunder?"

"The jukebox," replied Joe. "Sam blew a speaker. Dad'll love that."

"Sounded more like a sonic boom," I said. "Those F-15s fly over sometimes." I walked onto the front porch, glanced out the front window, #10 barely visible in the distance. Kevin was on the basketball court, but he wasn't shooting baskets. Then I looked at the lake. In the fading dusk, about two hundred feet off shore—flames on the water.

"Holy shit!" I froze for a moment to be sure of what I was seeing. "Joe! Get Dad, right now."

On the silent surface of Red Wolf, the boat was aglow. I ran across the parking lot, past my stone-faced, wide-eyed brother. "Kevin! Come on."

We ran to #9's pier, jumped into the nearest rowboat, started the engine, and headed out. In the west, the day's last rays were fading. The flames, reflected off an oily film on the water, looked twice their actual size. And though the fire was not as high as it was at first, it was still enough to blind us to whatever was floating in the lake.

I idled the engine. "Kevin, get in the bow. See anything, tell me." The smell of singed hair and scorched rubber filled my nose. Strained voices echoed from onshore. I heard Dad barking orders, and then Nancy Stoker screaming hysterically from the end of the pier. Shadows ran along the shore toward the peninsula.

Kevin pointed at three heads bobbing in the water. "There. See 'em? Holy crap!"

A choking, raspy wheeze croaked from the right. "Help, over… here!"

"Grandpa, Grand…!" cried another.

"Oh, god."

A small boy with an orange, adult life preserver pushing up past his ears struggled toward the burning boat. I killed the motor. "No! Hey kid, this way, this way."

The kid flinched when he saw our rowboat. Then, in a panic, he reached for the gunwale and tried to pull himself out of the lake. We nearly capsized.

"Hold it!" cried Kevin. "Wait, I'll help you." The boy was terrified. Tears and soot mingled on his face. Kevin leaned toward him. "What's your name?"

The boy opened his mouth and sobbed.

From the other side of our boat came the sounds of struggle. "Gramp—"

"Here," wheezed an old voice, weak and thin. "No…"

A voice from somewhere in the water replied. "It's Rocky, you've got Rocky."

"Okay. Rocky, you hurt?" I asked. The boy held tight and shivered.

"Good. I'm gonna grab your life jacket and haul you in." Kevin moved to the other side to balance the boat. Rocky was light and almost jumped out of the water. Kevin guided him to the seat in the bow.

The fire receded. I saw a man, kneeling on the captain's chair, fighting the flames with an extinguisher. He stopped for a moment and said:

"Get Dad next, he's got bad lungs. There, with Jeff."

I knew the voice in the boat, it was Lloyd Stoker. A short distance away, Jeff Stoker was wearing the same type of orange preserver. The old man was gasping, clinging to his grandson with one hand, flailing at the water with the other.

"Grandpa, don't!" cried Jeff.

There was fear in the flesh of Grandpa's bony arms, panic in his wild, staring eyes. With no preserver of his own, Grandpa battled for his life. Every time he tried to rise above the water, he pushed his grandson under.

On the peninsula, a motor started; running lights came on.

Kevin used the oars to maneuver us closer to Jeff and the old man. The boy's head was above water, but only by the length of his chin. Grandpa twisted again. Jeff cried out then spit a mouthful of water.

"Don't push him. Grandpa, don't push Jeff," I said. "Hang on to the boat. There's a bigger one coming, they'll pick you up." But the old man wasn't listening, would neither let go of his grandson nor grab the gunwale, not even with his free hand. Water misted off the old man's pursed lips.

I grabbed Grandpa's flailing hand and put it on the gunwale. "There. Hang on." I handed him a floatation cushion. "Take this. No. Your other hand. Let go of Jeff. Take it."

"Where? Where is it?" croaked Grandpa. I showed him the preserver. With an unnerving swipe, he let go of Jeff, pushing him under one more time, and clutched the preserver.

"Good. Don't move." I looked at the other boat, still some ways off. "No! Grandpa, keep a hand on the boat." Then, to Jeff, "You okay? Can you paddle to the other boat?"

Free of Grandpa's grip and glad of it, Jeff pushed away and swam like a school of muskies were nipping at his heels.

Dad drove a runabout commandeered from one of the guests. Kevin yelled directions to Joe and Harry, crewing for Dad. Seconds later they hauled Jeff into the boat. "Grandpa, you're next," I said. "The big boat, just like Jeff."

The orange glow from the flames receded, replaced by a silvery cast from the sunset.

"I… I can't…breathe." Grandpa had run an arm through the straps of the cushion. The other hand was still on the gunwale. Doom etched his face. His parchment-thin skin was cut and torn in a dozen places, and red-rimmed, yellow eyes bulged in their sockets. Pulling him out of the water wasn't going to work.

"Okay," I said. "Hang on to the side of the boat. We'll go in real slow, till you can stand on the bottom. Then you can walk out."

The old man gasped something that sounded like a prayer. "Yeah… oh… paa…."

I restarted the outboard. We crawled along, my hand on the tiller, Kevin with his arm around Rocky on the middle seat. Grandpa's skeletal fingers clung to the boat.

I glanced at my brother. "Hey, Kev, have you seen Max?"

"Maybe in the other boat?"

"He's missing all the action." I shook my head. "Grandpa, are your feet touching?"

Grandpa grimaced. "No, yeah, a little." We were in about four feet of water when Kevin jumped in, swam under the old man's arm, and propped him with his shoulder. Cushion still clutched to his chest, Grandpa let go of the boat.

I left them and docked the boat. Rocky jumped onto the pier and ran to his mother's open arms. By then, the water was thigh-high on the old man and Kevin. I waded out, took the cushion from Grandpa, and got a shoulder under his other arm. We walked him in and set him in a lawn chair. By that time, the fire was out and Dad was towing the charred ChrisCraft to the pier.

The entire resort had congregated on the waterfront. Mom was trying to calm Nancy Stoker, who was a knot of nerves. Through the trees, from several miles away, the sound of the rescue squad siren was heard. Five minutes later, flashing red lights came down the road. Parting the crowd like a prow through water, the squad inched along and parked on the boat landing. A volunteer put oxygen on Grandpa Stoker. Nancy asked for a sedative, but they had none to give. From time to time, boats passed off shore to get a closer look at the spectacle.

I sat down on the ground, took off my shoes and socks, and

watched the rest of the recovery operation. Allison came by, handing out towels. I took one and dried my legs. The cool evening air gave me gooseflesh as I peeled off my dampened shirt. I stood up, picked up my shoes, started to walk away, and almost plowed into Diane and Max.

"Whoa!" I stepped back. Honestly, in the flashing red strobe from the ambulance, I didn't recognize her right away. She was dressed down in the way only she knew, but she had less make-up than usual and her hair was pulled back in a ponytail. I pinched out a smile. She answered with one softer, and for a moment, my mind went back to the month before when she made the lights flash before my eyes for an all-together different reason.

"Max!" I twisted my mouth. "I could have used you a few minutes ago." It was stupid for me to wonder where Max was. I knew all along. But how could he have ignored the sound of an exploding boat?

Diane looked me up and down. "Still in one piece?"

"Yeah, luckily, I wasn't cruising with Lloyd." I looked away. "Except Grandpa. Don't know about him. He couldn't breathe. Engine blew, I guess."

She looked around. "Really drew a crowd."

Max said, "We didn't know anything was happening till we heard the siren."

I nodded. The night air continued to cool, but I hardly noticed. I threw the damp shirt over my shoulder and turned toward the lodge. "Oh, hey, what's the time?"

Max looked at his watch. "Nine fifteen."

"Shit!" I looked past the milling crowd. The Eklunds' car was gone. A second later, so was I.

CHAPTER TWENTY-NINE
No Shirt, No Shoes, No—

Friday Night, June 21

The stars were gone, obscured by clouds. Number 10 was shrouded in darkness; the only sign of life a single light in the kitchen window.

I arrived wet shoes in hand, a beach towel around my neck and, in spite of the warm night, shivering. I set my shoes on the grass and knocked on the door.

Erin came from the kitchen dressed in the same oversized sweater from the morning, pink cotton shorts, and flip-flops. "Wow! I saw it. What happened? Were you out there? That was you in the rowboat, wasn't it?"

"Yeah. The guy from #9 went fishing and blew up the engine."

She looked over my shoulder and said, "Come in. Oh my God! Is everyone okay?"

"They took Grandpa in the ambulance." The cabin was stuffy and warm, but not hot enough to quash the gooseflesh that covered me from eyebrows to ankles. "And Mrs. Stoker, she had a shit fit."

"I would too." She grabbed me by the hand and dragged me inside. "Oh, your hands, they're like ice. You're not touching me with those." She looked at me now, in the low light. "No shoes, no shirt, lucky this isn't a restaurant," she said in a way I couldn't read.

"I know, sorry. It's just my hands. I can fix that." She smelled like a color, purple maybe. "And I'm carrying a shirt, does that count?" I threw it on an end table.

The linoleum in front of the kitchen sink was worn through to black. I held my hands under the hot water until the blood flowed again, then dried them. A soft breeze puffed at the screens on the front porch. All the lights were out except the one over the sink. Erin sat at the table, magazine in hand but watching me, legs crossed, the upper one moving up and down like the handle on a pump.

She closed the *Glamour*. "You okay? You look kind of crunchy. Want something to drink?" She went to the refrigerator and opened a cola.

She was close again, less than an arm's length away. In the low light her hair glowed, her eyes no longer blue, but moist and darkly transparent. "Thanks," I said.

"Let's sit."

As I turned, my shirt hit me in the face. She giggled.

I put on the tee and said, "Okay, this means war."

"Haven't you had enough explosions for one night?" She walked to the couch in the front room and sat down.

Explosions, yes, but fireworks, like between you and me... I thought, but never said. I followed, put the drink on the coffee table, and sat down. Hands on knees, I sighed.

"I suppose that's a weekly show," she said. "Thrills and chills for the guests?"

"Hmm, good idea. I'll discuss it with management."

We talked about the engine fire and Grandpa. In time, the talking stalled. I squirmed. Erin's leg was pumping again. Both of us were stuck, lost in embarrassment. And I was a little scared.

She shifted her legs toward me and put an arm behind my shoulders. "Thanks for taking me." I didn't know what she meant. "On the mission. It was a blast. You didn't have to. And thank Max too. I probably won't get the chance. You guys moved the date and everything."

"I will, I'll tell him." With thumb and finger, I traced the chain under my shirt. My throat was dry. I needed a drink. "Do you think your family will come up again next summer?"

"I don't know. We haven't talked about it. Why?"

"Because of you, of course, but also..." She turned toward me, so she must have sensed something in my voice. "Also, because, I just hope we'll still be here."

"Of course, you will," she said. "Why wouldn't you be?"

I didn't want to get into dreary bank talk. "No reason."

She took my hand and gave it a squeeze. "Do you like to dance?"

I shrugged. "I don't know."

"Oh, come on. Let's—"

"Dance? Here? There's no music, and I'm no good."

A corner of her mouth sagged. "If you don't want to."

Another landmine found, my toes curled. "It's not you. I mean... there's no music."

She pointed at the radio sitting on the kitchen counter. "What do you call that? Come on. Do a slow one with me." She popped off the couch.

Finally, something I could recognize. "Yeah, Fanny calls it a prom hang."

"Okay." She turned the knob, scanning the FM dial for a song. She found an "Oldies" station. "Color My World" was playing. It was so romantic, I thought the song beamed straight from the moon to our little cabin. The kitchen light flickered as the sink-window curtains tilted and waved in the breeze. She put her arms around my neck. My hands met in the small of her back. The song ended. I nudged her cheek; she looked up.

"So, who showed you how to prom hang? I'll bet it was Diane."

I felt a blush. "Maybe." In the middle of a trying-too-hard kiss, my hand went under the waistband of her shorts. Then, it happened. Her hand dropped and stopped mine. I sighed. *Shit, that's it. I blew it.* "What?" I said softly, almost begging in her ear, but I knew. She had changed her mind. My heart limped.

"Slow down," she whispered. Deliberately, she moved my hand up, under her sweater, across the curve of her waist. "Did she show you this?" She released my hand. There was no bra.

I was lost in the vapor of summer, in the scent of her perfume. There were certainly other songs that played that night, but I cannot now name a single one. She kissed me, softer, sexier than my attempt. Her hips were moving; swaying like the night I met her, when the Wurlitzer played that slow country western song. But now I was moving with her, and kissing her too. She pulled away, took my hand, and led me through the bedroom door.

The room was dark, spare, and hot. In the corner sat a wooden chair. On a chest of drawers, in front of the mirror, a candle flickered. I'd been in the room a dozen times, but always to work, always in daylight. The door closed behind me. She wrapped me in her arms and looked up. "Come on. We don't have long." She sat on the edge of the bed and pulled me next to her. The button on my shorts gave way, then the zipper. I pushed my shorts to the floor. Her eyebrow arched. "Do you have it?"

Shirt halfway off, I paused. "What?"

"The glove. Did you get it?"

"Wait, it's here." I rifled through my pockets. Just like the shorts, the Trojan foil packet was wet.

She said, "Good. I wasn't… sure."

"You don't know the half of it."

She pulled back the covers, sat again, and then touched me.

My stomach surged into my throat. She'd found the only part of me that wasn't mush.

My hands were sweating, the foil was as tough as a cheap steak, and slippery. I went from corner to corner, pulled and jerked at the package. It wouldn't tear. "Ugh!"

She kissed me, and then whispered in my ear. "Come on, Sam." She slipped off her shorts.

"I can't… it won't… shit!"

She said, "Here, let me." With a fatalistic gasp, I surrendered the condom. She rubbed the packet across the sheet to dry it off, felt for the nick, and tore the foil.

For the first time I touched latex, rolled at the edge. It was like nothing I had ever seen before, and I had *no* idea what to do next. How did it unroll? And which way? I pushed on the condom; it wouldn't move.

Hands roaming, her breath was heavy in my ear. I uttered something sorrowful.

"What's the matter?" She looked down. Taking the condom from me, she pressed a single finger against my chest and pushed me on my back.

The candle behind made her a silhouette, but I had some idea of what she was doing. She planted her palm on my chest, leaned forward, and whispered, "Don't move."

I sat up on the edge of the bed. She was next to me, her fingers combing through the waves in my hair, and whispered, "Never thought I'd say it, but Fridays suck." We both knew what that meant: in the morning, she would leave for home.

"Let's pretend it's Monday." I put an arm around her waist and we kissed.

She broke the embrace and stood. "I better check the time." She put on panties, a sleeveless top, and went out to the kitchen.

Erin returned, my cola in hand. "Thanks," I said. I took the drink. I got the briefs and khakis, sitting in a heap on the floor, and put them on.

"You don't have to leave *that* fast." She sat down next to me, elbows on knees, and said, "I'm gonna miss you. This place too, I mean like, what are you going to do next week? Sabotage the pump?"

I laughed. "Not going back *there*, but I'll let you know; in case we need a third person." I looked through the door at the kitchen table. "Did it hurt?" I asked.

Her head turned slowly toward me. "What do you mean?"

"When you grabbed my shoulders, was I hurting you?"

She turned to me and pressed her lips to my shoulder. "No Sam, it didn't hurt."

There was a short silence. "Oh, okay," I murmured, another dumb question. I turned toward her and came face to face with the tattoo. "You know, if anything," I put my fingertips on the rose, "it was this that almost had me running the other way."

"Are you kidding? My Jeanie tattoo? Why?"

"At first, I thought... it looks just like... Steve has one, a skull with a rose too. It freaked me out, that's all."

She raised her eyebrows in her knowing sort of way. "So why did you stick around?"

I scratched my neck and said, "Well, let's see… You smiled at me."

Then, suddenly, very close, there was the sound of a car engine. Erin pushed away. I jumped. There were voices, her parents, outside the back door. She pulled the blankets back on the bed. "You gotta go! The window, crawl out the window," she wheezed.

"What? No!" My hands shook as I tugged on the handle. "Shit! It won't move." I stuck my head out the bedroom door. "Front porch, front porch." Her folks were at the rear door, trying to open it. The hook and eye held. A small square of crumpled foil lay on the linoleum. I kicked it under the bed.

I grabbed my towel off the kitchen counter, and tiptoed past Erin, who was suddenly, incredibly, completely clothed.

"Erin," called Mrs. Eklund. "Erin, let us in."

She called toward the back door. "Be right there." As if to say 'stay put,' she grabbed my arm and then scanned the bedroom. Then she saw my shirt, splayed on the floor. She grabbed the cotton tee and threw it at me.

"Okay, go!" she whispered, her hand clutching her sweater. "When you're ready, I'll let them in."

I stole out the front-room door onto the enclosed porch and waited.

She walked toward the back of the cabin. "Oh, sorry, I locked you out," Erin said, loud enough for *all* to hear. The hook dropped, the door opened, then, "Come in. How was the fish?"

Ever so slowly, I opened the porch door and slipped out. The door squeaked as it shut. I crouched low around the corner of the cabin, the glow from the kitchen window just above. I crept to the back door, picked up my shoes, and went into the shadows of the nearby trees.

A towel draped around me like a cape, I walked to the promontory at the end of the peninsula and sat down. The stars were back in the sky. I hoped Erin would somehow escape and know where to find me. I opened my pants, pulled off the sheath, and threw it in Red Wolf.

Thirty minutes, sixty minutes, ninety minutes later, I was still alone. I reached into my back pocket, pulled out the buckle, and stretched out the fabric. Tracing the letters with my fingernail— er's Nu—I remembered the ultimatum sent from the bank. My folks had to deliver $990,027 by July 17 or face foreclosure. I counted it down in my head: three weeks and five days from now, this spot would be lost to me. My family would be homeless, the stake Mom and Dad placed on Noquebay gone because of the buckle resting in my palm.

CHAPTER THIRTY

No Mr. Clean

Saturday Morning, June 22

There was no understanding fate. Of all the days, in all the weeks, in all the years of my life, it was my turn to be Saturday Morning Grunt. Erin's family had checked out. She'd left without a good-bye. How did she feel about that? If she didn't understand why I wasn't there to see her off, well, then neither did I. Oh sure, I'd told her about the cabins, nine of them to clean every Saturday morning for the new arrivals. At the moment Erin was leaving for home, I was stuck in #2, a bucket of Mr. Clean at my feet, my head buried in a shower stall. *Mr. Clean*—yeah, right. For the last week, the irony wasn't lost. The second my mother and I got into #10, I'd be on the hunt for the foil, the last, known tell-tale sign of my manic night.

It took three cabins to clear the haze in my brain, but no matter: a well-trained gorilla could have done my job, and as well. I walked toward #10. Mom backed the SUV, laden with fresh linen and cleaning supplies, onto the spot formerly occupied by the Eklund car, which by that time was probably halfway to Green Bay.

The five-gallon pail swung heavy in my hand as Mom and I entered #10. To her: a cabin. To me: a minefield. The Trojan foil packet might still be out there. Eventually, I would have to enter, with Mom at my side, the very room where less than twelve hours earlier I'd had sex with Erin.

Would Mom be able to tell? Would she smell the sheets and know it was me? Except for scratch marks on my left shoulder, a wound I planned to cherish for as long as I shall live, I'd snuffed all clues.

Mom went to the kitchen. I started in the bathroom, shuffling through a bucket that should have had skull and crossbones on the side. Ammonia, a box of Spic and Span, Comet, Lysol, two scrubbing brushes. Sponge in hand, I traced along the fixtures. My head was somewhere else. Start the week all over, that's what I wanted. Now I was going on no sleep. All night long, two words echoed in my head, Erin's voice saying, "Don't move."

I squeezed a stream of acid under the toilet rim. The bowl turned lily-white. Then I got a blast of vapor and my nose was on fire. The cobwebs were finally gone. The toilet brush, a pass or two, then flush.

I looked in the vanity. My heart sank. Erin couldn't have been gone more than an hour, and already the place was picked clean. No empty bottle of perfume on the shelf, no used lipstick in the cabinet. Mom called from the kitchen and asked me to do the bedrooms. I went into Erin's bedroom first. Sheets were piled in the middle of the bed. The floor was bare—no Trojan helmet torn in half. The window looked fine, too, for that matter. The light was different, almost spooky because Erin wasn't there.

"Sam, did you bring the pillowcases?"

"No, they're in the car."

Mom's footsteps faded out the back door. I kneeled and looked under the bed. There it was, the torn foil. In a panic, I reached under the box spring, but the Trojan was too far away. Scrambling to the other side, I groped again. My fingertips finally found the packet. I jammed the evidence into my pocket, stood up, and listened. Still no sound. I touched the pile of wrinkled sheets. I grabbed a handful of linen, put it to my face, and drew in the pungent, peachy tang. Erin. I took stock of the rest of the room. My eye went to an unlit, half-spent votive candle sitting alone on top of a chest of drawers. I picked it up, held it in my hand, cool now.

A breath caught in my throat when I saw it, standing alone against the base of the mirror. Erin's lipstick. I picked it up, my hand shaking as I removed the cap and extended the nearly spent, rose-colored gloss, the one she'd worn last night. My eyes burned. Blinking my vision clear, I put the lipstick together and tucked it, along with the candle, into my pocket.

A weathered chair sat next to the dresser. The backdrop of brown paneling made the item draped over the chairback almost impossible to see, almost as if my mind saw it before my eyes did. I took two quick steps toward the chair and took the nylon in my hand, the twin to the one I had used as a disguise during Mission: Jeanie Blue. The cabin wasn't a minefield, it was a keepsake city. What I didn't know at the time was that keepsakes can turn into relics.

The backdoor slapped shut. I rolled the nylon stocking around my hand and hid it away.

Mom walked in, linen in hand. "Why isn't the bed stripped? What have you been doing in here?"

"Nothing."

"I can see that."

I swept up the dirty sheets and threw them on the chair. "I'll take them out when we're done."

The new linen set down on the dresser, Mom raised an eyebrow at me, then tossed the corner of the fitted sheet. I heard Dad's voice outside, on the pier. The stocking reminded me it was time to do something about the belt buckle. Though Max and I had come up with a plan forward that had us writing letters to law enforcement, after reconsidering the shaky situation at the resort I thought the plan was too soft, not bold enough for the situation.

"Mom, I gotta tell you something." She looked up while smoothing the sheet. I continued. "I found that buckle. Remember? The one I hooked out of Finnegan's Hole last spring?"

"You did? I thought that thing was long gone. Where was it?"

"It fell into a lunch bag when they broke into my locker. I thought someone stole it, but there it was, in my backpack."

She grabbed another sheet and gave me a corner. "Why were you looking in your backpack in the middle of summer?"

I felt a tingle in my neck. I had stepped on the first bomb in #10, and it had nothing to do with sex. "Well, ah, I was looking for something else, and it was still there."

She followed me to the end of the bed and we tucked the sheet. She said, "So all this wringing the hands over Steve wasn't worth it."

"Ah, right, right. Anyway, do you think I should give it to the police? You heard what Nadine said at the dinner. She thinks it came off of the uniform Jean Manticore was wearing, before she disappeared."

"Yes, I get it." She stood up and waved for me to get the bed-spread. "Have you talked to your father about this?"

I said no but that he was right outside taking care of the boats. She told me to call him in. She sat down at the kitchen table and asked where the buckle was now. Dad came in the back door in time to hear me say I had it hid in my bedroom.

"He's talking about the Manticore buckle," Mom said. "He's found it again and wants to know what to do with it."

Mom and Dad listened to the buckle history, the one I want-ed them to hear, including the connection to the murder of Jean Manticore six years ago. Dad reminded me there is no murder without a body, but agreed the buckle was likely evidence, and the sheriff should have it. Mom recalled Nadine's poor opinion of county law enforcement, and that they may be in Willard Manticore's pocket.

"Right." Dad rubbed his face with one hand. "Small-town politics are not to be ignored, that's for sure. We're finding out the hard way."

I swallowed dry. "What do you mean?"

"You might as well know, Sam," Mom said. "The bank sent us a foreclosure notice last week. Unless something changes, we may not make it through the summer."

"Foreclosure? Not make it?" I asked. "What does that mean? Do we have to leave?"

"We have a month, July seventeenth, to show why they're wrong," Mom said. "But we'll need a lawyer, and that costs mon-ey, too."

"It's the Manticores, isn't it?" I asked. "That's what you mean, small-town politics."

"There's no need for you to repeat that," Dad said. "But yes, probably."

"Should we have a lawyer present when we turn in the buckle?" Mom asked.

"Or cut off a piece to keep for insurance. Or just say that the newspapers have to be in on it, then they can't ignore it," is what I said. *Play hardball,* is what I thought. For three more weeks.

———

The meeting with the sheriff started out pretty well. As chance would have it, the sheriff had business in Walnut Creek at three p.m. and would be able to stop by the resort at four-thirty the very same day to talk about the buckle.

The sheriff's squad drove past the tavern parking lot and stopped near the back door of the lodge. Mom and I were sitting at the kitchen table when Dad showed Sheriff Bullens and Deputy Ponce in. Mom and I stood. We said hello and everyone had a seat. Dad sat to my left at the head of the table, Mom to my right. The two officers were directly across from me.

"Mr. Bullens, Mr. Ponce, thank you for coming," Dad said. "We won't take too much of your time. Sam has discovered, or recovered, something from the lake that may be of interest." He nodded at me.

Slowly, I pulled the buckle from my pocket and set it on the table. "I fished it out of Finnegan's Hole in May."

Mr. Ponce's collar looked a size too small and was ringed by a narrow band of sweat. He looked uncomfortable before we sat down. He was older than Bullens, too. When I dropped the belt buckle his head synched back and an eye pinched half-closed.

Sheriff Bullens was open collar and powder dry. A buzz-cut made him look military. His fingers were thick and laced together on the table. "All right. What am I looking at?"

"A belt buckle," I said, a little shocked I had to say the obvious.

"I can see that," Bullens said. "What I'm asking is, why should I be interested?"

I shifted in my seat. "It could be evidence—"

"What Sam is saying," Dad said, "if you look at the colors, letters on the belt, it looks like it came from someone who worked at Carter's Nuts and Candies."

Bullens raised one eyebrow. "Yes, I suppose that could be."

"And we're wondering," Mom said. "About the missing person from six years ago, Jean Manticore. She worked there. Couldn't this be hers?"

Mr. Ponce sat forward and smacked his lips. "Anything is possible, ma'am. But really, how do we know where this really came from?"

"I just told you," I said. "It was in the lake. I was fishing the bottom and—" And then it struck me. Nadine had warned us, and she had been sitting in the same seat as Ponce. "We should search the lake for Jean's body." Dad put his hand on my forearm.

Bullens tipped his head toward Ponce. "Let me put it to you this way. There is a problem with the evidence, if that's what this is. In fact, as law enforcement officers, we need more than your word as to where this came from."

I sat up. My chair skittered. "Max was there. He saw it too."

"Nothing personal, son. You get this Max person, we can have a conversation. But until then..." The sheriff spread his hands. "First of all, searching a lake is a very expensive proposition. You want me to reopen a cold case on a missing person based on"—he pushed the buckle back at me—"a flimsy piece of metal and fabric. Ain't gonna happen."

CHAPTER THIRTY-ONE
Jeanie Blue Redux

The Week of June 24

I barely remember the rest of the meeting, I didn't stand when the officers left. The remaining part of the day was a blur. When the sheriff flicked off the buckle like a troublesome fly, something flashed before my eyes—the last week, the previous two months, my whole life? I don't even know. More likely it was my plan. In a matter of seconds, the whole Mission: Jeanie Blue fiasco had collapsed. And with it, what else? Diane and Max would think I had failed. I remembered the two finger bones I'd harvested off the shore and I kicked myself halfway around the resort because I forgot to bring them out. But then I realized I was better off keeping them in my pocket. They would have blown them off with the same prejudice.

On Monday, I decided to write a letter to Erin about it. We'd agreed to keep in touch, but the details of how that was going to happen across two hundred and fifty miles was never worked out. I wanted to hear from her, of course, and worried about the tell-tale mention of John-John slipping back into the picture. My letter was a total downer. No investigation. No front-page headlines or newspaper clippings, much less a dragging of Finnegan's Hole for a forgotten victim. Texting her was tough, but we managed a couple times, both of them were pretty lame and full of NVM (never mind), TTYL (talk to you later), and IDK (I don't know). If I had any idea of sexting, and I did, the sterile responses from Erin put an end to that fantasy. Even the bland texts I had to do quickly and on the sly then delete so my brothers wouldn't see them. Calling was even tougher because our plan had a minute limit.

Thinking about the sheriff and deputy pissed me off. I wasn't going down without taking one more shot at the Manticores. I drove into town and stopped at the Walnut Creek Library. A recent renovation included a microfiche reader, which eliminated my biggest worry—wading through stacks of moldy newspapers that had been sitting in storage for five years or more. This new invention was a godsend. My research took a couple hours instead of days. When I left the building, I was dumbfounded by the Manticore-family web and who it entangled, and more troubled than ever as to how to explain it to Max. I didn't have time to figure it out. He showed up the next evening.

When Max docked his boat, the water was liquid lead, the sky like a moldy old sponge, the air heavy and cooler than it had a right to be in late June. Happy to see him, I ran to the pier and secured the boat. Even before he left the captain's chair, I could see a line in Max's face I had never seen before, an edge that could have filleted a walleye. He jumped onto the dock, slapped the basketball from under my arm and challenged me to a game of one-on-one. In the time it took to get the flavor of the moment, I was left behind. When I got to the court, he greeted me with a chest pass that damn near knocked me over.

"Go on," grumbled Max. "Start."

I told him no, I wasn't interested in basketball or any other game just then. I wanted to tell him about the visit with the Sherriff. Before I could bring up the buckle, he started shooting the ball, offering me points up front as an inducement. It was more an insult, of course. The verbal barrage kept coming.

"What's the matter, off your game, Sammy? Missing Erin? Awww. Man, you are sooo pussy whipped." He shot a twenty-footer. "Christ, forget her. She won't be back."

I was feeling bad enough about the resort, the buckle, and Erin. The last thing I was going to do was sit and listen to Max's venom. I grabbed the ball and dropkicked it toward the pool. "Go fetch, you salty bastard." I turned and walked away.

Max came after me and shoved me in the shoulder, hard, but somehow there was affection, too, or desperation; it was hard to tell. "You aren't gonna let that crap bother you, are you?" Max's voice was finally without anger. "Ten minutes, in the boat. Come on, you've been wanting a ride."

"Why are you such a shithead?"

"Come along and I'll tell you."

The boat approached the middle of the Narrows, slowed to a crawl, and he cut the motor. For a while Max did nothing but look at the water, his face twitching occasionally, like a polygraph. His hair sagged with humidity and perspiration. A thin layer of fog hovered just above the water; the evening chill had an early start. The lines of Noquebay Lodge were starting to blur.

I hugged myself and shivered. "Hey, you know, I got some bad news. We had Bullens over Saturday, the sheriff. What a horse's ass. I wanted to give him the buckle, like we said. He wouldn't give it a second look. Said he couldn't be sure about us, that we might be making up the whole story. What should we do now?"

No response from Max. I could have been talking to the fog. "Come on, man, this is important. I think we should write a letter or call one of those TV reporters."

"Go ahead." Max sat back in the captain's seat. "It's up to you."

The anger from the basketball court was gone. Max was somewhere else. "What's wrong, man?" I asked. "I can't figure you out." His look said *are you fucking kidding me?* I held out my hand. "All right, fine. I get it." But he wasn't the only one with a family to worry about, and he knew it. "Listen, there's something else. I went to the library and looked up Mitch Manticore. After Bullens left, I had to do something. I couldn't leave the Manticore thing alone. I looked up the accident that put him in prison. The girl that died in the accident, she was actually—"

"Nora Loomis."

"Right." That stunned me. He knew the name of a girl that had died in a car accident before he—we—were born? It made me wonder what else he knew. "Right, Nora. Turns out, he,

Mitch, did time for vehicular homicide. He was driving a convertible, car left the road, hit a stump. Nora flew out…"

I didn't know how far to go with this. The next piece of information would change us forever, and I still didn't know if I was ready to say it. I picked up a length of rope and fiddled with it. "Anyway, the thing is—"

Max looked away. "It was my dad's car." He stomped on a spider crawling across the floor of the boat. "Nora was his girlfriend, not Mitch's."

I nodded and watched the spider coagulate into a contracted blob.

Max flicked the spider's remains with his shoe. "And Dad was there." He looked at me. "That about cover it?"

No, it didn't. Not quite. Both J. Roman and Mitch were drunk, but when the police arrived, Mitch was the one behind the wheel. From what I knew of J. Roman, it didn't seem likely he would have been out on a date and let someone else drive his car. Did Mitch climb behind the wheel after the crash and take the fall for J.R.? Probably. But I wasn't going to bring that up, not now. "Yeah, that's it."

For a while there was nothing but the sound of the waves lapping against the boat.

"When did you find out?" I asked.

"Couple a weeks ago. After the dinner at your house I started asking questions and Dad…" Max heaved in his chest. "He wouldn't answer." Max waved his finger at the floor. "Nadine did, though, and she didn't hold back." He straightened in his seat. "Know what else she told me?" Suddenly, his voice had a new clarity. "The boat that blew up at your place last week? It wasn't an accident."

I felt like he'd struck me in the back of the neck. "Of course, it was. Lloyd Stoker is a terrible mechanic. He'd been fussin'—"

"I'm telling you—it wasn't Stoker." Max looked me hard in the eye. "Think back to the raid. The Manticores are on our ass. Where did they park their boat? Number 9's pier, right behind Lloyd Stoker's boat, the one he bought from your dad."

I tied a knot in the rope. "And 'Noquebay Resort' was written on the back, so suck-head Steve thinks it belongs to us."

"Nadine has connections in town. Word is, Steve set the engine to blow."

I slammed the rope on to the deck. "Someday…" I waved the knotted rope, then looked away. "I'm glad you already knew that stuff about your dad and Mitch—"

Max cut me off. "I can't talk about it. Lawyers." He reached into his pocket, pulled out something and held it in his palm. "Remember this?"

I turned. A shallow profile of my friend's brooding face was all I could see. "Don't know, show me." Max put the stem between two fingers and held the object like a dirty diaper. "Sort of, yeah. Pocket watch, you had it out here fishing."

"Got it from my dad, family heirloom, handed down from dad to son, from his dad to that, blah, blah, blah."

"Why'd you bring it out here?"

Max's hand swallowed the watch. "Been carrying it around for a couple days. I'm sick of it. Then, on the way over to your place it hit me—put this worthless piece of shit to rest. And where better than Finnegan's?" I must have frowned, because then he said, "Every burial needs a witness."

Max stood up and cocked his arm like Aaron Rodgers.

I stammered. "No, wait, hang on. That watch goes back to… who? I forgot."

Max's voice cracked. "King Arthur, to hear my dear dad tell it." Max sat down and looked away. "Great-great-grandpa, man." His shoulders slumped. "Ah, so what. The ones I know are assholes."

We'd talked about his father's absences before. I felt awkwardly relieved. "Max, your dad, bad shit, really. The arrest, the trial, but he's been trying. You said so yourself, spent more time with you, golfing, movies," I almost said, *since your mom died.* I swallowed.

"I'm a fuckin' idiot." Max tossed the watch on the dashboard, turned, and looked down. "Do you know *why* he's been doing that? Spending time? Do you? Would you like to know?" The mocking tone I knew well, but this time it sounded like he was talking to himself.

"Well, I will tell you why. He's doing it so he'll look good in front of the judge! Not because of me, or Mom." Max sucked tears off of his upper lip. "Overheard that jackass lawyer of his." Max punched the steering wheel, stood up and turned away.

The fog crept in, the shore on either side of the Narrows barely visible. I was lost. "What? How do you know?"

"Yesterday, they were in his office downstairs. Heard every word. Told Dad to keep up the act, that's what he said, 'keep it up, church, golfing, the kid, doing great.' Well ha, ha, ha." Max put his forearms on the top of the windshield and hung his head. "They're working a deal with the judge, or I don't know, the D.A. Heard it, man. Another scam, that's all it is. They'll go easy on the jailtime if there's a kid in the picture. Beautiful. Just beautiful." He walked to the back of the boat and looked at the sinking sun, barely visible, pale and cold. "Hope the bastard does time, I really do."

I picked up the watch and sat on the gunwale. "Ya can't let this tear you up. Someday you'll have a son. Give the watch to him. He'll only know what you tell him. Hell, by then it's ancient history."

"Me? A family? Name's Cherhasky, man, not Robel. It's in the blood." Max snatched the watch from my hand. "I might want to give my son a watch someday." In one motion, Max threw the heirloom into the air. "But it won't be that one."

I blinked the moisture from my eyes and tracked the timepiece, arching through the gathering dusk. The gold watch tumbled into a metallic streak, then sliced through the filmy veneer of the lake.

———————

The boat slowed. I grabbed the pier and jumped off the gunwale. "September fog coming early." I held on to the boat. "Don't go straight across. Follow the shoreline."

"Red Wolf is big, but it's not an ocean." Max shrugged with one shoulder. "Shoreline will never work. Lennon's Bight is too shallow. I'll just point it south by southwest and tie down the wheel. Bound to hit something eventually."

"It's your hide," I said. "So, what about you and Diane?" My mind was so focused on a heartache named Erin, I had to be careful not to forget—the last time I saw Diane was after the boat explosion, with Max.

"We broke up." Max looked down and played with the boat keys. "I told her yesterday. She's a great girl…." There was a new sadness on his face, not like the one from minutes earlier.

I shook my head, confused. "Broke up? How? I mean, did she break up with you?" I asked. For anyone who knew the history, it was the right question. If there was a break-up, it usually started with Diane.

"Who cares? It doesn't matter anyway." He didn't look at me when he said it. "I better get going,"

"If you say so." I put my hands on my hips. "Four weeks and a pre-season football meeting," I said with a sappy lilt. "God, how I love it."

"Love it like sand in your shorts." Max shrugged. "Then why go out?"

"I don't know." I tapped the post with my shoe. "We're gonna be good in basketball. I'll rebound, throw the ball to you, and you shoot. Just like last year."

"I don't think so." Max started the engine. "Find someone else. I'm not going out." The ties fell away. "Tell Coach for me."

"Tell him what?" For precious seconds, I was speechless. Then I mumbled, "Tell him yourself." Max hit the throttle. I yelled, "Tell him yourself! And the siphon. The bank shuts us down—" But my words were lost in the roar of the motor.

Max turned the wheel toward the open water. The boat vanished into the fog.

CHAPTER THIRTY-TWO

Zero Hour—Fifteen Days

Tuesday, July 2

I had to go into Walnut Creek for a "Preseason Football Meeting." Leave it to a couple of gung-ho seniors bucking for co-captains of next fall's team to think it up. This was something James would have swallowed whole, but not me.

Before arriving at Red Wolf High, I made a stop at the bank for Mom. Green bank bag in hand, I approached the front door and held it open for a man in a wheelchair coming out, being pushed by a younger guy. Only after they exited did I recognize who they were.

"Thank you, Mr. Robel," said the man propelling the chair. "Sam, isn't it?"

My throat had tightened too much to speak, so I nodded.

The old man in the chair held up his hand. "Hold on, Junior. You say this is a Robel?" He squinted up through wrap-around sunglasses. "Ah, yes. We've met. Out at your father's place." He was in a dark suit even though the day was hot. "That bank bag looks a little light. Your old man, he should have taken our first offer, way back in May. Now the fool is in foreclosure."

"Dad, I don't think—"

"Shut up, Junior." He raised his cane and rapped me on the hip. "You tell him, Willard Manticore has a new number for him: 850,000." He flared his nostrils. "He'll know what it means, because it's nothing good. Think you can remember that, *son?*"

My grip on the door tightened into a fist. I wasn't his son, and if I was, I'd have punched his lights out long ago. "I'll remember." I pushed past the chair and went into the bank.

———————

The chalk talk was Xs and Os swirling across the blackboard and my mind wasn't even in the stadium. After the run-in with Willard and Junior Manticore, all I could think about were money and mortgages and eviction on the seventeenth.

Eviction. Had we stayed in Burlington, if James hadn't gone off and got himself killed... *So patri-fucking-otic weren't you!* If anger were muscle I'd have been an All-State linebacker. I thought of Max and Diane too. I hadn't seen her since the boat explosion. And after the watch descended into Finnegan's Hole, Max dropped out, too. He was always impulsive, sounding off at will, but this idea of "find a new shooting guard" was bullshit. We were a team, time was wasting, and the Red Wolf Siphon was still sucking the lake dry. I had the phone today so I tried texting him, but I got nothing in return.

Break was called. I took my bag lunch, found a quiet place in the hall, and called Max's cell. Just as it had been for a week, there was no answer. I'd already left a dozen messages to call me back; I didn't leave another. Next, I dialed Diane and expected to get her voicemail as usual, but she answered. She hadn't heard from Max either, and was even more upset about it than I was. She agreed to come down to the school to meet me.

Then I called a Green Bay television news room "tip line." After going through the operator, the phone rang. I'd always pictured Max and me taking this step together, one hoarse-whispering in the other's ear. But the clock at the bank didn't stop ticking just because I couldn't get ahold of him.

The voice on the other end said, "This is the Tip Line. Tom Preen, what can I do for you?"

My palms were sweating, my throat dry. "Hi, ah, this is Ben, Ben Bigelow."

"Yes, I heard. What's on your mind?"

"Oh, yeah, well I have a... I know about..." I switched the

phone to my other hand.

"You still there?" asked Mr. Preen.

"Sorry, I'm kinda nervous."

"That's all right, Ben. What's this about?"

"You probably don't remember, but about six years ago a girl went missing in Walnut Creek. Her name was Jean Manticore."

I heard papers shuffle on the other end. "Yes, I do. They didn't find her, did they?"

"No. It's a cold case." I took a deep breath and wiped the sweat off my upper lip. "Anyway, I was fishing in Red Wolf and I hooked a belt buckle and it looks just like one that she was wearing last time she was seen."

"Okay. Why don't you take it to the sheriff?"

"I did. They blew me off. They didn't even take the buckle." I found the chain around my neck and twisted it between my fingers. "There was a smart-ass deputy, said they couldn't trust me, that I could have gotten it from anywhere."

"Listen, Ben, if the sheriff isn't going to play ball with you, I don't know how I can help."

"Wait, I'm not done! I think the reason they killed Jean is because she was going to divorce Junior Manticore. It got real ugly, and she threatened to squeal about illegal irrigation they're doing out of Red Wolf Lake." I stopped talking while a couple of kids walked by. "I had to quit for a second. You still there?"

"I'm here. I don't know, kid. How do I know you're giving me a straight story?" said Mr. Preen in a faraway voice. "This sounds too much like a conspiracy to me. You got to give me something solid here."

I nearly choked myself with the chain. "I can tell you what she was wearing when she disappeared, and that hasn't been released in the newspaper."

"No, that's usually off the record." Mr. Preen's voice was close again. "Okay, I'll bite. How did you find out about this pumping operation?"

"If, if I tell you, you can't repeat any of it or I'm done."

"So, we're off the record. Agreed. Go ahead."

"I snagged the belt off the bottom of Finnegan's Hole last spring. Before I knew what I had, it was stolen from my school locker by Steve Manticore, who hid it in the boathouse in the Manticore's garage on Red Wolf Lake." I took a breath to slow myself down. "Last month, I broke in and got it back. While I was there, I saw this huge water pump connected to an intake pipe right below the boathouse. It was sucking water out of the lake like a mother."

"Okay, stop here for a minute. There are a million questions, like how did you know where the cloth was hid? How did you get in to the boathouse?"

"Not going to answer that."

"All right, where's all the water going?"

"Easy. The Manticores are one of the richest families I ever saw. They're crop farmers, acres and acres of irrigated land, north of Red Wolf. Go drive down Highway W, you'll see what I mean."

Mr. Preen whistled. "Well, Ben, and I'm guessing that's not your real name, if this is true, it's going to blow up like an atom bomb. How do I get a hold of you?"

He had my cell number. He said to keep him up to speed and that he'd make a few calls but could give me no assurances.

I sat down in front of a sandwich and two cartons of milk. There was finally some cool dope to pass along to Erin; she'd want to hear about the call to the reporter, so I put it in a lengthy text and waited for a reply. And waited. The screen never blinked. I reached for a carton of milk when I felt a rude shove on the back.

"Hey Sam, where the hell is that friend of yours?"

I turned. "Diane, nice to see you, too." I bit into my sandwich, but then threw it down. "What's up?"

"Max, that's what. The shit, where is he?"

Even for Diane, that was harsh. I shrugged. "You tell me." She sat down and took a drink of my milk. I opened the other carton. "No one's seen him. Maybe he's sick." I stopped eating. "You look tired. You okay?"

"I didn't sleep too good." She looked away. "I think we should find out, about Max, I really do."

I was on board with that. I couldn't eat, so I told her about the fiasco with the buckle and the Sherriff. She wasn't a bit surprised, but the details on the phone call to the watchdog reporter from Channel 2 made her sit up.

She said, "Good move, great. Are you going to finish that sandwich?" I slid it sideways. She sat down next to me. "I'm glad someone's doing something about it. Max was talking big, but when the chips are down… he's nowhere. What did Preen say?"

"He didn't believe me either." I shook my head. "He'd make some calls. Said get back to him in a few days. For chrissakes, I don't have three days. I don't have three minutes. The bank takes the resort on the seventeenth."

She talked around the sandwich. "Shit! The mortgage thing?" She poked me on the arm. "You and me, Sam, we keep going on this, right?"

"I got nothing to lose."

"Except your weight. You're thin as a pin." She waved the sandwich. "You should be eating this."

"That's what they told me at weigh-in this morning. I have to put on fifteen pounds before practice starts or they're going to bust me to water boy."

"You're stressed out," she said. "Well, I'm sick, too. Sick of all the talk in this town about how my sister is at the bottom of the lake." She finished the sandwich and milk.

"I'm going to try his cell once more." Diane stood next to me, her eyes like polished, black stones, looking out the front door. After a dozen rings I hung up, dialed again, and rested my brow against the wall, the tone throbbing in my head. "Holy hell, doesn't anyone ever answer the phone?"

There was something gnawing a hole in my stomach, and it wasn't hunger. The co-captains called an end to lunch. No way. There was no way I would go back to football. "Screw this, I'm driving out to his house."

Diane shouldered the strap on her purse. "Let's go."

CHAPTER THIRTY-THREE

The Dog Didn't Bark

Tuesday Afternoon, July 2

It was visible from a quarter-mile away. I pulled off the road, stopped, and gazed at the "Lake Estate For Sale" sign that filled the side window of the SUV. A phone number from a distant area code promised more information. We looked at each other; neither of us had known.

I pounded the wheel. "Selling the house, and he doesn't call either of us. How can they do that anyway? The trial is still going."

"When did that ever stop J. Roman? I don't get it, I really don't."

"So, they're looking for a new start. Okay, maybe. But he's too busy to pick up the frickin' phone or drop a text?"

I got out and opened the gate. The drive down the winding asphalt tossed my stomach. The house grew from behind a line of tall evergreens. I parked in front of the garage. We got out of the car and marched up the back porch. A rap on the door drew no response, so I hit the doorbell—four times. Silence. I cupped my hands around my eyes and looked in the window.

Diane asked, "See anything?"

"Yeah, well, no." I pinched my eyebrows. The sparkling kitchen, the rarely used appliances, and the solid oak dining set: they were all as before. "Quiet as church on Friday night." I couldn't put my finger on it, but something *was* missing.

"Here, let me try." Diane pushed past me and banged angrily on the door. I looked at her in wonder. Her shoulders slumped. "Let's look out front."

I led the way, looking at everything and nothing, desperate for a clue that wasn't there. Diane followed a straighter path, hugging herself, looking at little but the grass and sky.

At the end of the pier a pair of Canadian geese sat basking in the sun. The boat was not there. The lawn was mown, the flower boxes fully tended, but the bird feeder by the front porch was empty. I looked at the window to Max's second-floor bedroom, waiting for a face to show. The drapes were drawn, as they were on all the windows. The place looked deserted. Roman could be in Green Bay or Chicago as he often was, and Nadine might be shopping. But what about Max? We continued around the house, turned the corner, and headed back to the car.

"Eeehh, shit!"

I turned. Diane had fallen to the ground. She went to a seated position, grabbed her elbow, and started to cry.

I knelt next to her. "Are you all right? What happened?"

"I don't know. I tripped." Tears tracing down her cheeks, she tossed her head back and checked her leg. "Scratched my ankle. Sonofabitch."

I felt misty, too, but didn't know why. A scratch, a bump on her arm too, maybe, that's all I could see—and yet suddenly she was a mess. I asked, "Your arm, can you move it?"

She dropped her head and put her face in her hands. "No, it's all right. It's just... never mind." She wiped away the tears, took a deep breath, and then extended a hand. "Help me up."

We stood together. I looked back. "Why did you trip?"

There it was: a stake in the ground, a dog chain next to it. "THAT'S IT!" I stepped on the chain. "Middie's gone. The dog, whenever anyone knocks on the door, she always barks like her fur is on fire. Always. And when they travel, they hire a house sitter to stay with the dog."

A brackish taste rose in my throat. I sat down on the back porch and wedged my chin between my hands. Diane sat, too, trying to be brave, hands like a prayer between her legs. She licked tears off her upper lip.

"They're gone, you know."

We startled. An elderly man in bib overalls and a wrinkled fishing hat riddled with lures stood a few feet away, bait pail in one hand and a fishing pole in the other. The man grinned, which kind of pissed me off until I realized that the old codger was making ready to spit tobacco juice.

He wiped his chin with the back of his sleeve. "Ed Schlitz, live next door."

I nodded and said my name and introduced Diane.

"Friends of the Cherhasky boy, I'll wager."

"We thought we were." My voice dripped with sarcasm. "Until a minute ago."

Ed nodded. "They moved, about a week now. Kind of a rush-rush affair. No moving van, piled in a car and left. Not even a U-Haul. Late in the day, too. Made me wonder." Ed spit again. "Asked me to keep an eye on the place, the bank that is. They own it, you know, paying me for upkeep. Boat and the cars, even that fancy red one, all for sale."

I shook my head.

Diane's dark eyes were intense, the bruised arm forgotten. "Where'd they go? They leave an address?"

"Hold on now, I'm just the neighbor. Never knew them much when they was here, and they didn't tell me nothing 'bout their moving plans. I doubt you'll see them back in these parts." A pair of sparrows quarreled in a nearby evergreen. Ed shrugged. "Well, I'll be going, hear the pan fish a-callin.'"

I sat for a minute more, and then jogged to the garage. I peeked in the window. Ed was right, everything was still there: Roman's Corvette, Nadine's car, even the trailered boat. Diane caught up and stood next to me. I said, "That's it, Roman jumped bail! They're on the run."

"Yeah, then how'd the bank get the house so quick?" Diane looked in too. "Wouldn't they have sold the cars 'n shit for some pocket change? And the newspapers, I haven't seen a thing. Would have been front page."

"No phone call." My voice, though just a whisper, ripped with anger. "Up and left. Just like that." I turned. Spine pushed against the door, I lifted my head, the July sun bleary through watery eyes. "All the nights you stayed at the resort, you're welcome, man."

"Enough already." Diane said. "You sound like you've been deserted or something."

"So?"

She snorted a laugh. "You don't know the meaning of—"

"And you do?"

Lips parted, she looked me in the eye. She was going to say something, but brought herself up short. She turned away and looked at the lake.

I hadn't seen it coming. The scope of my life was so expansive the night with Erin. Now, less than two weeks later, it was collapsing of its own weight into a small point of dim light flickering in a lonely corner of the sky. With an angry thrust, I creased the aluminum garage door with an elbow, and let my back slide until I sat on the concrete. What was this leaving? This... I hardly knew what to call it. Betrayal? Desertion? It felt like I was in front of the Manticore siphon again. Only this time, it was me on the grid, and it was sucking the heart right out of my chest.

Diane sat down beside me and put her head on my shoulder. A spot of moisture wetted my shirt. I thought she must be crying. She was taking the news harder than I was, busted up and heartbroken over a guy that had abandoned her. Or had he? I still hadn't asked who broke off with who. But even a socially dense, box-of-rocks like myself could take a guess—for the first time ever, someone had broken up with Diane Warren.

"So how am I supposed to feel about this?" I blotted wetness from my eyes. Now she had me doing it. "I sure as hell don't know. We were together, partners. He knows we have to nail the Manticores."

"Sam, for chrissakes. What if something bad happened?"

A flush of guilt ran through me like a shot. What if there was something wrong? Terribly wrong? "I know, you're right. He never calls. God, I hope the mob didn't—?"

"I'm not going there."

"Good." I put my hand on hers. "Me neither." But I couldn't help it. I remember thinking, *Did he ghost her? Did he ghost both of us?*

She was single again. And if the texts from Erin were a cold front, we'd have had snow in July. We were in the same boat, Diane and me. In that moment, I felt closer to her than ever. She sniffled and I thought she might be dozing off. Her hair smelled like violets, the softness on my cheek as sexy as any miniskirt she'd ever worn. I'd have been the Benedict Arnold of Red Wolf, but all I wanted to do was put my hands in her long brunette locks, lift her chin, and kiss her. But I didn't. I rested my cheek on the top of her head and felt the rhythm of her breathing. If I'm honest, I desired more than that, wanted to breathe the air she was breathing, to get lost with her in a tangle of arms and legs. I wondered if I'd ever have the chance to show her who I was, what I could be. But the words I'm able to write now were only seeds in the soil then, waiting to germinate. I sighed and remained silent. Her head was somewhere else. She was thinking about Max. I was the *Nowhere Man.*

I bent my knees and waited for her to stir.

CHAPTER THIRTY-FOUR

The Gathering Gloom

Tuesday, July 9

T-minus eight days and counting to the Noquebay Foreclosure.

Last weekend was busy, as it should have been. The Fourth of July was the peak for everyone in the resort business. I had worked up a couple of new ideas on the siphon, but nothing was going to happen on the Fourth. I took a drive-by in a boat, and the Manticore place was rocking. Their private fireworks show was anything but; visible everywhere on Red Wolf, I thought they were trying to pay in some small way for the water they were pilfering from everyone who could see the fantastic light and sound show. *Not enough, you assholes, not even close.*

———————

When I stopped at the Mobil station to fill the car, I noticed Ethyl Warren's old Chrysler parked in the side lot. As I was finishing up, a familiar voice called my name. I hadn't seen Diane for a week, but we'd texted a few times to check on updates regarding Max and the buckle, of which there were none. She had a bagful of junk food in hand and asked if I wanted anything. I said no. She said that was good because she was "hangry all the time." I probably made a poor attempt at a smile.

She put her hand on my arm and said, "How you doin, Sam bone? You look a little down, like you hit someone's dog."

A car drove in behind me. "You got a minute? I'll pull around." I pointed to a parking area. "Over there. I'll meet ya."

We parked on the grass in the shade of a big maple tree. Diane sat on the hood of the Chrysler, sipping a soda. I leaned against the fender. "It finally came," I said. "Yesterday."

"What's that?"

"Letter from Erin. Dad called it a 'Dear John' letter."

"Oh, one of those."

"Yeah. Didn't take her long." I looked away, embarrassed. "She said she was getting back together with John-John, blah, blah, blah. I should have known, all the stuff she left behind, she was saying good-bye."

Diane tugged on my shirt to pull me back. Her face softened in a way I'd not seen before. "I'm sorry. She's a… I'm not sure I know the word."

I crossed my chest with one arm. "The word, Diane? I've been wondering myself. Maybe it's me that needs a *word*, like bozo or neek." I stepped toward a branch running just above my head and grabbed it. "Go ahead, I want to know what you think."

She'd been looking at me the whole time, I could tell, but now her eyes were moist. She blinked. "I know how you feel, that's all. And I wasn't going to say anything awful, because she isn't, not from what I could see." She took a quick breath. "She knows what she wants. You should be happy about that, actually. She had one hell of a vacation, and my guess, so did you."

"You know." I straightened. "Okay, but fifteen days, fourteen hours and twenty-three minutes after she leaves I have a letter in my hand…"

She smiled but not in a humorous way. "But who's counting?"

"Well, you said a dog got run over. That dog was me." I dropped my hands off the limb. "We're starting to get cancellations at the resort too. Someone must be talking about eviction or some such shit. Once a rumor starts… We got four calls last weekend, all asking for their money back." I sat on the fender, shoulders slouched. "In another couple weeks it won't matter whether they come or not. One less cabin to turn. Thanks again, James. See you at the next Assholes Anonymous Meeting."

She looked away for a second, then at the chain dangling from my neck. "And yet you still wear his dog tags."

I closed my eyes against the burn. "How do you know about that?"

"Max told me."

"Yeah, my awesomely-fantastic brother. Got himself killed over there and look where it put me, us, the whole family."

She put her hand on my knee. "You know he didn't—"

"Yeah, I know… but still here we are. It won't take long for the bank to sell it."

"What? The resort?"

"Yeah. Simpson says—"

"Simpson?"

"Former owner; we bought Noquebay from him. He told Dad the Manticores have been after our place for years. Who knows, probably set up another siphon. Five years, Red Wolf will be no more than a puddle."

She poked me on the shoulder. "And now that old bastard Willard figures he can get it by having the bank foreclose on you guys." She sat forward, put her face between her palms, and said, "You have to give it up."

"Give up what? Giving up the buckle didn't work. And the resort's a goner."

She raked her fingers through her hair. "Wrong both times. Neither are yours to give or take, are they? So forget it."

"Ah huh, easy for you to say." I pressed my lips into a fine line.

"What I'm sayin' is tougher so I'm not going to demand immediate compliance."

"There's something else? How generous."

"It's who I am." She paused. "Your brother, Sam, you can't be angry with him forever. He's been gone almost two years. Time to understand what he did, accept him for who he was." She pushed some hair away from my face. "From what I've heard, he wouldn't be holding any of this Manticore crap against you. Time to return the favor."

I chuckled without humor. "Return the favor. Sure." Neither of us said anything for a second. Then she said:

"Getting the buckle wasn't enough, but the Manticores are so arrogant, there has to be something they've overlooked, or forgotten."

It took a while for her words to sink in. "The buckle isn't enough." It made me recall a question Erin had asked me. "I gotta ask, because it's been bugging me. Your sister married money. Why did she keep working at a minimum wage job?"

"She didn't keep working. When she got married, she quit. But when things got bad between her and Junior, she went back. She'd signed a pre-nup, and not a good pre-nup, not for her."

"Oh, so there goes the money motive."

Erin must have still been in my head, because one other thing she mentioned rose to the surface—going back to the pump. Suddenly, my gaze found Diane's. I shook my head. "Jaysus Katie Key-rist. You're brilliant!" I grabbed her by the shoulders, pulled her close, and kissed her.

She slid forward and punched me. "What was that for?"

"Ouch! That's what I get for giving you a compliment?"

A corner of her mouth pulled sideways. "You have an idea. What is it?"

I looked back toward the pumps. "Meet me at Walnut Creek Lumber."

We went in the front door and took a hard left past a section of small kitchen appliances to a wall of paint. Diane grabbed my arm and whispered:

"Oh, come on. Sam Robel, vandal? What you gonna do, paint their house pink? Do black and white skull and crossbones?"

"Very funny, but not as far off as you think." I bent closer to the labels. "Where is the exterior latex? I want the cheapest one." Diane directed me to the next section. I looked at the price tags and groaned. "That's it. End of story." She couldn't believe I didn't have fifteen bucks for a gallon of paint. "Yeah, but I need ten gallons, at least, all the same color, something bright like orange or red. And I don't have one hundred and fifty dollars."

Putting her hand on my chest, Diane slid into a wave of giggles. "What the hell…" Laughing. "Are you going to do…" I shushed her. "No, wait, wait," she begged. "You're going to walk in…" she took a breath. "A seventeen-year-old guy just walks and buys ten gallons of *RED* paint. Oh my god, Sam. In a small town, don't you think someone might notice? You're fuckin' hilarious."

I had to admit, she had a point, but I was damned if I'd say it out loud. I leaned into her and laughed at her laughing. "Well, no cash so the point is moot."

"Oh, it's moot all right," Diane said.

"So mute your moot." Were we the first couple to walk out of a hardware store laughing? I don't know.

"Okay, I'll bite. What the hell were you going to do with all that fucking paint?"

I waved my finger at her. "Twenty would have been better. It would have worked too. The place next to the Manticore Mansion is heavily wooded with a little, tear-down cabin on it. It's not being watched, there's nothing there to steal. And it's only fifty feet away."

"Fifty feet to where?"

"The boathouse. Then, all we'd have to do is sit and wait."

"Wait for what?"

CHAPTER THIRTY-FIVE

Paint the Town Red

Thursday Night, July 11

At first, I thought it was a dream. Tapping, then a voice calling my name. I opened my eyes and looked about my darkened bedroom. The alarm clock read a quarter to midnight. I'd imagined it, that's what I thought, so I settled back into the mattress.

"Sam, wake up." More tapping on the window. I sat up on the edge of the lower bunk, the upper berth empty ever since Max left. In the adjoining rooms my brothers and sister snoozed. I went to the window and pulled up the shade. On the other side of the screen, hair pulled back under a baseball hat, her face strangely unfamiliar without make-up, was Diane.

"Diane. What the hell?" I whispered.

"Yeah, that's what I thought you'd say." She looked toward the bar, then back at me. "Whitey tighties, very nice. Get dressed, long pants, long sleeves."

"Why? Where we going?"

"Meet me by the car in five. I found the ammunition." She took a step, then came back. "Bar's still open. That's good. Oh, bring a hammer, screw driver, and a pliers. And a pair of gloves."

"Diane, I can't—"

"My car, in five." And she was gone.

———————

I wrapped the tools in a work rag and set them on the floor as I got into Diane's car. We pulled out of the resort.

"So, what's this all about?"

"We're the Red Wolf Midnight Runners, Sam. Robin Hood, Wonder Woman, and whatever all wrapped in one."

"What the hell is that supposed to mean?"

"Okay, right. Truth is, I talked to Fanny."

"Fanny?"

"Yeah, about my sister." Diane looked straight ahead, focused, concentrating. "She'd only heard bits and pieces about the latest, the belt, the sheriff's b.s. So, I told her. She's been with me through the whole thing. The early years, when Jean disappeared. Back then we both thought she just up and left."

"And now?" I watched for deer in the ditches. "What did she say?"

"She said it's time to wake up and smell the coffee." She turned left onto highway W, away from Walnut Creek. "And I told her about your paint job."

"What! You didn't." I looked closer at her. She smiled. "Sonofabitch, you did, you told her."

"Damn right, I did. And you know what she said? She said 'Do it!' It's a perfect plan. And you know what, if Jean is in the lake, I don't want one-single molecule of her going to fertilize Manticore soy beans."

Getting the thumbs up on this paint job from Fanny was a shock. "All right. Where are we going? And what ammunition?"

"In a minute." She accelerated. "You know how when you're so pissed at someone you just drive to their place to look around, you get there, and it's like, okay, now what?"

"Yeah, usually, it's 'nothing' and you drive home." On our right were soy beans and wooded tracts of land. On the left, her headlights bounced off rows and rows of the healthiest corn I'd seen in our four-county corner of Wisconsin. Manticore corn.

"Exactly." She slowed. County Road X approached. "I did that tonight. I cased Manticore Farms." She put on the blinker.

"We're not going there."

She side-eyed me. "You sound way too confident, given you're not behind the wheel."

"Holy shit. Come on."

As if the devil had whispered in her ear, she smiled.

We rolled past endless acres of beans and corn. "The best crops Red Wolf water can grow," I spat.

"Keep that fire burning." She lowered her chin. "You're the muscle of the operation."

"Me? The muscle? Then we got no chance. Listen, riding through the night with you is a lot of fun, but I can't be pinched on a felony. I told you that before."

"Ten gallons of paint? Misdemeanor at most. And remember, everything's legal as long as you don't get caught."

"Oh, now I feel better." Out my window, the Manticore place appeared.

She killed the lights. The silos rose next to the barn. Yard lights shone between the sheds and the house. The car slowed to a crawl. There were no lights inside the barn. In the far pasture cattle were grazing under a full moon.

"You see that tarp over there? It's covering a pallet full of five-gallon cans. Guess what's in them?"

Parked right behind the tarp, I noticed an eighteen-wheeler, CCT branded on the door. Cherhasky Capital and Transport. I hadn't seen nearly as many of the big rigs on the road lately, but then I hadn't been off the resort much either. Seeing the truck made me lonesome and worried for Max. If we were planning any kind of mission against the Manticore empire, it didn't seem right to do it without him. But neither was it right seeing the Cherhasky name in the Devil's Lair.

"Sam! Did you hear me?"

"Yeah. I don't know. What's in them?"

"Paint, of course, Einstein. And what's more, its *red*, for the barn."

I was stunned. "Oh my god… it's perfect. Shoot them with their own ammunition. No, we'll never… We'll get caught. They'll lose their shit. They have a dog."

"The dog died a month ago. The new one is just a pup, and I know him. You get the paint. I'll take care of the rest."

"The dog! You even know the dog? Is there anyone or any-thing in this county you don't know?"

She shoved me in the shoulder and said, "It's because I'm so charming." Luckily the doors were still closed because we both laughed out loud.

Lights off, she pulled ahead until she was pin high to the pallet. She got out first. The dog raced from the porch, barking as he came.

Diane got down on one knee and stage whispered, "Spike, here boy." She held out a piece of beef jerky. The dog slowed, stopped barking, and started to wag its tail.

Quietly, I got out of the car and opened the trunk.

CHAPTER THIRTY-SIX

Good to the Last...

Early Friday Morning, July 12

While Diane occupied the dog, I crouch-crawled to the far side of the paint. A rope skirted the base of the tarp, secured by a knot tied so tight I needed a screw driver to pry it loose. The dog growled. Diane whispered something I didn't catch. Yanking the rope side to side, I managed enough slack to expose one of the corner cans.

"Ow, damn." I'd scraped a couple knuckles on the metal edge. Inch by inch, I shoved the tarp around the circumference of the top bucket until the can was free; and so was the next one. I had my ten gallons, but I wasn't done. There was plenty of give in the tarp now. I grabbed two more pails, pulled the tarp back into place, and grabbed two of the handles.

Swag had come to the party; secret sauce was in his arms. The buckets felt so light, I damn near waltzed them from palate to trunk. Twenty gallons later, I clicked the lid shut. At the same moment, in the farm house, a light came on in an upstairs bedroom.

"Sticks! Let's go."

Shooing the dog away, she was back in the car a second after me. She started the engine. The lights downstairs brightened the kitchen and front porch. I ducked and swore. Tires skidding, she fish-tailed the Chrysler into a U-turn and floored the accelerator. I turned in the seat, watching for headlights.

"Sam, you called me 'Sticks!'"

Even with the 20/20 vision of looking back, if I try to

describe the look on her face in that moment a dozen times, they would be all wrong, and entirely correct. Was she glad or mad about the nickname? I didn't know, but it looked like she'd won something.

"What did you expect? I can't use your real name. Like 'Hey, Diane Warren of Wasko Road get over here and help with this felony!'"

"Misdemeanor."

"Really? How much is twenty gallons of paint worth?"

"Twenty? What the hell. You said ten." She looked at me, tipped her head back and laughed. "It's finally happened, built my very own Mr. Hyde."

The clock on the dash read 1:11 a.m. as we passed the Manticore Mansion. Diane slowed and turned into the drive. The headlights illuminated the house to the left and straight ahead, the garage. Security lights installed since Mission: Jeanie Blue surrounded the front porch and the garage.

"Whadda ya think?" asked Diane.

"Dead as a fly in a window well. Let's go."

She backed out, continued down GG, and took the next left into the heavily-wooded lot. The gravel driveway twisted through the woods until we came to the cabin, already half demolished. A dumpster marked the end of the drive. She killed the lights and the engine. I grabbed the tools and went to the trunk. She met me there and popped the lid.

"Can you carry two?" I asked.

She pushed up the sleeves on the old sweater and elbowed me aside. "Huh, can you?" She grabbed the handles on two buckets and walked toward the lake.

I got the other two and shut the lid. There was a well-worn path through the woods to the water but the rest of the lot was untended trees and underbrush. I showed her a dilapidated boat I'd spotted on a previous look-around. We turned it over and pushed it toward shore. She asked if I thought it would float.

"Hell no." She gave me a serious frown. "Well, sure, for a while."

There were no oars so I jogged back to the cabin and salvaged a six-foot board from the demolition site as a substitute. Before loading the paint in the boat, we loosened the tops. The hammer worked best, the claw side bending up the dozen or so tabs that held the metal lids in place. I left three tabs in place until we were ready.

We climbed into the rowboat. Sitting midship, I paddled with the board toward the Manticore boathouse. Security lights lit the house and garage but not the lake. The moon was full, and there were clouds. The wind was up, but this close to shore the waves were only moderate.

The rickety dinghy bumped against the launch ramps extending from the boathouse. I directed the bow out, put the stern within a couple feet of the concrete wall I knew was below the boathouse doors. It was then I realized how much had happened in less than half a summer. In the years since, this moment has become indelible, marked in memory because so much was at stake. To start with, Erin had almost lost her life here, stuck helplessly against the intake grate a few feet below. Those moments of panic, and the fact that both Diane and I would soon be felons, made me acutely aware of everything: the smell of paint mingling with seaweed drying on the shore. Erin sliding beneath the boathouse doors, the cool breeze goose-bumping my skin, and except for lapping waves, silence.

Diane took my place on the middle seat and grabbed the launch ramp. I went to the back, put the first pail between my legs, sat on the back seat, and waited. She asked how we'd know when to start.

I had ahold of the launch rail to my right as well, steadying the boat. "You can hear it," I nodded toward the building. "The pump sucks more than Freshman English. If I fall overboard with the paint, don't come after me. It's too dangerous. Anyway, I'll get out."

She knew Erin's story. Diane was not a strong swimmer and didn't argue.

Thirty seconds later, the quiet of the night was broken by the sound of a deep, throaty hum. "That's it. Hang on; that thing will try to suck the boat and everything else within twenty feet."

Diane latched tighter to the iron. "Jesus, Sam bone, get going."

My shoes mushed in water oozing through the hull. The transom was centered over the intake grate. I grabbed the handle, lifted the pail, and started to pour. With suction pulling for acres upon acres of corn, the paint sank, a red-ribbon snake diving right into the gullet of the Manticore irrigation monster. The bucket emptied. I set it aside.

"Can't you go any faster?" she asked.

"No. Too fast and it could damage the pump or jam the sprinkler nozzles. Then we *are* talking jail time." I tipped the second pail and held it steady. Fatigue set in. My back complained, but my forearms and shoulders were really bitching.

Diane had gotten on her knees and draped her right arm over the near rail. "You're not painting the fuckin' Mona Lisa, for chrissakes. Hurry up."

I lifted the empty pail and stretched my back. "Empty! Number three next." I turned and said, "How you holding up?"

Wincing, she tightened her arm against waves hitting the bow. "Are you shittin' me?"

"All right. All right." The buckets got heavier. The boat rolled with the swells, my feet stumbled over the seat, but still I was able to center the pail on the stern. The wire handle dug into my palm as I tilted the mouth of the paint can forward. Halfway through number three, my back seized up. A knee buckled. The pail slipped. I lost control. The grey bucket went overboard. I lunged for the handle and lost my balance. I pitched forward into—

Diane leapt, grabbed the back of my shirt, and yanked me back into the boat. I sat down on the seat, my shirt pulled sideways, all but two of the buttons gone, bucket number three dangling in my hand over the transom. The smell of latex filled my head.

I swallowed and said, "Thanks." I looked behind the boat and then at pail number four. The lids had made a holy mess in the bottom of the boat. Bucket two had tipped over and was dripping. I grabbed the last handle.

Diane sat down on the middle seat, barely hanging on. "Haven't you had enough?"

"What am I gonna do with five gallons of red paint?" I poured this one to choke the monster. "Okay, Jean. This one's for you."

"Slow down. Remember what you said—"

The last plop of paint hit the water. A terrible screeching sound coming from the pump house split the night. I dropped the bucket, covered my ears, and looked at Diane. She wedged her head between her hands. Like a bomb dropping from the bay of a B-52, the pitch of the screeching dropped.

Then, the pump was dead.

CHAPTER THIRTY-SEVEN

Off the Hook

Afternoon, July 12 and 13

Sleeping after the paint job was impossible. On our way home, I'd repeated my immunity theory about the Manticores—because the siphon was illegal, they wouldn't report the vandalism, so Diane and I had nothing to worry about. And then thought if I'd believed my own bull shit, I'd have slept a lot better.

My appetite was still AWOL. A glass of milk and two Oreos, that was breakfast. I was too spooked to eat lunch, and my parents were getting worried. They'd noticed my poor appetite for a couple of weeks, so I started wearing loose cloths to avoid questions about my weight. Right after lunch I was on the lawn tractor, mowing around the pool when Diane drove in and parked under the twin pines. I got off the mower and jogged over to meet her.

"Hey, how's my partner in crime?" I asked. She popped out of the car, slammed the door, and told me things were looking up. Ever since her mom heard Diane was trying to track down the truth about her sister's disappearance, she was letting her use the car and even slipped her some gas money. We slapped skin on that but my news wasn't so good. I kicked the tire on the car and said it would probably be the last time I'd have to mow grass. "Foreclosure happens next Wednesday."

"Don't scramble your eggs before they're hatched, Sam bone," Diane said. "That's why I came. There's a minor sensation on Highway X. I drove by on the way over."

"Whadda ya mean?"

"I mean we're rock stars. Number One on Billboard with a Bullet. Eighty acres of waist high corn is now the prettiest pink you ever saw, the nozzles bleeding red right above. And it's right there, right next to the road." She backhanded me on the belly. "The cars are lining up to get a look. We've hit the big time."

"Wait. You're kidding, right?" I straightened up. "Don't joke about this, Diane."

She put her arms out.

"It's true?" I asked. "We made it rain red in August. Just like Moses!"

"Well, he did a river, but..." She paused then yelled. "It's true!"

I wrapped my arms around her. We jumped and hugged and hugged and jumped.

"But Sam, wait. Wait, Sam…"

"What?"

"My brother told me, he saw them, they're hookin' up the plows. We gotta do something before they bury the evidence."

I got out my cellphone and turned away from Diane. I didn't want her to hear the fake name I was using with Tom Preen. She would think it was stupid, or even worse, funny. "Ben Bigelow calling for Tom Preen."

"Who you calling?" She spun me by the arm. "I want to hear."

I heard Preen's voice. "Yes, put him through." The line clicked. "Hello, Ben. I was starting to wonder if I'd hear from you again. How are things up at Red Wolf?"

"Not good, Mr. Preen. Not good."

"I did some inquiries about that buckle you told me about. Hit a stone wall. Nothing I could move on. Sometimes that's how it goes."

"What about the siphon out of Red Wolf?"

"You set me up on that one, Ben. I got laughed out of the restaurant and I hadn't even finished my pie."

"Let me tell you something even funnier. You ever seen pink corn?"

"You mean like in the store?"

"No. Field corn. Come up quick 'cuz they're plowing it under—"

"Wait, in July?"

"I know. Right? Someone dumped red paint down the siphon intake yesterday." I winked at Diane. "That's all I'm saying."

"Was it you?"

"That's all I'm saying."

"Pink corn? How much?"

"About eighty acres." I didn't really know. I smirked at Diane. She laughed silently.

There was a whistle, then a pause on the other end of the line. "I'm clearing my schedule. Looks like I can drive up tomorrow morning."

"That'll be too late." I almost hissed into the phone. Diane put her hand on my forearm and gave me a gentle squeeze. "I mean… you, your station, has a helicopter. It would be perfect. Everyone is seeing this from the highway. There's eighty acres of pink corn surrounded by another four hundred that's still green. It's a traffic jam out there. And by the time you're up here, a tractor plowing, but only the pink stuff!"

Diane shook a fist. "Good. Keep going. Keep going."

"Then you land the chopper, stick the microphone in Willard Manticore's puss and ask, 'Hey, Big Daddy, how'd you grow such pretty corn?'" Diane put a hand to her mouth, laughing.

Preen laughed too. "Okay. Okay. It's a strong case. The visuals are compelling, *if* they are as you describe."

I looked at Diane. She nodded. "Come now, and I guarantee it."

"Hang on a second." He put the phone to his chest, I think, then he said, "Keep an eye on the sky. If we make the dots connect, film at six and ten."

"Holy shit!" I covered my mouth. "Oh, sorry. Excuse me." But Preen had hung up.

Even though I'd laid down heavy hints to my family about the Manticore story, only Kevin joined me to watch the six o'clock news. Before she left, I asked Diane to come back and watch with me, but as the broadcast started, she had not arrived. I took a quick look out the back door to check for her, then went back to the couch.

The anchorman said, "And now with Breaking News…"

"Damn it, Diane, where are you?" I grumbled. I always thought the "Breaking News" lead was bullshit. How can there be such urgency every night? But of course, this was the exception.

"Come on. Come on." It was Allison's voice, coming down the hall from the bar. She entered the kitchen and said, "He's right there."

I saw Diane and stood up. "Great. Hurry. Preen is just starting."

Allison walked ahead of her and sat right next to me, so Diane would have to sit next to her. "Allison," I said. "Get your own spot."

"This is my spot."

Kevin chuckled at the three of us.

The report started with pictures, taken from the air, of cornfields, especially the pink stuff going under plow.

"There it is." Diane pointed at the screen. "That is so sweet. We are killing it, Sam."

"Killing what?" Kevin asked.

"What you are looking at," Preen said, "are hundreds of acres of remarkably healthy corn. Remarkable because most of the crops in this part of the state are stunted due to lack of rain. But not these…"

"Get to the pump," I said. "The siphon out of the lake."

Diane reached over and slapped my shoulder. "Shhh."

Allison elbowed me. "Yeah. Shhh."

The video was awesome and so was the report. Willard Manticore refused to be interviewed, and a family spokesman issued a "no comment" to all of Preen's questions. Perfect. The Manticores offered no formal statement, therefore my explanation of the pink corn was the only one. At the end of the report, I caught a glimpse of Allison's blond locks and Diane to my right. In the last few days, the dark-haired one had fallen asleep on my shoulder, then made a midnight call to my bedroom window. I'd actually fallen for her a long time ago, when she said hi to me in history class, then walked away. I reached behind Allison and gave Diane a high five. "Dragon slayers," I said. She smiled.

———————

T-minus four days and counting to the eviction. The Tom Preen story went off the hook. Saturday morning the Manticore Mansion was crawling with state and federal agents. With only ten minutes of free time, I could have buzzed over in a fishing boat to gloat, and taken in the sight of killer ants taking over a hornet's nest.

The chop of the helicopter was back in the afternoon, this time over the Manticore lake property, so I knew there'd be an update on the Preen Report: Special Weekend Edition. He'd promised more, and he delivered. I managed to escape the resort, but Dad allowed only time enough to watch the news at Diane's house. Sitting on the floor of her living room, backs against the couch, we watched again, this time thighs touching, holding hands. Now we had her mother to contend with. Suddenly energized by the story, she was in and out of the living room, cleaning the kitchen after making a rare meal. I wanted to kiss Diane. At that moment, wanted it more than anything else in the world. So why, of all days, did Ethyl have to wake from her extended hibernation?

"Walnut Creek gossip is going nuts on this, you know," Diane said. "I heard Steve was out at Tonto's Tap last night raising hell. You better be careful."

"About the buckle or about you?" I asked.

"About everything." She bent her knees and turned toward me. "He's going to lose his shit if his father goes down. Sure, he hates the bastard, but Steve knows who controls the money, and it sure ain't Junior. Mitchell, okay, he's made his bones, but he could care less about Steve. And now there's nothing left of his blackmailing plan *and*, if that's ever discovered, he goes to jail."

"If he wasn't such a horse's ass, then I'd feel sorry for him. Thanks for warning me." I kissed the back of her hand.

She closed her eyes halfway. "You're welcome." We moved closer.

Ethyl stepped in. "Is Preen on yet?"

Diane rolled her eyes. "No, Mom. We'll call you."

"Okay. Don't forget."

I waited until we were alone. "I'd give anything to see them tear out that pump."

"Let's do it. Let's go in a boat and watch from the lake."

"I can't, not right now. Monday, Mom and Dad are going to the bank for one final meeting to negotiate some extra time before they evict us."

"Shit!" Just then, a picture of Willard Manticore came on the TV. "And to think it all started because of that bastard." She turned her head. "Mom, it's on."

The Saturday night report was better because it suggested a connection between the now discovered siphon and the disappearance of Jean Manticore. Preen mentioned that, "Separately, TV 2 News has information on evidence discovered two months ago, that could help solve the six-year-old mystery. Ironically, the evidence may have come from Red Wolf Lake itself."

"Yes!" I cried. "Lay it on them. Fuckin' Sheriff." A knot let loose in my belly.

Diane's mother was still in the kitchen.

I felt Diane's other hand tighten on my upper arm. "I bet you'll have visitors tomorrow. County brownies."

I leaned closer and smiled. "County brownies?"

Now her forefinger was tapping my chin. "Yeah. You never heard of them?"

Every tap of her finger sent a charge through me. "I heard of 'em." I leaned closer and put my lips on hers. In four and a half seconds, I knew she was the best kisser I would ever know. I wrapped my left arm around her waist and—

"What was that? Something about the buckle?" Ethyl came in the room, saw us and said, "Diane! Sam! Have some respect. They're talking about Jean."

CHAPTER THIRTY-EIGHT

Zero Hour

The Week July 15

A few days later, Tuesday evening, T-minus one day to eviction: the boat brigade watching the dismantling of the Manticore property was modest, half-dozen boats or so. Wednesday evening, I heard the number tripled, but at Noquebay we had our own problems. In twenty-four hours, would we have a roof over our head? Should we be packing our clothes? Why keep operating the resort if we weren't going to be around to collect the rent? The meeting with the bank on Monday morning had gone well but not well enough to get an extension on foreclosure. On the other hand, the President of the Bank stuck his head in the door at the end of the meeting and said the board was meeting in a special session on Tuesday evening, the night before our eviction was to go into effect, and that Willard Manticore's position at the bank would be discussed.

Thursday morning. Zero hour. I had no idea what to expect. I was prepared for nothing. The boxes Mom put in my room for packing were empty, she knew it, and hadn't said a word. Joe and Allison had packed a few things. Kevin was with me on the denial train—when the sheriff slapped a lock on the front door of the tavern, then we'd start packing... maybe.

What would be the first sign of the apocalypse? A caravan of county deputies? A single executioner bearing a piece of paper?

Mom and Dad didn't seem to know. They'd never been through anything like it, but I think they pleaded ignorance because it was easier than explaining.

Every car that drove in was watched to see if it had official or police markings. At ten fifteen a.m. we were still in business when a Buick sedan parked in front of the bar. I was in the laundromat folding sheets. I looked through the screen window and saw a man in a three-piece suit get out of the car, look briefly at the tavern door, then walk toward the backdoor entrance to our living quarters. A flush ran through me. He looked lost, so I went out and asked if I could help.

"Good morning. I'm looking for the home of Jim and Elizabeth Robel. Am I getting close?"

Okay, so here he was, Doctor Death in a suit and tie. I wanted to tell him he had the wrong place and send him back down the road with some salty, side-eyed directions to the middle of nowhere. "We live right here." I nodded toward the lodge.

"I'd like to speak with them. I'll only take a moment, but it's quite important."

I showed the man, rather stocky with a hitch in his walk, into our kitchen. Mom was at the table, doing the bills. When she saw who was with me, her eyes widened, she dropped her pen, stood and said:

"Mr. Wentz, good morning. Sam, get your father; he's working in the bar."

As soon as he heard the name, Dad hustled down the hall like the place was going to explode. He shook hands with Mr. Wentz. "What brings you out here, Bill?" Dad asked.

"Good news, I think. I'm very pleased to bring it to you and your family." Wentz held up both hands. "The board voted Tuesday night to withdraw the foreclosure—"

"Yes!" I shouted.

Dad shook hands with Wentz again. He probably said something, but I don't recall. I gave Mom a hug, which was a good thing because it felt like she was about to collapse.

Wentz continued. "The terms of your mortgage remain the

same as before. No penalties or fees." He paused and looked down. "Also, you deserve to know, Willard Manticore was dismissed from the board. I can't say more but…" He nodded sideways. "I think the county inspector and his assessment against you is under review as well."

Mom had tears streaming down her face, the first time I'd seen them since James died. Dad looked as if a ton of lead had just been taken off his shoulders. "There'll be a party at Noquebay tonight," he said.

"One question," said Wentz. "I heard you have Finnegan's skull in your tavern. Can I get a look?"

———

The phone about busted in my hand. "Diane, they're not going to do it. The bank, they fired Big Daddy. We've got to celebrate." We set the time; she'd be over after lunch.

And what better way than by watching the demolition of Manticore Manor from the water. I went out to the rowboat with a small outboard and got ready to go. A moment later, a well-worn Chrysler 200 rolled to a stop in front of the lodge and out came Diane, a satchel over her shoulder. I stood in the boat and waved.

Half-a-minute later she was on the pier, dressed in blue jeans and a light sweater. I held up a hand. "Come in." She grabbed hold and sat on the middle plank. "What's in the purse?"

"This is not a purse. I'll show you when we get there." She put on her hat and sunglasses. "This is too good to miss."

"Move over." She did. I sat next to her. "Before we go, I want to tell you something. The thing is, I've noticed the only time I feel all right is when you're around." She parted her lips, as if she was going to say 'I like being around you, too' or something friendsy like that. I put up my hand. "Let me finish, or I'll screw it up. Probably will anyway… So, and it hasn't been for a little while, I mean, not just since Max left." I took a breath. "A while. Anyway, I know you don't have to…"

"Don't have to what?"

"Boys, obviously. You have them all over the place. But none of them know what I know, about how you feel about your sister, and how you and I painted a field of corn." She smiled at that. "You're fascinating, and you keep me guessing and…"

"And…"

If I waited any longer, I'd bust a blood vessel somewhere important, so I blurted. "I think we should, you know, date." I didn't want to see her reaction, so I looked straight ahead. "I know I don't own a car. I'm not Max. I can't—"

She put her hands on my face, turned my head, and kissed me. When finally she let me go, she said, "I can't answer you, not right now."

I froze for a second. Any answer besides a yes was a no. "Oh. I thought—"

"You thought the kiss was the answer. Someday… I can't tell you why, except it's nothing to do with you. And I wish I could say yes, but I can't."

There were a million possibilities racing through my mind. The one I thought of first was likely correct. It was too soon. She wasn't over Max. "I don't know if I'll have the guts to ask again." I handed her the binoculars, grabbed the pull start and gave it a yank. The engine came to life. We were both looking forward so I couldn't see her face, couldn't read her reaction to my question, if any. And maybe that was best. We headed for the Back Bay.

A light breeze at our backs, I pointed the boat east under skies streaked with high clouds. The temperature was comfortable. We found a spot among the small throng of boats about a quarter mile offshore. I threw the anchor. I sat on the floor between her legs, facing away.

She was fussing at something, then I heard a bottle top pop. She tapped me on the shoulder with a Lite. "Now we've got something to drink about."

I took the beer and looked up. "How'd you get this?"

"I have my sources." She threw her hair over her shoulders. "One way or another, you'll know why I asked you to wait for my answer. How long, I don't know, but you'll know. And by the way, do you think I kiss every guy that way?"

"What, like just now?"

"No. When you were at my place, watching Preen." I shrugged. "Tell you what, if we ever kiss like that again, we're going steady. Deal?"

"Deal." I raised my bottle. "Here's to Noquebay Resort." We tapped bottles.

We watched with and without binoculars as the pump house came down and the siphon pipe to the lake was filled with cement.

"Hi, folks."

Diane had seen the boat approach apparently, because her bottle had disappeared. I dropped my beer into the bottom of the boat, turned quickly, and sat up on the back seat. A middle-aged man wearing sun glasses, dressed in khakis and a polo shirt approached in a boat captained by another man. There was another passenger in a back seat. The boat came within a couple feet. The well-groomed man said:

"Quite a show. Are you two interested observers or just curious?"

Without a blink, Diane answered, "Both."

The man grinned. "I'm not from around here. Can you tell me, what construction company are they using? They're doing a good job, and quick."

I wondered why that was important. "No idea." The man looked familiar.

The captain inched the boat closer. The man said, "Mind if I grab hold for a minute?"

"Guess not." I grabbed the gunwale of the other boat; he did the same for ours. The lake remained calm, so the boats didn't pitch.

The man looked toward shore. "I was told this is all about a family scandal?"

I pointed with my free hand. "It was on TV a few days ago. The family that owns the mansion is in big trouble."

"I gathered that from the demolition."

"That was cover for a pumping station. There is a water pipe right below it. They were pumping water to irrigate their crops."

Now he was looking at me, squinting with one eye, even though the sun wasn't shining in his face. Even with the sunglasses, I could tell. "You know, I was told the exact same thing about ten days ago." He paused. "On the phone."

I froze for a second. He held out his right hand. "I'm Tom Preen."

I shook his hand. "Sa—" I coughed. "Sam Robel, this is Diane."

"Ah, then I'm wrong. You're not the guy."

I let out a breath. "What do you mean?"

"Maybe you've never heard of me, but I did the expose on the Manticores, the one you saw on TV; and I got a tip from a fella. I guessed from his voice he'd be about your age. When I saw you this afternoon, I followed a hunch."

Diane took her feet off the gunwale and sat up. "What was his name, this 'fella?'"

"He gave me Ben Bigelow."

Diane erupted in laughter.

I rolled my eyes and pointed a thumb at her. "She has a strange sense of humor."

Mr. Preen smiled widely. "And she's not afraid to share it. I love your laugh."

Diane settled herself down. "Thank you."

"Well, listen," Mr. Preen said. "If you run into Ben—"

Diane laughed again. The two other guys in the boat did, too.

Preen sucked on his lips, then continued, "Tell him I'd like to do an on-air interview with him. Now that the whole story is out, the risk is minimal, and there's still a big human-interest angle. The public would eat it up. Now, we'd have to have permission from both parents, should Ben be underage."

Diane crossed her legs. "Oh, he's not eighteen. Give me a second and I'll tell you exactly how underage *Ben really is.*" She tapped the beer bottle with her foot.

I stared at Diane. "How'd you like to swim back to the resort?"

She uncrossed her legs, leaned forward, and said, "Sam, you're such a beast. Just because you're a football player, you think you can throw me in? Is that it?"

Again, the men in the boat guffawed.

I turned back to Mr. Preen. "You see what I have to put up with?"

Mr. Preen said, "Are you two brother and sister?" He was close enough to pat me on the back. He lowered his voice. "Because if you're not, I have only two things to say—number one: you poor bastard, and number two: whatever you do, don't let her get away."

"You don't know what you're asking," I croaked. He smiled with half of his face. I let that sink in a moment. "I don't remember hearing Ben's name during the TV story."

"No, and you never will." Preen's face was suddenly stern. "Our conversation was off the record. Not even a judge can get his name out of me." I nodded. Preen took a look toward shore. "Oh, I wonder if you've heard? Yesterday, the F.B.I. raided the offices of Square M Construction."

A breath stopped in my throat, "Holy shit, I mean crap. Sorry."

"He meant shit," Diane said. Again, laughter from the other boat along with a request from one of the guys for her phone number if she was unattached, which she waved off.

"Arrested the owner too." Preen squinted. "What was his name?"

"Mitch," I said. "Mitch Manticore, also known as Tapper."

"Really?" Preen smiled. "Thanks. There were several charges, the worst was interstate transportation and sale of stolen goods. It was connected to another big case from up here, but the company is from Chicago—Cherhasky Capital and Transport. Ever hear of it?"

A ball of ice formed in my chest. I let go of Preen's boat and set back on the seat. The baseball cap, the matchbook found in the grass, somewhere along the twisted storyline I never wanted to believe. Heard of it? I might have known, had I not been so close to Max.

"Also called CCT. Maybe you've seen them in the news?" Preen asked again.

It took me a moment to realize he was still talking to me. I looked up and said, "No."

Diane sat forward and grabbed my arm. "Sam, are you all right?"

"Yeah, fine. Just the last few weeks. You know."

"They had a system, CCT would transport goods stolen from construction sites in Illinois up to Square M, who used the stolen material on their own jobs." Preen raised his hand. "Okay. I've taken enough of your time. You, I mean Ben, has my number. He can call me anytime."

Preen pushed off. "Oh, one other thing. The search for the body in Finnegan's Hole started two days ago." The engine started and they were gone.

Dumbfounded, I looked at Diane. "Can you believe that? Tapper and J. Roman tied up in, I don't know, what do you call it?"

"Organized crime." She looked toward shore. The wind came up and a moderate chop rippled the lake's surface. "Stolen construction stuff from Illinois ends up in buildings in Northern Wisconsin. That's probably why Square M was making out like a bandit. Literally."

"And they're already searching for Jean's body. It must be a dive team." I wondered how Diane would feel about the search finally becoming fact. "Are you all right with that?"

"I told you, I've had it with guessing games." Diane looked at me and shook her head.

I spread my arms. "What?"

"You're so full of shit. Ben Bigelow?"

I just smiled, looked ashore. "You think that's why they wanted our place. To put in another siphon?"

Diane nodded. "Maybe. Yeah. They've got crop land right down the road from you." She paused. "They'd 'ave shut down the resort, sold off the land for private homes—just like everyone else is doing. Made a killing doing it, and kept one spot for themselves."

"Exactly!" I said. "Well, not on our watch, you assholes." Diane and I slapped skin. "I've seen enough. Let's go in."

By the time I got the anchor weighed and the engine started, the waves were hitting the aluminum hull of the rowboat with a middleweight punch. To get back to Noquebay we traveled just off the northeast wind, which slowed our progress. About halfway home a larger, faster boat approached from the rear. I didn't bother to look at the vessel until it came dangerously close to our port bow. The spray off its hull doused both of us. I scowled and looked at the driver, who cackled loudly, and moved off.

"Shit!" I gripped the tiller tight. "Knock it off, Manticore."

Diane whipped him the finger. "Suck it, Stevie."

Steve circled, increased his speed, and took an acute angle toward my bow. "What the? Hang on!" I pushed the throttle arm left, the boat veered right. Again, we were drenched by wash off the boat. I slowed down.

Steve slowed with me and yelled, "Chicken shit."

Diane grabbed my knee. "Ignore him. Just get us home."

Steve accelerated, pulled away, and I took a breath of relief. Keeping a wary eye on his boat, I accelerated as much as I could which, given the rough water, wasn't much. The runabout bumped and banged through the waves in a huge circle. Instead of heading away, he turned and, like a torpedo, took a bead on us. I went to the running back tactics I used to avoid tacklers in the open field.

I stayed on the same tack until Steve was so close I could see blood in his eyes. The bow of his boat raced directly for our port side.

"Turn, Sam, turn. He'll cut us in half."

CHAPTER THIRTY-NINE

The Battle of Red Wolf Lake

Thursday, July 18

Diane screamed. At the last second, I pushed the tiller. The boat pitched. The big outboard yowled as Steve tried to match our turn. He missed us by inches. The wake from the runabout rocked us like we were a paper cup.

Diane grabbed the gunwale. "Sam, he's gone crazy."

I set course for shore, a quarter mile away. Steve carved a smaller circle and took aim. He wouldn't fall for the same scam twice, so I went into a zig-zag tack. I yelled, "Put on a life jacket." She grabbed for a preserver, but lost her balance, slid to the floor, and scrambled back on the seat.

In the next instant, the back end of Steve's runabout slammed into the mid-section of our boat. Diane was thrown from her seat and landed at my feet. The blow put a huge dent in our left gunwale and tipped us dangerously, right-side down. Diane flew into me, a belly-flop onto my bent knee. She cried out, collapsed, then rolled onto the floorboards near my feet. Finally, the wind blew the boat upright.

I cut the engine and said, "Diane!" Curled in a fetal position, she groaned, was unable to stand. "Diane, what happened?"

Her was face contorted in pain. Tears flowed from closed eyes. Her mouth was open but she made no sound.

Rage pounding in my chest, I looked for Steve. He had turned his boat around and was making a quarter-throttle victory pass-by. Beer in hand, sitting on the top edge of the captain's chair, he gloated over us, the vanquished.

While passing he said, "Hey, Robel, you suck more on water than you do on land."

I grabbed an oar and swung it like a Louisville Slugger. The edge of the flat end creased across the windshield then into Manticore's chest. The bottle of beer went flying and so did he, into the back seats. He got up spitting and swearing.

I put the motor in neutral and helped Diane to her seat.

"It hurts, Sam. Like cramps."

"Okay, honey, I know. I'm getting you home."

The bow of the runabout loomed over us. But instead of coming in at ramming speed, it tapped our transom. Steve stopped the engine and appeared on the prow.

I pointed a finger at him. "What the hell is wrong with you? Look at Diane! For chrissakes, she's hurt…bad." I sat her on the middle seat.

"That's your fault. She's with you. She's no friend of mine. Whatever she gets she deserves." He curled a rope in his hand. "Once I dispose of your ass." He looped the rope around my small outboard. "Everything 'll be fine." He lassoed my engine and then found a cleat on his hull. "Everything." He tied the rope so that the boats would not separate. "Now, I'm going to bloody your ugly face."

I stood between Steve and Diane. There was literally no-where to run. If I'd been alone, I might have taken my chances in the water. But I had Diane. The next thing I knew the sole of Steve's boot was planted in my belly. Knocked off my feet, glasses flying, I plowed into Diane. We fell in a heap near the bow. Her cry was weak and mournful.

"Come on," I said, as I helped her to the front seat.

"That's it, Sir Crap-a-lot." Steve, suddenly there, grabbed my collar. His fist, my cheek. My vision flashed.

Eyes closed, I ducked, wrapped my arms, and threw him down. Metal hull, edge of wood. Creasing pain. Rolling. I smelled oil and fish bait. A knee in the groin. I buckled.

He stood over me. "You smart-ass types"—he kicked

me—"never know"—he kicked me again—"how to fight." He cocked his right leg.

Still on my back, I kicked his left knee.

He buckled. "Ow! Lucky… fuck. Who told you to get up?" His elbow, my temple. My head banged the hull. I was on my back again, Steve astride my belly. I grabbed his shirt. His hands around my throat. I rammed my knee into his ass. His head jerked forward.

He grinned. "Way off, man."

Pressure in my head. I let go of his shirt. My hands behind his head and pulled. At the same time, my knee, his ass, again. His forehead slammed the edge of the gunwale.

"Shit!"

My knee once more. The heel of one palm under his chin, I pushed. Steve, face-first into the gunwale. His nose cracked. Blood flowed. His grip loosened. My palm thrust into his broken nose. He cried out and broke the hold.

I grabbed the motor's throttle bar and swung it into the side of his face. "Ah!" Steve grabbed his cheek and stumbled to his feet. So did I.

"Oh, my god," Diane croaked weakly. "That's enough. Both of you, stop."

He threw a wild left hand. I grabbed him. Steve tried to push me overboard. I lost my balance, grabbed his shirt, went into the water and took him with me.

I popped to the surface right away, the water somehow bracing. Steve was disturbingly close, thrashing. I kicked him in the ribs, then swam to the rowboat, pulled myself to the top edge, and draped my arms over the side.

Diane came to the middle plank. "Sam, are you okay? Your face! Jesus Christ."

"I—guess—so," I said through heaving breaths. She couldn't see Steve. I threw my head toward the other boat. "Over there, I don't know. Once…in… the water, the fight… over."

She sat up straight. "Did you see him get out?" I shook my head. "Sam, go get him."

"He just beat the shit out of me. He can 'get' himself."

231

"No, he can't. He can't swim."

"Tough shit. He better learn."

Diane dragged herself in front of me, on her knees. She grabbed my hand and bought her face close to mine. "Sam, I know he hates you. I saw what just happened. But can you let him drown? Is that who you are? Because that's what's going to happen."

I pulled myself up. "Yeah, sure. You know the story. I go after him, he grabs me and we both drown." She said that wouldn't happen to me. I punched the hull with the side of my fist. "For you, not for him." I pushed away, kicked off my tennis shoes, and swam to where I thought he might be.

Below the surface, the water was churned from the waves but there was plenty of light from above. I swam first toward Steve's boat. Very soon, a dark outline appeared, pitifully, weakly struggling against himself and the water. I went up for a breath, then under again. By the time I got directly behind him, he was barely moving. Wrapping my right arm around his chest, I paddled for the surface. He was limp. We broke the surface fifteen feet from the rowboat. Mist flying from my lips, I yelled, "Steve, Steve, breathe, breathe."

There was no response. I wrapped my left arm around to meet my right, and squeezed his chest. "Breathe, you fuckin' moron." I squeezed again.

"Is he alive?" Diane asked.

"Don't know." I paddled us toward Diane, and then grabbed the gunwale. "Hang on to his shirt. Can you do that? I'll push him in." She looked pale and weak, but she nodded. "One, two, three, go." I grunted and pushed. The strain on Diane's face made me ache. "He's too heavy. Wait a second." Diane could see signs of breathing. "Good. Hang on." I went under and untied his work boots and let them float away. "One more time," I said. This time we got his torso over the top. Diane held him steady, half in, half out of the boat. I grabbed his feet and swung them over the gunwale. As soon as Steve was face down, flat on the floor of the boat, he started to cough. Then he vomited what looked like lake water and beer.

"Oh, gross." Diane pushed his hips, trying to get him on his side.

"Yeah, good." I reached over the gunwale, grabbed his far shoulder, and pulled it toward me. Together we got him lying against the hull.

Diane grimaced and collapsed onto the bow seat. "Jesus, these cramps."

Once back in the boat, I retrieved my glasses, loosed the rope from around the motor, and let the runabout drift free. The waves had pushed us well off shore.

I looked at Steve's twisted body. "For chrissakes Steve, Junior isn't worth this shit."

Gasping, heaving, Steve looked at me through the corner of his eye. "You dumb bastard, it's not Junior after your ass. It's not even my old man." His face spasmed. He puked again then put his head down, exhausted.

"Then give me a name." I punched his shoulder, harder than I had to, more vicious than I should, but I needed to know what he knew. His abdomen contracting, knees jerking, Steve cried out:

"You suck, Robel!"

"The name."

He opened his eyes into wise, arrogant slits, and through a manic grin of clenched teeth he said, "Jer-e-mi-ah."

I couldn't think. What the hell was he talking about? How many Jeremiahs did I know? Only one, and he—

A foamy, bubbling laugh dripped out of the corner of Steve's mouth. "What's the matter, Sammy Suck-up?" He choked and spit, the drool oozing to the boat floor. "Cat got yer tongue?" He took a wheezy breath. "You know who... heh, heh, heh." Then in a sing-song voice. "Jeremiah was a bullfrog—"

"Liar!" I slammed my foot into his belly. He passed out.

I yanked the starter chord on the engine so hard the rope broke.

"Hurry, Sam," Diane said, a hand on her belly. "I'm bleeding."

My head snapped around. Blinking twice, three times, I looked her up and down, but could see no red. "Bleeding? Where?"

She looked down at her hands, holding her belly. "Down there."

Chapter Forty

Visiting Hour

Saturday, July 20

The Rescue Squad took two people to the Walnut Creek Hospital that day. One, a near drowning, the other with abdominal pain and bleeding. Not long after, the sheriff's cruiser was parked outside the bar, again. I gave a statement about the altercation, including a blow-by-blow description of the fight, dueling boats, and how I pulled Steve out of the lake. As to Steve's motivation for starting the melee, I pleaded mostly ignorance, but guessed since Diane had broken up with him weeks earlier, and she was now spending time with me, it was a jealous rage. I left speculation on the Manticore situation to them.

A couple days later, Steve Manticore was still in the hospital. Sarah Crimmins and I talked once a day so she could keep me up on the local scuttlebutt. Mom took one look at the bruises on my face and my swollen cheek and almost put me in solitary confinement. Most of all, I couldn't get my mind off Diane. I wanted to see her Friday but Mom wouldn't let me leave home. I called her twice but she didn't pick up, she must have been sleeping. Finally, Sarah got the details. I asked her to come over to the tavern. I got her a soda, we sat on the porch, and I asked her to fill me in.

"What have you heard?" Then she looked closer at me. "Yeah, in a minute. I mean, your face. How are you?" I looked worse than I felt, as I was telling everyone. I asked about Diane again. "She had to have surgery yesterday." Sarah glanced out the windows.

My throat went dry as dust. I wanted to know more than that. What kind of surgery? What was her condition? "I don't know much about that kind of stuff. But I think she's okay. The nurse told me family visits only. How you going to get around them?"

"Gotta think on that. Thanks, Sarah."

I walked around the rest of the afternoon with rocks in my gut. I ate a small supper. It was still light out, so I shot hoops on the basketball court. I dribbled the basketball lazily. Leaves skittered by, pushed along by a soft, warm breeze coming off the lake. There wasn't a sound in the air save the slap of the basketball, which echoed off the lodge, the pool house, and the tree line. The sun was still warm. Looking across the Narrows, there wasn't a powerboat to be seen, only a handful of fishermen looking for luck around the island. After a busy day, the resort was at rest. A dark sedan drove by and parked by the back door. I took little note, dribbling then shooting.

A rebound veered sharply toward the lake. I didn't notice Dad walking toward the court, the man from the car right behind. "Hey Sam, come here." I put the ball under my arm. Dressed in a dark suit and white shirt, the stranger's square jaw, narrow waist, and sunglasses put a shiver through me. I'd seen him before, in June, in Max's kitchen. Then, the man was carrying files and boxes. Now, he had only a manila envelope and a familiar guitar in hand.

"Sam," Dad said. "Mr. Jorgenson brought something for you."

"For me?"

The sedan drove away. I handed the ball to Dad, slid my thumb under the tab, and opened the envelope. It contained a single piece of stationary. My eyes coursed down the page, fingers ever tighter, my mind racing faster with every line. "Holy shit." I handed the paper to Dad. "Read this."

I paced, then stopped, ran my hands through my hair, and paced again.

Dad nodded. "Explains a lot, doesn't it? There's one other thing Mr. Jorgenson told me. You should know. It's going to be released to the public tomorrow. They found the body in

Finnegan's. It's so decomposed, they have to do DNA analysis to identify it."

"Holy shit. They found Jean Manticore."

Dad sighed. "Well, it appears so, thanks to you. We'll see."

"I gotta have the car. I want to see Diane. Dad, she's the one in the letter. I gotta."

"I know. Go ahead. Take your *time*. There's no rush. Better put the guitar away first."

Walnut Creek Memorial Hospital was small. There was no security for me to check through. The light behind "3" lit up. The bell rang, the door opened, and I stepped off the elevator. A small, unmanned nurses' station stood to the left, flanking a hall that extended straight-away before me. A second wing went to the right. I checked the sign for the room numbers and turned.

Diane's room was third down on the right. A sign on the door said "Family Only." I took down the sign, tucked it behind the manila envelope in my hand, and rapped on the door.

A voice I knew well, though softer than I'd ever heard, said, "Come in."

The room had two beds; the one closer to the door was empty. A single overhead light shown from behind a partially drawn curtain, separating the beds. All was quiet. Treading lightly, I walked in and peeked around the edge of the curtain. Diane had the head of the bed up, knees bent, a paperback novel in hand.

I raised my eyebrows and said, "Hi, how are you?"

"Sam!" She pushed herself upright, put out her arms, and cringed.

The envelope and the sign went on a bedside table. I wrapped my arms around her and squeezed, but not nearly as hard as she hugged me.

"Oh, come on," she said. "I won't break."

I laughed a little and wrapped her up. "I'm so glad to see you."

She sat back and looked at me. Sorrow filled her eyes. "Come here." She raised her hand and lightly touched my cheek. "Does it hurt very much? The bruise?" I shook my head. Then she poked my arm. "How about this. Do you hurt here?"

"No."

She punched me in the shoulder.

"Ouch! Hey! What was that for?"

"Saturday night, Sam Robel. I've been here for three days—"

"Well… two."

"Feels like ten. And you don't come to see me until now? Do you know what it's like? Lying here, with no one here, after surgery, after that whole boat thing?" Her eyes misted.

I grabbed her hand. "Hold on, Diane. I wanted to come. Mom grounded me for a day. And I called the nurses, they're drill sergeants out there. They told me no visitors except family."

"What? I never said that. How'd you get my room number?"

"Sarah told me." I pulled the sign from under the envelope. "I'm here illegally. I took this off your door when I came in." I showed it to her. "Anyone asks, my name is Ben Bigelow."

The laugh that came out of her started too low in her belly. She cringed again. "That was a good one." She took the sign. "Mother, dear." She handed it back to me.

She looked at the book, now closed, resting on her lap. "Have you heard anything from Steve?"

"No. Do you think I will?"

"Guess not. He's leaving tomorrow morning, the hospital, I mean. That's what I heard." She flipped the edge of the pages. "Thanks for pulling him out. I know he'll never say it, and I know you didn't want to…"

"Come on, Diane, give me a little credit. I wouldn't have let him drown."

Her grin was as muted as the light, but I could see it, and this one made it to her eyes. "No, I don't think you would have let him croak. I talked to him yesterday, you know. He gave it to me straight about J.R. Had to, 'cuz he was stoned on pain pills." Two hands held the book now. "We had the blackmail thing right, Sam, but it wasn't Manticore. Steve was trying to milk money from Cherhasky. Makes sense when you think about it. He hid the buckle in the Manticore garage. But if J.R. was the mark then he had to be the one squeezing the resort. He had the money and connections. He could have done it."

"So that's what he meant," I said. "When he said Jeremiah was the one after our ass. But why?"

"Why did J.R. squeeze you guys?"

"No. Why did Steve blackmail J.R. What was his motive?"

She shrugged. "We never got around to that, but with all that's gone down, if I ask, he would probably tell me." She picked at the book. "Sam, there's something I have to tell you."

"Oh, I almost forgot. I have something, too." I picked up the eight by thirteen envelope. "You won't believe it." I opened the tab, then looked up at Diane. Her eyes held something I couldn't figure out. They always had the power to stop me, and they did again. I closed the tab. "You first. Tell me your thing."

Her hands stopped. Paperback firmly in hand, she said, "No, I should go after you. What's in there?"

A little deflated, I went with the small news first. "They found the body." Her dark, almond eyes were so wide, I almost forgot the second part, the harder part. "They can't be sure who it is, you know. They have to identify, so it's not for sure."

"When will they know... for sure?"

I shrugged "Dad said they're using DNA." She was quiet for a while. I felt like she was melting inside, and I couldn't bear it. "It could be a while." I had no idea, of course. "That brings me to this." I pulled the letter from its sleeve. "I got it today. It's from Max."

She pulled the book tight against her belly and for a moment, she didn't breathe. "Where is he? Where did he go?" She grabbed the envelope.

"There's no return address. He's in hiding. The whole family is. Something called Witness Protection. I think you should read it."

She whacked me with the envelope. "This a joke? Well, *not* funny."

I flinched. "No, it's not. Look for yourself." I handed her the letter.

Her eyes softened, and then just as quickly, she looked petrified. She threw off the blanket, lowered the railing. "Help me sit up." Her hand in mine, she swung her legs around and sat on the edge of the bed. "Where is he? Where is the bastard?" Again, I told her there was no address. "What?" She scanned the letter. "Shit. The envelope, give me the envelope."

"You already looked." I turned the manila envelope over and showed her the front.

Where there might have been a return address, it said: Federal Marshall, Department of Justice, Milwaukee, Wisconsin.

Her voice was still strained. "What the hell, what's that supposed to mean?"

"They delivered it today. Read it. It's already almost a month old. You'll see why."

She dropped the envelope and started to read, her gaze swallowing the words in what looked like spasmodic gulps. After the first line or two, she misted up and couldn't go on. Eyes closed, she pressed the letter against her stomach and bent in half, as if she'd been punched. She handed the paper to me. "Read it for me."

I sat down and put my arm around her. "Is something wrong? Should I call the nurse?"

"Oh Sam, you're such a nag, you really are." She glanced at me. The expression almost made me laugh. She nudged me with her shoulder. "I'm okay. Really."

I took my arm from around her, and held the letter with both hands:

June 2013
Somewhere, Planet Earth

Dear Sam,

I have no idea when, or even if, this letter will get to you. Some ■ *secretary, who'll probably fix my grammar, will type it, and by the time you get it* ■ *will have chopped it to bits. I guess* ■ *know we left town.*

I can't tell you much more than you already know. My family is in the witness protection program because of ■ *gave to* ■ *.* ■ *mentioned* *the* ▉ *of* ▉ *from* ▉ *and* ▉ *is all I can say,* ▉ *who will* ▉ *, if you know what I mean. That's why I couldn't say anything to you before I left. We had to blow town in the* ▉ *and leave no clues. You can't believe what we've been through; I even have* ▉ *clothes. They weren't going to let me write this letter, but my dad negotiated with* ▉ *so I could. The phone call I* ▉ *between* ▉ *and* ▉ *was about this. You remember, I threw the watch into Finnegan's Hole right after that.*

You were right Sam; I wish I had the watch back. Dad bought me a new one to take its place. I won't be able to contact you ever again (you can't contact me either, don't even try).

I hope you keep the band going. About the only thing I was allowed to bring along was my guitar and my ▉ *dog. Brought along* ▉ *of course, but that's another story. I left the old acoustic guitar for you, Sam.*

I've been watching the news. We did it! We nailed the ▉ *. So glad we did that before I left. We were one bad gang.*

Show this letter to Joe and Kevin. Hey Joe—tip that outhouse once for me. Still breaking drumsticks, Kev?

And say goodbye for me to everyone at Red Wolf High, especially Diane. Hope she remembers me the way I remember her.

One last thing I want you to do, Sam. Get my name in the class annual. They're erasing everything else about us (they call it " ▉ *"), but I want my name to appear on something in that town. Just have them put "picture not available" where my senior photo should be.*

> *So long forever——*
> *Your friend,*
> *Max (P.S. not my* ▉ *anymore)*

I looked at Diane. Shoulders hunched, head down, she had a handkerchief in hand, wet with tears. This wasn't what I expected. I thought she would be happy about the letter, at least at the beginning. But there was none of that. She was tense and angry.

The letter, when read in Diane's presence, hit me a lot harder. The room closed in. I pushed back tears. I wanted to put my arm around her, hold her the way I should have when we visited Max's house.

I sucked on my lips. "You really miss him." It was hard to say, because seeing her that way, knowing her anguish, I realized even thought he was gone, she cared for him more than me.

"There's more to it." She shook her head. "All along I thought it would work out, we would find him, or he'd come back, or… shit, I don't know."

My stomach was in a knot. The hospital smell was sickish. My hand holding the letter started to shake. "Or what? What is it?"

"I've suspected for a couple weeks." Her chest heaved, then a shudder. "I missed my period, Sam. I'm pregnant, or was."

I don't know why, but all I could do was look at my hands, the letter quivering in one, the other twitching just like my lips. Then I looked at her. Did she say pregnant? What the hell did I know about that? I blinked twice. "You said 'was?'"

Diane got up and sat in a bedside chair. "I gotta say, if Max has anything, it's timing." Diane dabbed her eyes with a tissue, then balled it up in her fist and tapped the end against her lips. "I figured there'd be two I'd have to tell, you and Max. Now it's only you."

I put the letter back in the envelope and took hold of the bed railing. "Tell what?"

"Don't you know why I was bleeding? Or why I had surgery?"

I shook my head. "Don't even know what kind of surgery you had. And I'm worried that I, you know, caused it." My eyes burned. "I hurt you bad, in the boat. You were fine until I kneed you in the stomach. I figured I ruptured your intestine, or something."

"Oh, Sam, we make quite a pair, you and me. I've been blaming myself, and really, it's dip-wad Manticore we ought to string by the thumbs." She shifted her weight in the chair. "This chair sucks. Help me back to bed."

I took her hand, but she didn't need much assistance. She straightened her gown, pulled the sheet, and then said, "Let's strike a pact, you and me, no more blame game. Deal?" We shook and sealed the deal. She sighed deeply. "I wasn't peeing blood, and the operation wasn't on my colon." She paused, for my benefit, I suspected, to let the information sink in. "I had a D and C. It's done whenever... when a..." She cleared her throat.

It finally hit me. Her intense reaction when we cased the Cherhasky house and found it deserted. Then tonight, uncontrollable emotions in the face of a simple piece of paper, written by a former boyfriend. And the timing was right. "You lost the baby."

She sucked on her lips, looked at me, and nodded slowly, once. "Max's baby."

She nodded quickly, half-a-dozen times.

My throat tightened, my legs felt like sticks of butter, unable to bear the heat that suddenly filled the room. I sat on the edge of the bed and looked down at the floor. I'm not sure, but it must have been fifteen seconds or more before my breathing returned to normal. During those seconds, the hours, the weight of the summer came down on me, then just as quickly melted away. For the first time in a long time, I thought of James Jr. I had forgotten him not for days but weeks at a time. What kind of brother does that in less than two years?

Diane's hand on my forearm sent a scribble of voltage up my neck. I remembered where I was. My eyes jolted toward her.

Cheeks flushed, she held her other hand over her mouth, to cover a trembling chin. "Sam?" She inhaled deeply through her nose. "What are you thinking? Do you hate me? You do, don't you?"

"Hate you. What?" I turned toward her, held her tight, and said softly into her ear. "I'm sorry. I was somewhere else."

She took a couple of deep breaths, then looked out the window. "This changes things, I know."

"Something is changing every day between you and me lately." I sat back. "This is why you couldn't go steady with me. You thought you were pregnant." She bit her lip and nodded. I mimicked her nod and tapped my hand against my thigh. "Well, how about now? Swipe right?"

"Of course!" She lowered her chin. "It's not legal to kiss someone like that in a hospital."

"Legal?" I put my finger under her chin. "I'm not even supposed to be here."

We kissed until alarm bells went off, literally, in the room next door. She said, "Speaking of alarms, I want to get the hell out of here."

She looked great to me, and if she was going home tomorrow anyway, then why not just blow out of there tonight? It was easy.

Finally, she laughed. She ran her hand through my hair and sighed. "Easy Sam Robel. So, tell me, Mr. High-Falutin Pool Boy, what's the next step?"

Now I laughed. "You remember last Memorial Day weekend? You promised me a day of fishing—"

"Promised?"

"Ah, yeah. Then you dumped me and went shopping for *shoes* with Fanny."

"Got some real nice ones too. High heels. I'll wear them for you sometime."

Suddenly, I was a little breathless. "I've heard that one before."

She raised an eyebrow.

"All right, then. High heels beat fishing every time."

CHAPTER FORTY-ONE

A Proper Burial

Thursday, July 25

The fishing date, arranged two months ago, was finally going to happen. Diane escaped the hospital and within days was as good as ever. Around the resort it felt like the rebirth of spring in the middle of summer. There was even an overnight rain shower to rejuvenate the flowers and grass. I watched the Channel 2 News twice every day for the latest developments on the Manticore/Cherhasky situation. Tom Preen and I had talked a couple of times. He now had my real name and phone number in case there were any breaks, be they the CTS/Square M Interstate Organized Crime charges or the missing person found on the bottom of Red Wolf. I was interested for obvious reasons but most of all because I still didn't know why J.R. Cherhasky was so set against me doing anything with the buckle. My goal all along was to find out about Jean Warren Manticore and whether she was on the bottom of Finnegan's Hole. Why should he care about that?

Our fishing "date" was set for one week after the disaster with Steve Manticore. As it happened, I got a call from Preen that morning that could ruin the fishing all together. I wanted to tell Diane the news before we got in the boat, but in daylight the resort had surprisingly few private places. A boat on the water was the best choice. For the first time ever, she was right on time. While loading the boat with bait and tackle, I did my best to hide the sputtering in my chest. I noticed the absence of the satchel.

"What? No beer this time?"

"Kind of a bad luck charm for us last time," she said. "Plus, you don't like it anyway."

"I do when there's a pretty girl attached."

She hooked a finger into one of my belt loops. "Get in the boat."

I stopped the boat well west of Finnegan's Hole. I didn't have nearly enough rope to drop anchor, but the breeze was light, the sky smeared with wide splotches of purple-white clouds. Diane and I had dressed for the weather, which was a little cooler than typical for August.

"Before we do any fishing, I have to tell you, I got a call from Tom Preen today." Together on the middle seat, she turned to face me. I said, "He had a lot to say and I want you to hear it from me."

Leaning forward, elbows on knees, she said, "Okay, I'm ready."

"I was too, but not for this." I rubbed my neck. "It's not your sister, the body."

"It's not?" She raised up. "Not Jean? Who then?"

"They don't know." I coughed and looked away. "They don't have the DNA back yet. Did you or your mother give a sample?" She had done it days ago. "They didn't need DNA for Jean. The dental records didn't match."

"Well then I'm right back where I started." Her expression sagged. "Will they start searching again? They obviously found the wrong person. There's another one down there. Otherwise, where'd the buckle come from?"

"Probably won't start looking again until they have a positive I.D. on the one they have, and with DNA, that could take a long time, especially if they don't sample the right people."

"I guess. Something else Steve told me since he got out of the hospital. Turns out it was *J.R.* called the County Inspector on you, got the septic ruling against the resort. He opened the door for the Manticores to buy you out."

"Sonofabitch." A speedboat passed. Its wake rocked us for a

bit. The sun rose higher. I took off my shirt. My brother's dog tags dangled from my neck. "They probably were planning another siphon, just like we said."

"Definitely." Diane rolled up the sleeves on the unbuttoned cotton blouse she used for a cover over her bikini top and shorts. "That leaves only three questions. Who is the body? Why would J.R. care about the buckle? And why did Steve blackmail J.R.? I can only answer the last one."

"That's one better than I can do."

"This talk in the hospital, it reminded me of something. I blew it off; thought it was the Vicodin talking. But now it's starting to make sense. Something the WAGS came up—"

"The WAGS?" I asked.

"The Wild Ass Guess Society, the gossips of Walnut Creek, whatever. Anyway, their story is that Willard Manticore is not Steve's father. The way the old bastard treats him, it sorta fits."

"Yeah, I heard that one."

"Well, a couple days ago Steve said so too. And guess who he named as the sperm donor?"

"Oh, no." I looked at her, knowing there could be only one answer. "No. No!"

"Yes. The one and only J.R. Cherhasky, who has never, ever acknowledged Steve or had anything to do with him, that I know of. Might cause a bit of anger, lead to a touch of revenge, even… blackmail."

"Holy shit, Max has a half-brother and doesn't know it." I let that seep into my gray matter for a moment. "Okay, we have to explain why the buckle would scare J.R., and I still don't get that."

She nodded. "Creepy, nasty people." Diane rubbed her upper arms. "And now J.R. is gone. How do they question him if he's in a protection program?"

"They don't." I shook my head slowly. "Poor Max. Jesus, what a fucked-up family."

"Sam, what if he sees this in the paper? He's gonna see it."

My spine straightened. "You said it. He'll be as surprised as we are." I saw her pretty brown eyes and thought of how, at that moment, I wouldn't have traded places with anyone. The tingling skin, the shared mischief, and the gnawing tug that drew me to her even before we were dating were much worse when she wasn't there, wasn't near, and now made a daily encounter with her, even if only for a few minutes, a fix I could barely do without. No, I wouldn't have traded places, least of all with Max and his family and whatever amount of money they escaped with. "So, either there are multiple bodies in Red Wolf, or Jean is somewhere else, dead or alive." She wondered how the divers could have missed a body.

"I asked Preen. Two bodies in Finnegan's? Preen said the sheriff was sure the divers did a complete search. But it could happen; there's no light down there."

She sniffed dismissively. "How the hell can they tell? In all that water?" I agreed. She said, "It's not like there's a sign pointing, 'body over here' for chrissakes." Silent assent. "Shit, Sam." She put her face in her hands. "I don't know what to think. What to hope for."

I wrapped an arm around her and bought her head to my shoulder. For minutes neither of us spoke.

"What should I do?" she asked. "I'm not talking to the cops. What about Preen? Would he be able to help?"

I rested my chin on her head. "I don't know. Let's think on it. You don't have to decide right now."

She nodded and pulled away. Looking in the water, I saw a fish surface for a bug. The vision of Max's watch and how he put the family legacy to rest right here in this part of Red Wolf suddenly came to me. I slipped my fingers between the strands of chain in front of my chest and twisted. Slowly, it tightened around my neck.

Diane noticed. "Sam." I turned my fingers again. "Sam! What are you doing?"

I made a fist around the woven chain. "When I was talking to Preen a few weeks ago, I pulled on this so tight it gagged me. I was hating on my brother for putting our family in a huge pile of shit." I squinted into the distance. "I was wrong."

She got off the seat, onto the floor boards, and kneeled in front of me. She wrapped her hands around mine and the tags. "It's digging into your skin. Let it go."

I met her eyes. "Exactly. You told me weeks ago, but I didn't listen. I can't wear these for the rest of my life." I flexed my arm.

"No! Don't. Not because of me."

"I know." I put my left hand behind her neck and kissed her forehead. "You're right. It's time."

My fingers interlaced with the chain, I yanked it free. The dog tags rested on the palm of my hand. I ran my finger across his name, James Arthur Robel Jr. one last time.

The boards creaked as I joined Diane, kneeling there. One arm around her, the other palm extended over the water of Finnegan's, I said, "Goodbye, James…"

I turned my hand. The tags dropped and found their proper, final resting place.

Acknowledgements

This is a work of fiction, but anyone familiar with my background will readily note I have borrowed freely from my experiences growing up on a resort much like Noquebay, albeit fifty years ago. My thanks to all the people who came into my life through the resort and added color to the novel.

I came to writing comparatively late in life and have benefited immensely from the criticism and encouragement from my writers group Author's Echo. Some of the members have heard every word of this novel several times over. I am lucky in too many ways to list here, but I must mention three. My family, wife Barb and children Peter, Michael, Rebecca, Renee, Kimmi, and Kerri are a daily source of inspiration. Second, writing is an avocation for me, without the stress of economic need weighing on my pen. And finally, many thanks to David Ross and Kelly Huddleston at Open Books. Without their faith, dedication, and expertise this book would not have been published.

Made in United States
North Haven, CT
03 January 2024

47030763R00152